"Chief of Neurosurgery is a long way from a small practice in Slate Hollow, Kentucky, Adam. Almost a different world."

Leah wondered why she'd said that. It sounded almost as if she was asking him—what? To leave Chicago and come to Kentucky with her? Wasn't that what she really wanted? For him to make a commitment to her—and the baby he didn't even know she was carrying?

"Leah, my son is coming to live with me. We've been apart for a long time. I have to concentrate all my energy on Brian."

His energy. Not his love. His words took her breath and sent a stab of pain through her heart. Adam would never open himself to love and to being loved. Once more she realized how close she'd come to caring too much for this man. The decision she'd agonized over since learning she was pregnant was made in an instant. "I understand. I really have to be going."

"Leah, if there's ever anything I can—"

Leah took a step backward, avoiding his touch. She wasn't made of stone, even if he appeared to be. "There's nothing you can do for me."

Or our baby.

ABOUT THE AUTHOR

Carol Wagner and Marian Scharf—the award-winning writing team of Marisa Carroll—are sisters living in a small northwest Ohio town, where they are surrounded by five generations of family and friends. *Winter Soldier* is their twenty-ninth book.

Books by Marisa Carroll

WINTER SOLDIER
Marisa Carroll

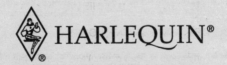

HARLEQUIN®

TORONTO • NEW YORK • LONDON
AMSTERDAM • PARIS • SYDNEY • HAMBURG
STOCKHOLM • ATHENS • TOKYO • MILAN • MADRID
PRAGUE • WARSAW • BUDAPEST • AUCKLAND

ISBN 0-373-70841-6

WINTER SOLDIER

Copyright © 1999 by Carol I. Wagner and Marian F. Scharf.

This edition published by arrangement with Harlequin Books S.A.

Look us up on-line at: http://www.romance.net

Printed in U.S.A.

These are the times that try men's souls.
The summer soldier and the sunshine patriot
will in this crisis,
Shrink from the service of his country,
But he that stands it now,
Deserves the love and thanks of man and woman.

—Thomas Paine, December 23, 1776

CHAPTER ONE

THAN SON NHUT.

Even above the roar of the jet engine he caught the echo of the pilot's words, felt them snag the edge of his consciousness. *Than Son Nhut.* For almost twenty-five years, more than half his lifetime, Adam Sauder, had returned to that place only in his nightmares. Today, he was actually going back.

Before he heard her voice he smelled her perfume, a light, lemony fragrance had tantalized his senses. "Dr. Sauder?" He pretended to be asleep. Maybe she'd go back to her own seat, leave him alone. God, it had been such a long flight. Thirty-six hours from Chicago to—

She spoke again, a bit more forcefully this time. "Dr. Sauder? Are you awake?"

Damn, she's persistent.

He rolled his head toward the well-modulated but demanding voice, but didn't open his eyes. "I'm awake," he said in the don't-tread-on-me tone that had struck fear into the hearts of interns and residents at St. Barnabas Medical Center for the past five years.

"I thought so." She sounded neither cowed nor embarrassed. "We'll be landing in Saigon in a few minutes. I thought I should introduce myself."

She could have done that anytime since they'd left

Chicago. Why did she have to pick now, when he had almost willed himself to that gray nothingness between waking and sleeping that was the only place he seemed to find peace? *Saigon. Than Son Nhut.* The names wouldn't die, just like his memories of the days he'd spent there. "I thought they called it Ho Chi Minh City now."

She chuckled, a sound as light and pleasant as her perfume. "No one calls it that. Even our luggage tags say Saigon."

The laughter was irresistible. He lifted his heavy eyelids and looked at his tormentor. Clear hazel eyes, neither green nor gold, stared steadily back. He blinked and her face came into focus. She smiled, and like magic her deceptively ordinary features turned from plain to pretty. "I'm your gas-passer," she said.

Gas-passer? She must have been raised on M*A*S*H reruns. "You're my anesthesiologist?" She didn't look a lot older than his nineteen-year-old son, Brian. She sure as hell wasn't old enough to be a doctor.

"Nurse anesthetist," she clarified.

They didn't give out advanced nursing degrees to teenagers, either. Mentally he added ten years to her age, pegging her somewhere close to thirty.

"I'm Leah Gentry." She held out her hand. He took it automatically. Her handshake was as firm and no-nonsense as her voice and, surprisingly enough, as potent as her smile. He pulled his hand from hers and her smile disappeared. "I'm in practice with Caleb Owens," she said more formally.

He knew who Caleb Owens was, although he'd never met the man. He was a friend of a friend—or an ex-friend. Adam directed a sour glance at the back of B. J. Walton's head, as his old Marine buddy lolled, snoring away two rows in front of him.

B.J. had made it big in computers in the eighties. He had more money than he could count—not that he didn't put a lot of it to good use. He'd sponsored half-a-dozen private medical-aid missions to Central America, Africa and even Russia over the past ten years, and he'd badgered and bullied and made a damned pest of himself until Adam had promised to be part of the next one.

B.J. had made a big deal of Adam's moment of weakness. He'd called a press conference and talked up the humanitarian mission of top-notch nurses and doctors taking time from their busy lives and careers to help the less fortunate. Then he'd promised a bundle toward the new spinal-injury rehab center if St. Barnabas agreed to let Adam come along. St. B's knew a good deal when they saw one. They agreed to supply all the specialized equipment Adam needed and offered to send technicians to keep it running at peak efficiency. It was a hell of a public-relations coup, the hospital administrator had told him. And it wouldn't do Adam any harm in his quest to be the next chief of neurosurgery, either. And then B.J. had dropped his bombshell.

This time they were going to Vietnam.

"Caleb was so disappointed he couldn't make the trip. He was looking forward to assisting you."

Adam continued to scowl at the back of B.J.'s head a moment longer, then shifted his gaze. "I'll manage without him. But what about you?"

She looked puzzled. "I'll be fine."

"I mean, are you up to operating with me? Owens is a general surgeon. You're probably used to gallbladder and uterine excisions, not keeping someone under and stable while I tinker around in his brain for eight or ten hours."

"Caleb does a little of everything. Slate Hollow's a small place. You have to be flexible." A hint of defensiveness had crept into her voice. Adam suppressed a momentary twinge of conscience. She was a colleague, a professional. They'd be working together for the next three weeks. He was barking at her as if she was a not-too-bright first-year intern.

"Ever scrubbed for brain surgery before?"

"You mean other than bashing a patient on the head with a hammer, while Caleb drilled through his skull with the Black and Decker Two Speed to let out the evil spirits?"

"I didn't mean—"

She cut him off. "Yes, you did." She was right. He couldn't deny it without lying through his teeth, so he kept quiet. Neurosurgeons were considered the glamour boys of medicine and had a reputation for being arrogant and imperious. He'd just reinforced the stereotype, big time. "The answer is yes, Doctor. I have worked with your kind before."

Your kind. The emphasis on the words was so slight most people wouldn't have noticed, but he did. He almost smiled. She was a fighter. Good. They would need that kind of grit and stamina where they were going. "I apologize," he said. "B.J. told me he always gets the best people for these jaunts. He was right. What I should have asked you was if you'd had experience operating under...less-than-ideal conditions.''

He'd almost said battlefield conditions. What had made those words pop into his head? Was it because, below a sleeveless white tank top that molded itself nicely to her breasts, she wore desert-patterned utilities, fatigues to everyone but an ex-Marine, and combat boots—a look that was decidedly military. Or because the past was growing stronger with every mile they flew, bringing long-guarded memories dangerously close to the surface?

She glanced down at the U.S. Marine Corps emblem tattoo on his left forearm, partially visible below the rolled-back cuff of his shirt, a souvenir of his first liberty after boot camp at Parris Island all those years ago. ''I've been around the block a few times, Marine. I won't bug out on you.'' She gave him a mocking little salute and headed down the aisle toward the front of the plane.

He closed his eyes but could still see the proud tilt of her head, the sway of her hips in the baggy utilities that tried hard but couldn't completely hide the fact she was all woman. Three weeks in close proximity to Leah Gentry was going to be very interesting. And maybe, just maybe, it would be interesting enough to keep him from losing what was left of his mind.

''MAY I JOIN YOU?'' Leah asked Kaylene Smiley, the mission's head nurse, as she came abreast of the older woman's seat. She and Kaylene had met for the first time in the lounge at O'Hare the evening before. Dr. Roger Crenshaw, the anesthesiologist Leah would be working with in Dalat, and Kaylene were playing gin rummy on a folded-down tray.

"Of course. Roger just won my last nickel. You've saved me from losing another hand and being in his debt," Kaylene said.

"It's a good time for a break," Roger agreed. "I'm going to use the lavatory before the plane lands. If you ladies will excuse me." The elderly physician stood up, pocketed his small pile of winnings and with a courtly gesture offered Leah his seat.

"What do you suppose it will be like there? Saigon, I mean. The only pictures I've ever seen are from the war. And in the movies." Kaylene was looking out the window as she spoke.

"They make most of the movies in Bangkok, you know. There are parts of it that look like Saigon did during the war." Shielded by the high back of the airplane seat, Leah tried to shake the feeling that Adam Sauder's eyes were boring burr holes into the back of her head in preparation for taking it off her shoulders.

"Really? I didn't know."

"I have three brothers, all making a career of the military, and my dad just retired after thirty years in the army. So I know about war movies." Leah also leaned forward and looked out the window at the green tangle of jungle and rice paddies visible below.

"You're wearing dog tags," Kaylene observed. "Were you in the service, too?"

"Yes, I'm an army reservist now."

"My brother was here in 1967. He was stationed near Dalat, where we'll be staying. I never thought I'd come here." Kaylene returned to looking out the plane window. "According to the travel books, Dalat's supposed to be a beautiful place. The brass from both sides vacationed there during the war, but my brother can't imagine why I wanted to come on this mission. He said he'd never come back—never in a million years."

THE PLANE ROLLED to a standstill, the stairs were drawn up and the door opened. Brilliant sunlight poured into the cabin as Adam walked out to meet his past. Much had changed. Oh, yes, there was still the same heat, the same stifling humidity, the smell of hot oil, metal and concrete baking in the sun, and the guard posts between the runways he'd manned as a nineteen-year-old Marine corporal still stood. But the sandbags were gone. And the skeletons of crashed and burned aircraft that had made takeoffs and landings so dangerous toward the end of the war had been hauled away. Most of the other buildings he might have recognized were gone, destroyed in the final hours before the airport had been abandoned to the conquering Vietcong.

But it was the sounds that were the most different. In fact, it was the lack of noise that marked the biggest change. There wasn't another aircraft in sight. Their chartered Air Vietnam jet was the only plane landing or taking off. It was quiet, eerily so. Absent from the scene was the drone of helicopter blades, the whine of fighter jets taking off and landing, the roar of cargo planes evacuating load after load of civilians....

Adam shut down his recollections with an efficiency that was the result of long years of practice, retreating behind the buffer zone of reserve most doctors learned to erect around themselves early on in their careers, or else they risked losing their sanity. From that perspective he could view Than Son Nhut from a place outside himself where he observed, but didn't participate in, what was going on. He spent a lot of time in that limbolike state these days, and every time he went there he found it harder and harder to come back.

"Damn, Adam. Did you ever think we'd be back?"

It was B.J. at his elbow, a duffel bag slung over his shoulder, a wondering look on his face. B.J. was a millionaire fifty times over, but you'd never know it from the way he looked or dressed, or from the luggage he carried.

"No," Adam said truthfully. "I never expected to come back."

"It's friggin' spooky. I half expect a MIG to come screaming out of the sky the way it did that day and strafe the runway, or a sniper to start taking potshots at us when we unload the plane." His expression darkened as he looked around him, but a moment later his usual good-natured smile returned. He mopped at his red face with a blue bandanna he pulled out of the back pocket of his jeans. Then he tied the four corners of the bandanna into knots and put the makeshift hat on his balding head. "I'm going to have to get myself a cover. I forgot how friggin' hot the sun is here." He looked sourly at Adam's full head of hair. "Some guys have all the luck."

Adam and B.J. had gone through boot camp and infantry training together, and ended up with the same duty assignment, attached to the embassy in Saigon.

A cushy assignment anyplace else on earth. In Saigon in 1975 it was the stuff of nightmares. They'd arrived in country just before Christmas in 1974 and left in April of '75. B.J. on an Evac flight after a sniper's bullet hit the tire of a jeep he was driving, causing it to flip over on him, and Adam aboard one of the last helicopters off the airfield. But at least they'd gotten out alive; many hadn't.

"Yeah, all the luck in the world," Adam said.

"Mr. Walton?" It was Leah Gentry again. She was wearing a boonie cap in the same shades of brown as her utilities and mirrored sunglasses. She had a decidedly unmilitary, traffic-stopping, lime-green backpack with a picture of Minnie Mouse emblazoned on it slung over one shoulder, and in her other hand she carried a large, locked, fire-engine-red toolbox. "Sir, I was wondering if I could speak to you for a moment."

"Hey, don't go calling me sir." B.J. grinned.

"Yes, sir, B.J." Her lips tightened momentarily, then curved into a heart-stopping smile.

"Never made it past PFC, myself. Adam here was a corporal, though. No wait. You ended up with sergeant's stripes before you got out, didn't you, Marine?"

Adam ignored his friend's question. "I think she's deferring to your age, not your rank."

B.J. laughed loudly enough to turn heads in their direction. "That's a low blow, buddy." He turned to Leah. "And even more of a reason for you to cease and desist, Captain, ma'am."

"Captain?" Adam repeated.

"Officer on deck, old pal," B.J. said, slapping

Adam on the back as he made his little joke. "Ms. Gentry here's an officer in the United States Army."

"You're active duty?" He hadn't expected that. He'd noticed the utilities, but had her pegged for a military wanna-be or maybe a weekend warrior, not regular army.

"Reserves since '94."

"Desert Storm?"

B.J. answered first. "And Somalia and Bosnia. I told you I only get the best. Leah knows the ropes. And she's not going to go into a screaming panic if the lights go out or some ex-Charlie bureaucrat with delusions of grandeur starts hasslin' us about our paperwork. We're damned lucky to have her, so don't go giving her a hard time."

"It's too late," Leah said mildly. "Mr. Walton, could you spare me one of the interpreters to run interference with the customs officer?" She lifted the big metal case a few inches. "I've got everything I need to work in here. I don't want any of it confiscated by some round-butt desk jockey with an overactive sense of duty or a quick eye for a bribe. If I don't work, Dr. Sauder doesn't, either. Or anyone else, for that matter," she concluded with a grin.

"I'll walk you through myself," B.J. said, suddenly all business. "It's liable to take some time to get us all through the red tape, so we might as well start with you. The commies may have lost the cold war, but they won the paperwork one. Then I'm coming back to ask for volunteers to stay with the plane. I don't intend to see any of our stuff get 'liberated' by any of those desk jockeys you mentioned and end up on the black market. Can I count on you, Captain?''

"Certainly. Just tell me when.''

"I'd like to get everyone squared away at the hotel ASAP. Would you be willing to take the first shift with the plane? I'll leave Adam here with you. Got a problem with that, Marine?'' B.J. asked in a softly challenging tone. He had made his peace with the past. He knew Adam had not.

"No," Adam said. "No problem.''

"Great. It's settled, then. I'll make sure the government liaison guy they promised to have waiting for us gets us some guards. Once they're stationed around the plane all you have to do is stick around a while to make sure they stay honest. Piece of cake.''

Adam wasn't so sure of that, but maybe with Leah Gentry to keep him company, he could fill the silence of the present with the sound of her voice and keep the horror of the past at bay.

CHAPTER TWO

ADAM WALKED OUT onto the balcony of his hotel room to greet the sunrise in a country he'd hoped never to see again.

"Good morning, Doctor. You're up early."

He swung around. Leah Gentry was standing on another postage-stamp-size balcony next to his. She looked fresh and rested, even though they hadn't gotten to their hotel rooms until after midnight the night before. "Good morning. Is that coffee you're drinking?" He'd given up alcohol years ago, cut down on his red meat and smoked only the occasional cigar, but he'd refused to give up coffee.

"Yep. I made it myself." She laughed, the wonderful, lilting laugh he'd found himself beginning to crave as though it were...coffee. "I'm not fit for human company if I don't get my fix in the morning, so Mom sent along one of those little coffeemakers and every conceivable electrical adapter. Luckily one of them worked. The wiring in this hotel is... eccentric," she finished diplomatically. "Would you like a cup? The door's unlocked. Help yourself."

"Thanks, I'll be right over," he heard himself say, and wasn't as surprised as he would have been only twenty-four hours earlier.

The time they'd spent together at Than Son Nhut

hadn't been as bad as he'd expected. True to his word, B.J. had gotten Leah and her tackle box full of anesthetic drugs and instruments through customs in under an hour, some kind of record in Vietnam. And true to his word, the Vietnamese official had shown up with his armed guards—sober young men dressed in dull green fatigues and pith helmets that sported a red star. With AK-47s slung over their shoulders, they took their places on each side of the hangar door.

Left alone in the vast echoing space, he and Leah had made small talk, played gin rummy on Leah's tackle box and listened to the drumming of rain on the metal roof. It was November, the tail end of the rainy season, so the downpour lasted for less than an hour, instead of half the day.

The sun was setting when the rain stopped. The air had cooled ever so slightly. Leah produced apples and oranges, peanut butter and cheese crackers and bottled water from her backpack. They shared their makeshift meal with the guards, who spoke English far better than Adam spoke Vietnamese. As darkness fell, a little battery-powered lantern materialized from yet another pocket of Leah's backpack. It fought the darkness to a standstill in a small circle around them.

As the hours slowly passed, he'd kept her talking about her work, about growing up an army brat and about her family. He'd learned her parents were retired, her father after thirty years in the military, her mother after a career as a teacher. One brother was a U.S. Navy SEAL, one a navy chaplain, the third an army Green Beret.

And in return he had given up a few details of his own life during the dark minutes before midnight—

broken home, one brother, who lived in California, he saw only now and then. Both parents dead. They'd lived hard and died young, he'd told her. She hadn't asked for more details and he hadn't offered them. He told her about the judge who'd given him the choice of joining the U.S. Marine Corps, or going to jail for a joyride that had resulted in a totaled car. He'd taken advantage of college courses the Corps offered, found he was a good student and went on to medical school. And then the unrelenting grind of a neurosurgical internship and residency, followed by one marriage, one son, one divorce and all the nightmares he could handle. This last he hadn't spoken aloud.

Than Son Nhut he'd faced and survived. This morning it was Saigon. The city had fallen to the victorious enemy only one day after his helicopter had lifted off the airfield. He wondered if Leah's company might be as potent a talisman against the past today as it had been yesterday.

He walked the few feet down the hallway to her room and pushed open the louvered door. Her accommodations were identical to his—high ceiling, white walls, sheer curtains at the French doors. The place had once been a villa that belonged to a South Vietnamese general, B.J. had told him. Now it was a hotel, a joint venture between the Vietnamese and an Australian firm. They were trying hard, but they hadn't gotten it quite right yet. The rooms were clean, the toilets worked, and there was hot water, but no soap and only one towel in the communal bathroom. The electricity was eccentric, as Leah had said. To turn on the ceiling fan, he'd had to hook two bare wires together, and there was no such thing as room service.

Leah must have heard him enter the room. "There's whitener in those little packets," she called from the balcony.

"No, thanks. Black is fine." He couldn't help himself to her coffee and then just leave, walk back into his room and stare at the walls, so he made himself move through the doors onto the balcony to stand beside her.

Saigon was up with the sun. The dusty, tree-lined street below was crowded with bicycles, motor scooters and *cyclos,* the bicycle-rickshaws that served as taxicabs and couriers everywhere in Vietnam. There were also a few cars and buses, but completely absent were marked lanes and traffic signals, at least none that anyone was obeying. Traffic moved in both directions on both sides of the street. It was every man for himself.

Leah was leaning over the railing watching what went on below. She was wearing a flowered cotton skirt that ended just above her ankles and a short-sleeved pink blouse that complemented her creamy skin. Her mink-brown hair was pulled back into a French braid so complicated he wondered how she could accomplish it on her own. There was nothing even vaguely military about her appearance. Today she was all woman.

"How does anyone manage to cross the street safely?" she asked.

"Like that," Adam pointed with his coffee mug. A man with two young children in tow waded, undaunted, into the traffic. Miraculously, bicycles, *cy-*

clos, motor scooters, even a bus, swerved to miss him and the children.

Leah let out her breath in a *whoosh.* "They made it," she said, turning to Adam with amazement on her face. "You just start walking. Show no fear. It's like my dad said it would be."

"Your dad was here?"

"In '65 and '68," she said.

"He was in the country during the Tet offensive?"

She nodded. "That's where he got his Purple Heart. He wants to come back, but Mom says no more. She's never going anywhere that requires a passport again. We moved eleven times in fifteen years. I'm sorry. I told you all this last night, didn't I."

"I enjoyed it," he said. She blinked. He'd spoken too tersely. He was out of the habit of making small talk with a woman.

"I'm going to do some sight-seeing right after breakfast. Dad wants pictures of the embassy and Chinatown, and I want to tour the presidential palace. They've kept it exactly as it was the day the North Vietnamese marched into the city. Want to come along?"

"No." Again, too terse. "I mean, I...I hadn't thought about it."

She rested her hip against the stone railing and looked at him over the rim of her coffee mug. "Of course, you were here before. You said so last night." She turned her head, her gaze moving in the direction of the abandoned American Embassy. "It's so different—not what I expected at all. My impressions were shaped by those videos of the last days—pictures of tanks and soldiers with guns, mobs of terrified people fighting to get out. But this... It's as if the war never happened.''

"For most of these people it didn't,'' he said. "Vietnam is a young country. Half the people here were born after the war. They don't want to look back. They want to move forward.'' Good advice. Too damned bad he couldn't follow it himself.

B.J. appeared on Adam's balcony. "Hey, buddy, there you are. You left your door unlocked, did you know that?'' He waved a greeting. "Good morning, Leah.''

"Good morning, B.J.''

"Leah has coffee.'' Adam moved to the edge of the balcony and surveyed his friend across the few feet separating them. B.J. was wearing jeans and a Hawaiian-print shirt in shades of pink and orange. His red baseball cap was emblazoned with the Marine Corps emblem in gold.

"So does the hotel restaurant, old buddy. *Café filtre* and baguettes. Delicious.''

Leah laughed and held out her mug. "You mean I dragged a coffeemaker all the way from Kentucky for nothing?''

"Nope. I'm only saying they've got great coffee in the hotel. Hospital coffee is the same the world over—not fit to drink. I doubt it's any different at Dalat. You'll get plenty of use out of it there.''

"Any word on when we'll be moving out?''

B.J. poked at a piece of crumbling balcony railing with the toe of his shoe. "That's what I came to tell you. The trucks pulled up at the airport about an hour ago. If there's any sight-seeing you want to do, I suggest you do it this morning. We'll be leaving here before noon. Don't want to get stranded overnight somewhere along the highway. Luckily the day starts early here. Most of the shops are open by seven, the museums, too. Some of the others have already left the hotel. If you apply yourself, you should be able to see a little of the city and at least hit the antique shops on Dong Khoi Street."

"An excellent plan, B.J. If you gentlemen will excuse me, I'll be on my way."

"Why don't you go with her, Adam? Take her to the embassy and the presidential palace," his friend suggested.

"No." His voice was harsh. Striving to soften it, he added, "I figured I'd go back to the airport with you. Make sure everything's okay."

"Not necessary. I've paid all the fees and a few plain, old-fashioned bribes. Nothing's going to go missing. Head out with Leah and get a souvenir to take home to Brian. Have your picture taken in front of the embassy. Better yet, have a beer on me if you can find the Tiger's Den."

"It's too early for a beer, and I doubt the Tiger's Den survived the reunification." The panic-filled streets of the defeated city he'd known were long gone, but he wasn't interested in trying to find the bar he and B.J. and their buddies had hung out in.

"I don't need a chaperon," Leah said. "I'll find my own way."

"I know you will. It's Adam I'm worried about. Lousy sense of direction. Gets lost all the time. Why I remember one night in Norfolk—"

"Stow it, B.J. You lead," he said to Leah. "I'll follow."

She stayed where she was. "But I thought—"

"I changed my mind. I'd like to go if you're willing to put up with my company."

She studied his face for a moment and he endured the scrutiny. He had the feeling she could see all the way to the center of his soul, but that was ridiculous. If she could really see what was inside him, she'd turn and run like the sane and sensible woman she was. Instead, she said, "Okay, let's go."

LEAH WALKED DOWN the vaulted hallway with Adam Sauder on one side and B. J. Walton on the other. She was glad none of her brothers were around to see what she was up to. They'd teased her about picking up strays all her life. Usually it was the four-legged kind, puppies with sore paws or homeless kittens, but she tended to do the same thing with people. Most of the others probably couldn't see the pain behind Adam Sauder's dark gaze, but she did, and it should have warned her to stay away. Instead, she found herself riding down to the lobby in the elaborately grilled elevator, saying goodbye to B.J., hailing a double *cyclo* and moving out into the bewildering stream of traffic with him still at her side.

Their *cyclo* driver was a young man of French and Vietnamese descent who spoke excellent English. He maneuvered them skillfully through the heavy traffic, taking them directly to the abandoned American Embassy, a concrete-and-glass fortress every bit as ugly as it had looked in the news footage on TV. The building had a sad, defeated air about it, Leah thought. Someone had hung laundry in one of the old guard towers. She sat quietly for a moment, Adam equally silent beside her. Then they climbed out of the *cyclo* and stood by the gates where she had seen videos of refugees trying to climb over, of grim-faced young Marines on the wall pulling others into the compound, of overloaded helicopters taking off from the roof.

She'd brought her camera, and without her asking him Adam took her picture in front of the gates, and then their driver took a picture of both of them together. Her father's ghosts were close. She could feel their eyes on the back of her neck. "Were you here?" she asked Adam.

He shook his head. "I never got this far." His expression appeared set, his jaw clenched. Leah didn't ask any more questions about the past.

They didn't stop to tour the presidential palace. She didn't know what she was going to tell her dad when she got back, but she'd think of something. Most likely the truth. *I went there with a Marine who was in Saigon at the end. He didn't want to go inside, so we didn't.* Her dad would understand.

Instead they took B.J.'s advice and went shopping. Their driver took them to a small, bustling marketplace. It was alive, wall-to-wall, with sights and sounds and smells that were raucous and tantalizing, unfamiliar and fascinating. Leah stood for a long minute just looking around. Street vendors peddled their wares on every corner. Food stands crowded storefronts, shoppers jostled one another as they ogled the merchandise. Vietnam was still a Communist country, and poor, but you would never know it by the stacks and boxes and cartons of VCRs, televisions, CD players and microwave ovens piled inside the tiny stores, spilling outside onto the sidewalk, lashed to *cyclos* and bicycles, and stacked in pushcarts.

She bought a pale blue silk *ao dai,* the traditional slim dress and loose pants worn by Vietnamese women, for her mother. Exactly like the one her father had brought home thirty years ago, but three sizes larger. Then she bought a mint-green one for herself. She chose greeting cards with beautiful, silk-screen paintings of craggy green mountains and mist-covered valleys that she could frame for Caleb Owens and his wife, Margaret. Also one for Juliet Trent, the pregnant teenager she had befriended. That left only her brothers, and for them she bought carvings of elephants and of smiling old men smoking their pipes and wearing the traditional conical hats called *lo nan.*

Adam stayed by her side saying little, waiting patiently. He didn't buy anything, not even for his son, Brian. She knew his name, knew he was nineteen and a sophomore at Harvard. Adam had told her that much the night before. But she knew nothing beyond those few facts, certainly not why his father wasn't buying him a gift from this exotic and fascinating place.

Like the stray animals Leah had rescued in the past, once or twice she'd become involved with stray men—men with haunted eyes and sad smiles like Adam Sauder. Trying to heal wounded souls was much harder than healing wounded bodies, she'd learned to her sorrow. His hurts and heartaches were none of her business. This time she wasn't going to get involved. She was going to protect herself for a change. She saw him pick up a watch, turn it over, then put it down again.

"Do you suppose it's really a Rolex? For only a hundred dollars?" There was a sign in English above the table of watches. There were a lot of signs in English, nothing in Russian. The few Russians who came now didn't have money to spend. The Americans and Australians did.

"I doubt it, but it's a very good knockoff."

"It would be a nice gift for your son."

He picked the watch up again, unbuttoned his shirt pocket and took out a money clip. The shopkeeper appeared in front of them as if by magic. "You like?"

"I'll take it." Adam peeled off five twenties and handed the man the money. He didn't bargain for a better price.

"Engrave for free," the smiling shopkeeper said. "Remember Saigon always."

"I don't need a watch for that." But Adam handed it to him, anyway.

"What do you say on it?"

"For Brian—" Adam began.

Suddenly there was a small stampede of sandaled feet, and from out of nowhere came a whole gaggle of children of all ages, all sizes, from toddlers to young adolescents, who swirled around them. Street children. There were many of them in Saigon, some orphaned, some not. Left behind in the headlong rush to prosperity, they roamed the streets living hand-to-mouth.

"*Nguoi My! Nguoi My!*" It meant American. Leah had learned it from her phrase book. "Friends, give us money—dollars."

She wished there was more she could do to help, but she'd learned the hard way you couldn't save the world all by yourself. At least, she could do her small part and make today a little better for them. She slipped her hand into her skirt pocket to fish out a couple of dollar bills she had stashed there.

The children became even noisier when they saw the money. They began to jump up and down, laughing and giggling, demanding more. The shopkeeper waved them away. They ignored him, crowding around Adam and Leah and plucking at their clothes. A couple tugged the straps of her backpack. Leah laughed and tugged back. The shopkeeper picked up a broom resting by the door and made sweeping motions toward the children, still scolding in Vietnamese. The boys shouted. The little girls squealed, and one of the smallest started crying.

Leah glanced over at Adam. His face was as white as his shirt. A look of pure horror.

The shopkeeper shooed the children out into the street. Leah held her breath and watched them until they were safely on the other side of the narrow, crowded roadway. She turned back as the ebb and flow of Saigon street life surrounded her again. She was alone. She looked around. Adam was already a hundred feet away and walking fast. Surely he hadn't turned tail and run because a group of kids had hustled them for a couple of dollars. Then she remembered the look on his face and thought maybe he had. She watched him go, a head taller than everyone else around him.

"Adam, wait! Your watch." She might as well have saved her breath. The level of street noise made it impossible for him to hear her. She didn't think he would have stopped if he had. He'd left her alone in the middle of a strange city without a word of explanation. She had every right to be angry with him, but she wasn't. Being stranded didn't worry her—she could take care of herself. What bothered her was the memory of that look on his face. She wanted to know what had put it there. She wanted to help take it away—and that bothered her most of all.

CHAPTER THREE

A DELIVERY-TRUCK DRIVER made a U-turn in the middle of the street two blocks from the market, tying up traffic in every direction, when Leah was heading back to the hotel. It took her driver almost an hour to maneuver his *cyclo* through the snarl. When she finally arrived, the bus to take them to Dalat was waiting, engine idling. She paid the driver and hurried to her room. While packing, she listened for sounds of movement from Adam's suite, but heard nothing. She couldn't stop wondering where he was and what he was doing. She couldn't forget the horror she'd glimpsed on his face—an old horror, familiar and long remembered. It sent a shiver of dread up and down her spine. When she left her room, she knocked on his door. There was no answer. She hadn't really expected there would be.

Adam wasn't in the lobby. He wasn't on the sidewalk outside the hotel. He wasn't on the bus. She shoved her duffel bag into the overhead bin and looked around. The passengers were all women, except for Roger Crenshaw.

"Glad you're here, Leah. Only two more to come," he said, putting a tick beside her name on the clipboard he was holding.

"Join me. We're almost ready to leave." Kaylene smiled and beckoned from across the aisle.

"Where are the others?" Leah asked, sliding onto the cracked leather seat beside the woman she already considered a friend.

"B.J. and most of the men left for the airport—" Kaylene glanced at her watch "—half an hour ago."

"Dr. Sauder, too?"

"Yes, I believe I saw him with the group."

Leah was relieved to learn that Adam had made it safely back to the hotel. Something of what she was feeling must have shown on her face, for Kaylene looked as if she wanted to say more. But just then the bus doors screeched shut on unoiled hinges behind the final two members of the group. Moments later they pulled out onto the street, parting the waves of opposing traffic like a whale in a school of shrimp.

The ride to Dalat was one of the most nerve-racking experiences of Leah's life. The highway out of Saigon was crowded with all manner of vehicles, from eighteen-wheelers to high-wheeled carts pulled by water buffalo. There were seventies-era American cars, Japanese motor scooters, Chinese trucks and buses, cyclists and pedestrians, and no one paid any more attention to the traffic laws here than they had in Saigon. There seemed to be only one rule of the road: have a horn and use it. It was a long, harrowing drive, and even the beauty of the mist-washed hillsides was not enough to take Leah's mind off their driver's suicidal tendency to pass other vehicles on the winding stretches of narrow roadway with sheer, unguarded drops only inches from the bus's wheels.

The sun had set and the short twilight had almost

faded when they arrived at the hospital compound in the jungle, several miles outside the hill-country city of Dalat. Father Gerard, the French Canadian priest in charge of the hospital, and two of the nuns, whom he introduced as Sister Grace and Sister Janet, came out of the square, two-story, brick building to welcome them.

Leah took a moment to look around and get her bearings before following the white-cassocked Father Gerard and the others on a tour of the compound. To the west of the hospital was a church made out of the same dusty-red brick, its copper-roofed steeple green with age. Grouped between the two buildings were half-a-dozen thatched-roof huts. Smoke from cooking fires curled through holes in the roofs while small children played outside in the dirt, among chickens and potbellied pigs. Here, Father Gerard explained, as he led them to their rooms in two larger communal huts, the families and friends of hospital patients stayed while their loved ones underwent treatment.

They drew names out of a hat for room assignments, and Leah and Kaylene found themselves paired up, an arrangement that suited them both. Their room was at the end of the long building closest to the hospital. Barely big enough to turn around in, it held two hard, narrow beds draped with mosquito netting, a small table and one chair, a metal washbowl and pitcher. A single bare lightbulb hung from the ceiling. The hospital had electricity provided from Dalat, but in the compound there was only an aging generator that produced electricity for two hours at dusk and one hour in the morning. Showers and toilets were in the hospital building. The kitchen and refectory were there, too.

The evening meal had been held for them. They took their places at the long benched tables and the Vietnamese nuns brought them soup thick with noodles and bits of pork and chicken. It was spicier than anything Leah had ever eaten, but delicious. The rest of the meal consisted of steamed rice, stale French bread, dried fruit—and tea—no coffee. Adam wouldn't like that, Leah thought. When they'd finished eating, they toured the wards and the operating suites. It was dark by the time they returned to their rooms to unpack. The generator shut down at eight as advertised. They undressed by candlelight and were in bed by nine.

Leah was so tired she ached in every muscle, but still she couldn't sleep. Where were the supply trucks? They should have arrived by now. The highway they'd traveled was treacherous enough in daylight. At night, with only the moon to guide them, it would be even more dangerous. She stared into the darkness and listened to the unfamiliar but comforting sound of Kaylene's gentle snoring. She found herself straining to hear the sound of trucks laboring up the steep grade to the hospital compound. What if something had happened to them? To B.J. and the others? To Adam?

She forced herself to relax. There was nothing she could do to get the trucks and their occupants here any faster, and tomorrow was going to be a long, busy day. The two operating suites would have to be evaluated and arranged to the surgeons' satisfaction. The electrician would have to get the generator that would power all their high-tech equipment and computers up and running. All the surgical instruments had to be checked and checked again. There would be patients to evaluate, operating schedules to draw up. But still she couldn't sleep. Instead, she watched the luminous hands of her travel clock creep forward in slow circles until at last her vigil was rewarded with the unmistakable sound of heavy trucks pulling into the compound.

They were here. They were safe. *He* was safe. Leah closed her eyes, but it wasn't until she heard the low rumble of Adam's voice as he exchanged greetings with Father Gerard that she relaxed enough to fall asleep.

THUNDER RUMBLED in the distance, barely audible above the steady roar of the generator on the other side of the wall. Adam looked out the operating room's one small window, saw the dark clouds rolling down from the mountains and knew they were in for a downpour. He would be surprised if they didn't get a thunderstorm at this time of the afternoon every day for the next three weeks. He saw Leah Gentry glance over her shoulder to the same spot and then continue her conversation with Roger Crenshaw.

He'd been avoiding her all day. He owed her an apology and an explanation. The apology he could handle; the explanation he wasn't so sure about. Adam watched as Leah and Roger inspected a pressure gauge they'd just unpacked. Roger would oversee the larger operating room next door where the orthopedic and general surgeons would set up shop. He and Leah would work together here. The generator's staccato beat stuttered and faltered. The lights flickered and dimmed, then steadied again. Leah dropped a screwdriver on the cement floor and mumbled an apology in his direction.

He acknowledged it with a nod and went on checking his own instruments, thousands of dollars' worth of specialized scalpels and retractors, drills and clamps. He hadn't bothered to keep them with him on the plane, as Leah had with her red toolbox. If they'd been lost, he wouldn't have to operate. He could have turned tail and run back to Chicago. He closed the case and set it on the table by the antique autoclave in the corner. From now on they were Kaylene Smiley's responsibility.

Roger Crenshaw left the room, and Adam found himself standing at the head of the operating table watching Leah work. "Everything check out okay?" he asked.

She was apparently so involved in what she was doing it took a moment for his words to sink in. Then she looked at him and blinked. There were dark smudges beneath her eyes, as though she hadn't slept well. She probably hadn't, if her bed was as hard and uncomfortable as his.

She smiled tentatively, obviously not quite certain how to handle him after yesterday's disappearing act. Her hair was in the same French braid as before, but today little curling wisps had escaped to brush against her cheek and the nape of her neck. "The humidity is giving me fits. Everything's sticking or jumping around." She tapped one of the gauges with the tip of her fingernail.

"B.J. said they'll have the air conditioner installed

soon.'' Even though it was cooler in the hills this time of year than in Saigon, the humidity would play havoc with the delicate instruments on which both he and Leah relied. The air conditioner was a necessity, not a luxury.

''I'll run one more check when it's up and going. Then I'm ready whenever you are.''

''We start patient evaluations first thing in the morning. Would you like to sit in on mine?'' Back at St. B's he let his residents do most of the face-to-face work. These days he kept his distance from his patients, especially the youngest ones.

''Thank you, I would. Caleb and I work together that way. I like to have a feel for the patient. There's more to anesthesia than just checking height and weight, and looking up dosages on a chart.'' She tilted her head slightly and smiled at him.

Adam had been waiting for that smile, and the realization made him angry at himself. He took it out on Leah. ''This isn't going to be fun and games. It's triage. The oldest, the youngest, the sickest—those are the ones who can't beat the odds, the ones we'll have to pass over.''

Her smile disappeared. ''I know that.''

''B.J.'s done a hell of a job getting me what I need to operate here, but it's still a Third World setup. No heroics. No miracles. Some are going to make it and some aren't. Can you handle that, too?'' He looked down at his hands, balled into fists on the metal table. He sounded like the soulless medical machine he was becoming.

''I can live with the tough calls,'' she said quietly. ''Can you?''

He ignored her question. Losing your soul didn't mean you had to behave like a jackass. "I'm sorry," he said. "I shouldn't have talked to you like that. We'll do our best for all our patients. We'll do fine together."

"I always give my patients one hundred percent. I'm sure you do, too."

She didn't sound completely mollified, but he forged ahead. "And while I'm at it, I also want to apologize for leaving you stranded yesterday."

"I can take care of myself."

"I know you can. That has nothing to do with it. My behavior was uncalled-for."

"I have your watch," she said unexpectedly.

The statement and the change of subject caught him off guard. "My watch?"

"The one you bought for your son."

He'd forgotten all about it. He'd forgotten everything but the past the moment he heard the smallest of the street urchins begin to cry. Leah reached into the pocket of her shorts and pulled out the wristwatch. She handed it to him. It was warm from the heat of her body. "Thanks," he said.

"I had the shopkeeper engrave it."

Adam turned the watch over. *To Brian. With Love, Dad. Saigon, 1999.*

With love. How long had it been since he'd told his son he loved him?

She waited as the silence grew between them. A frown creased her forehead. "It's my turn to apologize, it seems. I'm sorry. I shouldn't have presumed. I'll pay to have the inscription removed."

He stuck the watch into his pocket and twisted his

mouth into a smile. "No, it's fine. Thank you for taking the trouble. Thanks for everything." He turned to walk away. Leah reached out and laid her hand on his arm. A current of energy had passed between them when his hand had brushed hers moments before. He'd ignored it. This time he couldn't.

"What happened there at the marketplace? Why did you take off like that?"

"It was nothing. Not enough sleep and too much sun."

"It was more than that."

The storm had rolled down off the mountain. Now the thunder crashed directly overhead. She didn't even flinch. He knew he was going to have to tell her something, perhaps even the truth, or at least a portion of it.

"Was it being in that marketplace? Or was it being in Saigon?"

Damn, she's persistent. "It was—" The lights went out. There was no blinding flash of lightning or crash of thunder, but the room was suddenly dark except for the small rectangle of light coming from the window. The rain still pounded on the roof, but the rhythmic stutter of the generator had ceased. It was a distraction, the answer to an unvoiced prayer. "The generator's out," he said unnecessarily.

"Do you think it was hit by lightning?" There was a quiver in her voice.

"No. It's right outside the window. I think we would have known if lightning had struck it."

"Of course. How stupid of me. It probably just ran out of gas." He heard Leah suck in a sharp breath, saw her turn toward the light.

He smiled. He couldn't help himself. "Don't tell me you're afraid of storms."

She slid off her stool, looking at him over her shoulder. She moved toward the window, a darker silhouette against the pale rectangle of murky light. "Of course not." She laughed a little self-consciously. "But I'm not very comfortable in the dark. Isn't it silly? I'm thirty-one years old and I sleep with a night-light."

"Don't tell me you lay awake all night staring into the darkness to keep the monsters at bay." Why had he said that? Because it was what he did every night?

"I'm not sleeping alone," she said.

"Does it help not sleeping alone?" He had a sudden vision of her in bed with a man. He didn't like it. Some of what he was thinking must have seeped into his voice.

She spun around, bringing them within a step of each other. He reached out and steadied her with his hands on her shoulders. He couldn't see her blush, but he was certain she did. "I didn't mean it that way. I mean, having a roommate. Besides, I have a clock with an enormous fluorescent dial. It's practically as good as a night-light." She turned the tables on him. "What comes for you in the dark?"

"No, Leah." Then he stopped her from saying more with his mouth. He'd meant only to silence her, but her lips were so soft and warm....

She pulled away. "You don't have to kiss me to shut me up. I won't insist that you explain to me what happened yesterday," she whispered, her breath warm against his lips.

"I'm not kissing you to shut you up. Not anymore.'' She opened her mouth and let him inside to explore. She tasted of mint and cola. Her tongue touched his and something inside him flared with a white-hot flame, searing his heart. He pulled her close. Her breasts pressed against his chest, her softness against his sudden erection. He kissed her harder. He could go on kissing her forever, more than kissing her, making love to her over and over again. Adam found the fantasy taking hold of his heart and his brain. He wanted all of her, the way he hadn't wanted a woman for a long, long time. ''You don't have to be alone in the dark, Leah. Stay with me tonight,'' he said before the barriers of self-control could slam down on his need for her.

She shook her head, but didn't step out of his arms. ''That's not a good idea.''

He could hear voices beyond the wall, a mixture of French, Vietnamese and English. People were working on the generator. Before he knew it the lights would come back on. The intimacy of near darkness would be erased. ''What's wrong with both of us taking comfort from each other?'' He could feel her pulling back and he tightened his arms around her. ''Don't go,'' he whispered against her hair. It was half plea, half command. He found her mouth again.

She relaxed against him for a handful of heartbeats, kissed him back and then pushed away, her hands on his chest. Her breasts rose and fell with her quickened breathing. There was a look of wonder on her face, and he knew their kisses had affected her as strongly as they had him. It was a warning signal he should have heeded, but he did not. ''Stay with me, Leah.''

She shook her head. ''No. I don't sleep with colleagues. I don't do one-night stands.'' She took another step away. He let his palms slide along her arms, then manacled her wrists with his hands, keeping her close.

''This wouldn't be a one-night stand.''

''I'm not good at short, intense affairs, either.''

''Leah. I...'' He couldn't say ''I need you'' because she would demand to know why, and maybe he would tell her, and then the thin plate of armor separating him from his private version of hell would buckle and melt away, and he would be lost. ''We would be good together,'' he finished lamely.

''Another reason it's not a good idea.''

He felt a chuckle working its way up into his throat and didn't hold it back. ''Thank you, I think.''

She smiled, too, but it was a little off center. ''There is something between us, physically. I'm not denying it. But there are other reasons it's not a good idea. You're heartsore, Adam, and I'm not the woman to take away your pain. I know, I've tried before....'' She lifted her hand to his cheek just as the generator kicked in beyond the wall, and the lights flickered back to life. ''The truth of the matter is that I don't think we should be alone with each other outside this room anymore.''

CHAPTER FOUR

LEAH RESTED HER HEAD against the back of the old, canvas chaise longue and closed her eyes. They had been in Vietnam ten days. Tomorrow was Thanksgiving. There would be turkey, dressing and cranberry sauce, of a sort, freeze-dried and foil-wrapped. This was the first Thanksgiving she'd spent away from home since Desert Storm, but she was almost too tired even to be homesick.

Kaylene Smiley joined her in the screened hospital veranda, two cans of soda in her hands. "You look like you could use a drink," she said, handing Leah one. Kaylene had come straight from the surgical suites. She was wearing green cotton scrubs and a paper surgical hat that framed her round, good-natured face like an old-fashioned mobcap.

The soda wasn't cold, but it wasn't warm, either. Leah accepted it with a grateful smile, popped the top and took a long swallow. "Thanks, I needed that."

Kaylene sank into the chair next to Leah's. "I'm getting too old for this. I should be thinking about retiring and playing with my grandchildren, not hiking off to the back of beyond to play Florence Nightingale."

"I thought you told me you came on the mission to get away from your adorable crumb crunchers."

Kaylene had five grandchildren, all under the age of seven and all living within a few miles of her home. Leah had gathered from the pictures Kaylene showed her that the little ones spent as much time as possible at Grandma's house.

"I did. But now I miss them. I even miss my husband." She grinned and settled into the chaise with a sigh of relief. "Sixty-eight surgeries in eight days. It might not sound like an awful lot back home, but under these conditions we must be setting some kind of record. How's your pituitary tumor doing?"

Early that morning Adam had operated on one of the Vietnamese nurses whose infertility was likely caused by a tumor of the pituitary gland. The tumor was benign and the surgery had gone well. Their patient was already awake and alert. "Adam thinks she shouldn't have any trouble conceiving now."

"Another little miracle. Justifies my aching back and feet."

Leah murmured agreement. The sun had dropped from sight behind the mountains that surrounded the valley where the hospital and several small villages were located. The air had already begun to cool. At dusk the church bell would ring to call Father Gerard and the sisters and their flock to prayers. Evening here was the most pleasant time of day. It reminded her a little of Slate Hollow with the smell of wood smoke in the air, the laughter of children at play and dogs barking in the distance.

"I really should bestir myself to take a shower before the hot water's gone," Kaylene said a few minutes later.

Leah lifted her hand and brushed back a strand of

hair that had worked its way out of her braid. "That does sound like a good idea."

"The only problem is I'll have to get out of this chair to do it."

"You know you hate cold showers." The hot-water heater that supplied the showers was ancient and unreliable.

Kaylene took another swallow of her soda and swung her feet off the chaise with a groan. "You talked me into it. I also have to do some laundry. I'm not celebrating Thanksgiving with dirty undies. Hello, Doctor."

"Good evening, ladies."

Leah turned her head, but she didn't have to see him to know it was Adam. She nodded hello, not trusting her voice.

"Is there something you need in the operating room, Doctor?" Kaylene was from the old school of nursing. She didn't call any of the doctors by their first names.

"Everything's perfect in the OR and you know it," he said with one of his rare smiles.

"Just making sure, because once I get out of these scrubs, you're not getting me back into them for forty-eight hours." There were no surgeries scheduled the next day in honor of Thanksgiving.

Kaylene went back into the hospital, leaving Leah and Adam alone on the veranda. Leah stared down at her soft-drink can. Adam stared out into the compound. The church bell began to chime.

"It's time for mass," Leah said unnecessarily.

"Don't let me keep you."

"I wasn't planning to attend."

"Then would you care to come with me to the orphanage?"

The nursing sisters ran a small orphanage together with a school in another building about half a mile away. Leah, Kaylene and one of the doctors made the trip down the road at least once a day to visit the children and check on their patients.

"Has something gone wrong with My Lei's shunt?" The six-month-old girl had been born with a condition that caused fluid to build up on her brain. Five days ago Adam had implanted a shunt, a tube to redirect the excess cerebrospinal fluid. She had been doing well ever since, but any kind of surgery was risky for an infant, especially brain surgery.

"She's fine," Adam said quickly. "But I promised Sister Grace I'd check on her today. If you're too tired or you still don't want to be alone with me, just say so."

She'd hesitated too long in answering his invitation. He was impatient with personal interaction, she was learning, as though he spent little time in idle conversation. It was only a few minutes' walk. Surely she could keep her feelings under control and her hands to herself for that length of time. "I'm always tired," she said. "But I'm not worried about being alone with you." It was the first mention he'd made of that afternoon in the OR. The first for her, too. She stood up and walked to the screen door.

Adam stepped in front of her and held it open. Leah searched for a topic of conversation. "Have you seen B.J. today?" she asked as they passed the church and headed for the roadway.

"Not today, but it's obvious by the sound of your

voice he's hatching some new scheme, and he's got you as excited about it as he is. Am I right?''

"You seem to know him very well.''

"We've been friends a long time. What is it? A new program to revolutionize the Internet? Although I didn't have you pegged as a computer geek.''

"I'm not." She laughed. "I use one, but I don't understand it.''

"Don't tell me he's planning to try and fly a hot-air balloon around the world. No, that was last year.'' He smiled. "I give up. What is it today?''

"He told me he has a new project he's working on—containerized hospitals. They'll fit on the back of a semi-rig or you can sling them under a helicopter and drop them just about anywhere in the world. Pod-Meds, he wants to call them. Completely self-contained and fully equipped operating rooms with labs, X ray, physical therapy and even water and electricity.''

"What about a stable blood supply and competent follow-up care?''

"I didn't say there weren't problems. Big ones. But that's where people come in," she said. "To donate blood, solve the problems and teach others how to care for themselves.''

He looked at her and smiled, but it didn't lighten the shadow behind his eyes. "Never underestimate the power of a dreamer. You and B.J. are two of a kind.''

"I think it's a great idea.''

"I do, too. I hope he brings it off." This time his response seemed more genuine, heartfelt, and his smile took her breath away.

They walked in silence, listening to the sound of children's laughter carried to them on the smoky air. "I always marvel at how wonderfully happy these children are—except for love, they have so little," Leah said as they moved into the shade of the tall stands of bamboo that grew beside the road where the humid air felt ever so slightly cooler.

"Family is important to the Vietnamese. They'll do just about anything for their children. Even children like My Lei who haven't got much of a future."

"I wish there was something I could do," Leah said, thinking aloud.

"You've done plenty already." Adam's tone sounded harsh, resigned.

Leah kept her eyes on the track. "But it isn't enough."

"With a case like My Lei it's never enough." He shoved his hands in his pockets and lowered his head.

"Are you sorry you operated on her?" Leah asked. If he said yes in that same stony voice, she would turn around and go back. She thought of the happy, smiling baby. Her life was precious even as imperfect as it was.

"No," he said at last. "I'm only sorry I couldn't make her well and whole. There's still so much we don't know about the human brain. So much that can go wrong."

"And some things that can be put right."

They'd come to a place where a small runnel crossed the road. It wasn't deep, but too wide to step easily across. Adam held out his hand to help her. Leah hesitated. She didn't want to touch him. She remembered all too well the feel of his hands on her arms, the heat of his body, the taste of him in her mouth. A craving for his touch was part of what kept her awake at night.

A bird called somewhere off in the distance, another answered, calls as strange and exotic as the setting. She and Adam would be together only a little over a week longer, then he would go back to his world and she to hers. She would remember that and keep this attraction between them in perspective. She put her hand in his and jumped across.

"If Vo's family can't be located, perhaps I could sponsor them," she said, hoping he'd attribute her breathlessness to the steepness of the rise they were now climbing. Vo was My Lei's father, a young widower.

"You can't take on a responsibility like that. The child has no mother. Vo doesn't speak English. He has no marketable skills."

Leah thought of the dying old woman she'd befriended back in Slate Hollow, along with the woman's pregnant great-granddaughter, Juliet Trent, She had already made herself responsible for the two of them. Adam was right. She couldn't do the same for My Lei and Vo. "I was only thinking—"

"With your heart, instead of your head."

She turned on him, stopping him dead in his tracks. "Is that such a bad thing?"

"Yes, when it blinds you to the realities of the situation."

She started walking again. "I'd rather be blind to reality, if it keeps me from seeing things as callously as you do."

He reached out and grabbed her wrist, spinning her

around to face him. "I'm not blind, Leah. I've only learned the hard way how it tears you up inside when there's no more you can do than what's been done. I stopped believing in miracles a long time ago."

"You did work a miracle for My Lei. For the others, too. The old man whose pain you took away, so he can enjoy his last months with his family, and the nurse who will have babies to love and cherish now."

"Those weren't miracles, just damned good surgery. If they were miracles I could have cured the old man's cancer and given My Lei back what a misplaced gene took away from her."

Suddenly they heard the unmistakable sound of squealing tires followed instantly by a crash. "Oh, God, an accident!" Leah started running.

Adam was faster. He passed her within the first ten feet. The school came into view. Leah stopped at the gate for a moment to catch her breath, but Adam just kept running toward the sound of children's screams. "What happened?" she asked a Vietnamese nun on her knees in the roadway, her simple white habit torn and bloodstained, her arms around two crying, mud-splattered little girls.

"Our bus. It crashed," she said in French-accented English. She started to cry, just like the little girls clinging to her sleeves. "There." She pointed toward the road just out of sight beyond the high brick wall surrounding the school. "It is in the ditch. We came for help. Sister Grace is hurt. Hurry, please. The other children are still inside."

"Are you okay?"

"Yes," the nun replied. "I only hurt my shoulder."

Leah dropped to her knees, ran her hands over the little girls' arms and legs. "Can they tell you where they hurt?"

"They are okay. Just cuts and bruises. Go to the others. I'll take care of them." She began to talk soothingly to the little girls in Vietnamese.

"Send someone to the hospital. Tell them what's happened!" Leah yelled over her shoulder and started running again. "Tell everybody to come."

The orphanage bus, an old Volkswagen van, had gone nose first into a marshy ditch in front of the school. It had already sunk halfway into the mud by the time Leah arrived. Sister Grace and three more children were huddled by the side of the road. The nun was dazed and bleeding from a cut on her forehead. One little boy was crying lustily and holding his wrist. His hand was twisted at an awkward angle, the wrist obviously broken. The other two appeared uninjured, although they were wet and muddy and very frightened.

"How many are still inside?" Leah asked Sister Grace just as Adam braced his foot against the frame and literally tore the side door of the van from its hinges.

"I...there was nothing I could do. The tire blew out. I'm sorry. So sorry." She looked up at Leah with unfocused eyes.

"It's all right," Leah said. "It wasn't your fault. How many children were with you?" The nun was in shock. She would have to be checked for a concussion, but at the moment getting the rest of the children out of the wrecked van was the most important thing to be done. "Sister Grace?"

"I..."

"Adam, how many children do you see?"

"Two. Both girls. Are there any more, Sister?" Adam called.

Sister Grace responded to the command in his voice. "There were eight, no, seven children, and Sister Marie."

There were two little girls on the road with the sister and three more children here. That left two unaccounted for. Leah relayed the information to Adam as he hoisted himself through the door of the van. She watched the vehicle settle deeper into the mud. One of the children inside screamed weakly. Leah realized Adam would need help getting them out of the van, so she left Sister Grace and stepped off the shoulder of the road, immediately sinking into muck over her ankles. "I'm here, Adam. What can I do to help?"

"I'll hand them out to you. This thing is filling up with muck."

"I'm ready," Leah said.

"Come on, put your arms around my neck, honey," she heard Adam croon. "Thatta girl. Here we go." Adam shifted his weight and leaned out the door to hand a child to Leah. "Abrasions, contusions and possible broken ankle," he said. The van settled deeper into the mud. "This stuff's goddamned quicksand."

Leah held the little girl close, murmuring soothing nothings. The child's clothes were covered with mud. So were her face and arms. Marsh water dripped from her long black hair. She was conscious and whimpering with pain. "What about the other one?"

Adam's face closed down, and it was as though

Leah were confronting a machine. "It's bad. She's unconscious and trapped under the seat. I'll stay with her until the others get here. We'll need a backboard and we'll need an OR. She has a compound fracture of the left tibia and, God help us, I think she may have a broken neck."

CHAPTER FIVE

"LEAH, WAKE UP."

"I'm not asleep," Leah murmured. "I was just resting my eyes." She straightened from her slumped position in the unforgivingly hard chair, every muscle screaming in protest, to find Kaylene standing over her.

"I know, dear. I'm here to relieve you. I'll sit with the little sweetie while you go clean up and get some rest."

"What time is it?" The only light in the room came from the hallway and the pale green glow of the portable monitor by the bed. Automatically Leah checked the display. All the readouts looked good. Their patient was sleeping comfortably.

"Almost three."

The last time she'd noticed, it had been just a little past two. "I did fall asleep," she said ruefully. "I'm sorry."

"Nothing to be sorry for. It's been a very long day."

In unison they moved toward the child's bedside. The little girl slept quietly, her shattered left leg held immobile by a metal traction bar. Leah leaned over the bed rail and smoothed her straight, night-dark hair back from her forehead. She looked very small and helpless with her neck also immobilized, by a wide cervical collar. "Do you know her name?" There hadn't been time before to ask.

"Ahn Lyn. Isn't it pretty?"

"Very pretty. I wonder what it means." Leah touched the little girl's cheek in a gentle caress. "She moved her arms and wiggled her toes." Leah's voice was not quite steady. "Almost as soon as she woke from the anesthetic. There was no damage to her spinal cord."

"I know. Isn't it wonderful?"

"How are the others?" Sister Grace, the little girl with the broken ankle and the boy with the broken wrist were also in the hospital.

"We're still monitoring the sister, but her vitals are good. She had one heck of a knock on the head. The children are sound asleep. So, you go get some rest. I'll stay with her."

"You're as tired as I am," Leah protested.

"No, I'm not. I slept while you and Dr. Sauder were standing vigil. Now go."

Adam. Where was he? Two hours ago when the little girl woke up, moved her arms and wiggled her toes, he'd simply walked out of the room and not returned.

"I'll be back at 0600."

"No, you won't. We're not operating today, remember? It's Thanksgiving. Father Gerard and the regular staff will look after the children. Now go. Sleep till noon. All afternoon if you want. I'll save a drumstick for you."

Leah crossed the darkened compound with the aid of a pocket-size flashlight. In her room she lit a candle, grabbed a towel and a clean set of scrubs and headed for the showers. The water was cool, so she didn't linger beneath the spray. She dressed hurriedly and wrapped a towel around her head, then headed back to her room. She was so tired she could barely stand, and no wonder; she'd been awake for more than twenty hours. But even though she was exhausted she knew she wouldn't sleep. Not until she found Adam and assured herself he was all right.

He had barely let Ahn Lyn out of his sight from the moment she was lifted from the overturned van until the moment she'd opened her eyes in the tiny, ill-lit hospital room. Tests had determined that the injury to her neck was less severe than Adam had first feared. Surgery on her spinal column wouldn't be required, but he had remained in the OR to assist the orthopedic surgeon in the repair of her shattered left leg. He'd stayed by her bedside with Leah until she'd awakened, and then he'd disappeared.

She opened the door to the screened porch fronting the women's lodgings and stepped inside. The dim circle of light from her flashlight picked out the toe of a man's running shoe. She sucked in her breath.

"Don't scream, Leah. It's me." The voice was low and rough and male, the words quietly spoken.

She let her breath out in a rush. "Adam?"

He lifted his hand to shield his eyes from the beam of her flashlight. Leah switched it off. The moon was riding low among the clouds, but the candlelight spilling from the window outlined Adam sitting with his back against the wall, his legs drawn up to his chest. "I'm sorry. I didn't mean to frighten you."

She dropped to her knees beside him. "Where have you been?"

"Walking. I saw the light in your window, but you weren't here."

"I was in the shower."

"I can smell your soap." He touched her cheek. "Lemon. You always smell of lemons."

"Adam, are you all right?"

He dropped his hand to his knee, but not before she felt the faint tremor in his fingers. "I'm fine."

"I don't think so. If you were fine you'd be in your bed asleep, not sitting here in the dark."

"I hate to sleep." His words were clear but unutterably weary. He was still wearing the scrubs he'd worn in the OR. He smelled of hospital soap and warm skin.

"Why, Adam?" she asked softly. She covered his hand with hers. He had strong hands, with long blunt fingers, a surgeon's hands. She hadn't imagined the trembling when he'd touched her. He was shaking all over.

"It all comes back when I sleep," he said simply. "They're always in my dreams. Twenty-five years of nightmares. Back home I can deal with it. Here, they're too close. I hate this place."

So coming back to Vietnam hadn't been the healing time for him that it was for some vets. She had suspected as much, and now she was sure. "Did you hope coming back here would make the nightmares go away?"

"I came for B.J. I knew it wouldn't help. Nothing has helped."

"A therapist?"

"I've talked to the best of them. No one had a clue."

"Did you tell them the truth? Did you tell them you're suffering from post-traumatic stress dis—"

His words were like rapier thrusts. "What makes you think it's post-traumatic stress disorder I'm describing? I wasn't in combat, Leah. Not like the guys who went before me. I was only here at the end. One hundred and seventeen days to be exact. I never set foot outside Saigon. It wasn't war then—it was only cleaning up the mess." He didn't shake off her touch, but his hand had balled into a fist beneath hers. "Maybe I'm just losing my mind."

"Are you on medication?"

He gave a harsh bark of laughter. "Pills give me the shakes. I don't take them. No one wants a surgeon with the shakes mucking around in his brain."

"You're shaking now," she said.

"I know. For hours. It won't go away this time." He lifted his left hand, the one she wasn't holding and held it in front of him. "Children should never die."

The statement confused her, but she answered the desperation in his tone as much as his words. "All the children are going to be fine—all of them."

He came to his feet in one smooth movement, pulling her with him. "She didn't go sour after I left?"

"Ahn Lyn is awake and stable."

"Ahn Lyn. Is that her name?"

"Yes."

"When I saw her trapped in that damned van…" He lifted his hands and bracketed her face. "I can live with all the rest—the dreams of the shelling and the sniper attacks and the riots—but I can't live with the memories of the little ones dying. I can't.''

The hopelessness in his voice chilled her heart. ''Adam, please tell me—''

''No! I don't want to remember. I want to forget. Help me forget, Leah. Please, help me.'' He pulled her into his arms, lowered his mouth to hers, and she tasted his desperation and his desire. ''With you in my arms I can forget, at least for a little while.''

She knew some of the grief that gnawed at him. She'd had friends who'd died young. She'd seen children die. She could no more deny him now than she could fly. He pulled the towel from her hair and threaded his fingers through the strands, holding her face still for his kiss. Her mouth opened to the urgency of his. She wrapped her arms around his neck and kissed him back. She longed to take away some of his pain and sorrow and lose some of her own, which she kept locked away in a very small corner of her heart.

But somehow, in a heartbeat, the kiss changed and became completely sexual, purely a man and a woman and the fire that can consume them. She didn't let herself think, only feel, and her response urged him to do the same. They were as alone as they could be in the crowded compound. Kaylene would be with the little girl for hours. The others were asleep or keeping watch over patients in the hospital. Adam slid his arm behind her knees and lifted her as though she weighed nothing. She let her head rest on his shoulder and felt the wild beating of his heart against her fingers. She was naked beneath the thin, much-washed cotton of her scrubs; Adam probably was, too. She could feel the heat of his skin, the roughness of hair, the rock solidity of bone and muscle against the side of her breast.

He set her down on her bed and stripped off his shirt. She fumbled with hers and he helped her draw it over her head. Adam's hand went to the drawstring of his pants. The candle had blown out with their movements; now there was no light except the moon's glow through the window. She shimmied out of her pants, wanting nothing between them. He stood for a moment looking down at her, all moon shadows, darkness and secrets that could cause her pain, as well. When he lay down beside her and took her in his arms, Leah forgot everything but her desire for him.

His hands cupped her breasts. His lips covered hers and she felt his tongue inside her mouth. She returned the intimate caress with a hunger that matched his. Then Adam kissed her cheeks, her eyelids, the curve of her ear. He splayed his fingers through her hair and held her head still for another mind-emptying kiss. Then he moved his mouth to kiss her throat, her collarbone, the upper swell of her breast. His beard was rough and exciting against the softness of her skin. He took one hardened nipple into his mouth and Leah sucked in a breath, swallowing a moan. She reached up and held his head close to her, feeling pleasure arc along a glittering pathway from her breast to her womb.

She reached down and wrapped her fingers around him. He gasped, then entered her slowly, but when he realized how ready she was for him, he began to move more strongly within her. She met him thrust for thrust, each giving and taking what they needed from the other. His mouth sought hers once more, muffling her moans of pleasure. Finally he climaxed deep inside her, and his release pushed her into her own.

She had never responded to lovemaking this way before, going beyond thought, beyond reason in a realm of pure sensation. It frightened her a little, how well she read his desires, and he hers. But she didn't want to analyze what had just passed between them. She only wanted to feel. She became aware of the weight of Adam's body on hers, the fullness of him still buried within her. Then he shifted his weight and lay beside her. Leah listened to the deep evenness of his breathing. He was asleep, and in moments so was she.

ADAM AWOKE from a dreamless sleep with Leah in his arms. No, not dreamless he realized groggily, but sleep not filled with nightmares and the cries of dying children. Instead, his dreams had been filled with images and sensations of the woman beside him. He turned her head gently and kissed her awake. A small, cold corner of his mind told him not to do this, to let her sleep. Making love to her again, unprotected and uncommitted, was as wrong and irresponsible as something a boy Brian's age might do, but he couldn't stop himself. The taste and touch and scent of her had become as necessary to him as his next breath.

"Leah." He whispered her name in the darkness.

"I...I must have fallen asleep," she said, but her arms came around his neck and she kissed him back.

"So did I." He wanted to tell her what a gift it was, but was unable to find the words when she was so close, her breasts pressed to his chest, her legs tangled with his.

"I've never done that before. I...I never lose myself that way."

"I never do, either. Thank you, Leah..." He stopped himself from saying *my love*. He didn't mean it, and she would know he didn't. But somehow it sounded right and so he whispered it to himself.

"Are you okay? Really okay?" she asked, and he could feel her searching gaze on his face as her fingers moved to touch his mouth. He turned his head and kissed the inside of her palm.

"I'm fine." He wasn't, not really. Already the darkness was pushing at the edges of his thoughts, but when he covered her mouth with his, the darkness receded, and light, along with bits and pieces of longing and dreams that couldn't be, filled his thoughts. She was drawn to strays, the hurt and injured. If he told her everything he'd kept inside him for so long, she would stay and try to heal him. As much as he craved her solace, he wouldn't take advantage of her that way.

The kiss was long and hungering, and when it was over he was hard again and she lay panting beside him. "What time is it? I don't want Kaylene to find us," she said.

"It's very, very late, or very early. But still hours before dawn."

"I don't want the dawn to come," she said softly. He knew she didn't like being in the dark. He knew she was offering him a part of herself with those words, and it humbled him.

"Neither do I." He pressed himself against her and she opened her legs. This time their lovemaking was not so gentle, and was over more quickly. They didn't sleep afterward, but lay twined together. Her hands, moving in small circles over his back and shoulders, were almost enough to keep the demons at bay, but not quite, and he took her once more to hold back the darkness. She seemed to sense his desperation. She met him halfway, and they joined and melded and once more found oblivion.

A baby crying somewhere in the compound awakened him, and this time even the warmth of Leah's arms around him couldn't hold back the memories....

The Orphan Plane. It was April 4, 1975, a week after his nineteenth birthday; 243 children and sixty-two adults took off in the C-5A Galaxy cargo plane heading for new homes and families in the United States. He had helped carry the little ones on the plane, strapped them in the seats, two by two by two. An hour later he was helping carry their bodies out of the wreckage of the huge aircraft. It had crashed into a half-flooded rice paddy trying to return to Than Son Nhut with a malfunctioning hydraulic system.

All around him were dead and dying children, and there was nothing he could do about it. One little girl he remembered more than the others. He had found her alive in the wreckage and held her head above the water so she wouldn't drown. But she couldn't be saved and had died in his arms. He had watched her die, and then he'd gotten up and gone about doing what he could for the others. In one way or another he had been repeating those motions every day of his life since.

There had been good times, too. After Brian was born he held his son in his arms and thought he might be able to put the past behind him. But when Brian was ten he'd crashed his bicycle head-on into a mail-box. Adam had been out in the yard watching and rushed to his side and cradled his bloodied face in his arms all the way to the hospital. From that day on the nightmares had come back and never gone away.

He looked down at his hand. He was shaking like a leaf. What was worse, he was shaking inside. He couldn't operate in this condition. Hell, he didn't even know if he could set foot inside the hospital again. He had to get out of this place or lose what little was left of his reason and his soul. Adam slid Leah's arms from around his neck. Forced himself not to kiss her again. Pulled on his clothes and walked out into the night.

IT WAS DAYLIGHT when Leah awoke again. There were tears on her cheek, as though she'd been crying in her sleep, but she couldn't remember any bad dreams. And then she realized she was alone. She dressed in haste and smoothed the rumpled sheets on her bed, drawing the blanket up just as Kaylenè entered the room.

She looked a little surprised to see Leah up and around. "I thought I told you to sleep till noon."

"I guess my internal clock had other ideas," Leah fibbed. "I was just going to take a shower." Adam's scent, the scent of their lovemaking, clung to every inch of her.

Kaylene grimaced. "My internal clock can stuff itself. I've had my ice-cold shower, and I'm still going to sleep till noon."

"I'll make sure no one disturbs you." Leah wanted to ask Kaylene if she'd seen Adam. Perhaps he'd gone to the hospital to check on Ahn Lyn, but she didn't think so. He'd probably left her bed just to spare her the embarrassment of Kaylene finding them together.

"Who's sitting with Ahn Lyn?" She held her breath, waiting for Kaylene's answer.

"B.J. He relieved me about half an hour ago. She's had her pain meds and she's sleeping soundly. Still moving all her extremities. So far, so good. Sister Grace's vitals are stable, and the other kids are fine."

B.J. was with Ahn Lyn, not Adam. She stretched her mouth into a smile. "Thanks for the report. Pleasant dreams."

"Mmm." Kaylene was already in bed.

Twenty minutes later, showered and with her hair back in its habitual French braid, Leah faced B. J. Walton across Ahn Lyn's bed.

"You're looking for Adam, aren't you?" he asked her bluntly.

"Yes. I...I'm worried about him."

"He's gone, Leah," B.J. said, his sympathetic gaze taking in the dark circles beneath her eyes. "I found a note when I woke up this morning. It was too late to stop him."

"He's left the compound?"

"He's leaving Vietnam." His hand fisted on the bed rail. "Damn. I should have never talked him into coming back." Ahn Lyn stirred in her drugged sleep and B.J. lowered his voice. "He wasn't ready."

Leaving the mission? Leaving the country? She hadn't expected that. Her aching heart jerked painfully in her chest. *Gone. Out of my life.*

"What happened to him here, B.J.?" She had to know.

"He won't tell me. I have my suspicions, but he refuses to talk about it. Maybe it wasn't a bungee-stakes-and-jungle-patrols kind of war here at the end. But it wasn't pretty. Snipers, shellings, the refugees scrambling to get out. I'm sure it was hell being the last ones out of the only damned war we ever lost. I thought maybe you…"

"No," she said. "He told me nothing. Not even that he was leaving." But what had she expected? Adam was a stranger to her. He had taken what she'd freely offered and promised nothing in return. Once more she'd let her heart overrule her reason. She'd given a piece of herself unwisely. Now he was gone, and she was left alone to consider the consequences of her actions and, God help her, to want him back again.

CHAPTER SIX

"DOES YOUR MOTHER know you're here in Chicago?"

Brian Sauder shifted his attention from the view outside the office window to his father's face. "Not exactly," he answered carefully. "She knows I'm spending the weekend out of town." He'd driven seventeen hours straight to get to Chicago from Cambridge. His brain was nearly fried, but what he had to say to his dad was too important to wait until he got some sleep. That was why he'd come straight to St. Barnabas, instead of waiting for his dad at his condo.

"Out of town, but not out of state." Adam stood up and walked around his desk. Brian stood up too. *Jeez, I'm an inch taller than he is. When had that happened?*

Adam waved him back to his seat. "Are you in trouble, son? Is that why you came to me?"

"No, it's nothing like that."

His dad picked up a big piece of quartz he used for a paperweight and held it in his hands. "You're not having problems with your grades, are you?"

"Solid B's."

"Good." One corner of Adam's mouth curled up in an expression Brian couldn't quite classify as a smile. "I doubt even Elliot's connections would get you back into Harvard if you flunked out." Elliot Carlton was his stepfather, an investment banker in Boston where he lived with Brian's mom and his little half sister, Megan.

"Yeah, I know. He keeps reminding me what a generous donation he made to get me considered in the first place. That you and Mom made a big mistake sending me to public school all those years." His dad had gone to a public high school in Pennsylvania, and then on to the University of Michigan after he got out of the Marines. Brian thought it would have been good enough for him, too.

"A fact your mother pointed out to me many times as you were growing up." This time Adam did smile. His mom smiled like that, too, when she talked about his dad. They were still friends, sort of, and Brian was glad.

"She'd have a fit if she knew I was here."

His dad was still holding the big piece of quartz— tightly. His knuckles were white. When he saw Brian look at his hands, Adam put the rock down, then walked behind the desk and gazed at the snow falling in huge, wet flakes outside the window. "Why didn't you tell her you were coming to see me?" he asked.

"Christmas break doesn't start till the end of the week. I...left early."

"She won't like that." Adam turned and spread his hands flat on the teak surface of the desk.

"That's why I didn't tell her."

Adam frowned at his reply, accentuating the harsh new lines around his mouth. *Jeez, Dad's looking old.* He hadn't looked like that when he saw him last at the end of the summer. Was he sick? Did he have cancer or something? Or had he caught some weird disease in Vietnam? Is that why he'd come home almost two weeks before he was supposed to? Brian hadn't lived with his dad since he was eleven, but he loved him. He didn't want anything to be wrong with him.

"Why did you come here, Brian?"

Worries about his dad's health were forgotten for the moment. It was now or never. Adam had just asked the million-dollar question and he had to answer it. "I don't want to be an investment banker. I don't want to go to work for Elliot at Carlton, Lieberman and Carmichael. I don't want to go back to Harvard."

"Have you told your mother this?"

Brian snorted. "Are you kidding? She'd have a stroke. She'd have me committed."

"A lot of other mothers would feel the same way."

Brian stood up again and started pacing the width of the office. "I've given it a year and a half, almost. It's not for me."

"Math has always been your strongest subject."

"That doesn't mean I have to be a banker or, God help me, an economist."

"No, it doesn't."

"I don't know exactly what I want to do with my life, Dad, but I know it isn't following in Elliot's footsteps. I'm dropping out of Harvard at the end of the semester. I need some time to think things through. I'd like to come here and live with you. God knows Mom and Elliot would make my life miserable if I stayed in Boston."

"Brian, I don't know what to say."

Adam's hesitation hit Brian like a fist to the gut. He hadn't let himself believe his dad would turn him down. "It's okay, Dad," he made himself say. "I'll find somewhere else to live if you don't want me at your place."

Adam was silent for a long moment. "Why don't you try sticking it out until spring?"

"I've made up my mind, Dad."

"I think you're making a mistake."

"Maybe I am, but I'll never know if I don't give it a try. That's all I'm asking. The chance to make my own mistakes. I can live with the consequences." His dad had been a Marine in Vietnam when he was nineteen. All Brian wanted to do was figure out his own path in life. Surely he had a right to do that.

"Okay. Call your mother and break the news to her. I'll back you up."

Brian pushed away from the credenza, his heart beating madly in his chest. He wanted to give his dad a hug, but the desk was still between them, so he held out his hand, instead. "Thanks, Dad."

Adam didn't take his hand right away. Brian held his breath. Then his dad leaned forward and clasped Brian's hand in both of his. "I'm not giving you a free ride. You'll have to get a job, and you'll have to promise me you'll consider going back to school next year."

"I'll start looking for a job first thing tomorrow." He couldn't stop the grin spreading over his face. "Thanks, Dad. I knew I could count on you to see my side of this."

"I'm not looking forward to talking to your mother."

"Neither am I, but I might as well get it over with. Can I use your phone?"

"Dr. Sauder?" His dad's secretary opened the door between their offices and stuck her head inside.

"Yes, Camilla?"

"There's a young woman here to see you."

"I don't have any patient appointments scheduled for this afternoon."

That was odd, Brian thought. His dad always had patients scheduled on Wednesdays. He operated on Tuesday and Thursday, and saw patients on Monday and Wednesday. At least he always had.

"She's not a patient," Camilla said. "She says she's a friend. Her name is Leah Gentry."

"Leah?" The way his dad said the name caught Brian's attention.

"Leah Gentry," Camilla repeated. "Should I tell her you're busy?"

"No." Adam ran a hand through his hair. His expression didn't give much away, but Brian could have sworn he saw his hand shaking. "Send her in."

"You have a meeting with Dr. Fenimore at two-thirty, don't forget."

"I won't."

Camilla opened the door wider. His dad was staring at it like he expected a ghost to walk through it. Instead, a very ordinary young woman with dark brown hair in a French braid entered the room. She was wearing a military-issue parka, and she had a lime-green backpack slung over one shoulder. The backpack had a picture of Minnie Mouse on it, just like the one his little sister had. Her nose was red from the cold, and there were pale blue shadows under her eyes, as though she'd been awake for a lot of hours in a row.

"Hello, Adam," she said stopping just inside the door.

"Hello." His dad came out from behind his desk and took a couple of steps toward her.

"It's good to see you again." She held out her hand.

"It's good to see you, too. Welcome home, Leah." His dad came just close enough to take her hand. He held it for a long moment, and they stared at each other like they'd thought until that very moment they'd never see each other again.

Brian cleared his throat. The woman turned her head in his direction. Her eyes widened momentarily. She had very pretty eyes, all kind of green and gold mixed together.

"I'm sorry, I didn't mean to interrupt."

Adam dropped her hand and retreated behind his desk. "This is my son, Brian."

She smiled, and he smiled back. He couldn't help himself. "Hi," he said.

She held out her hand again. "Hello, Brian. Your father told me a lot about you."

"Leah was my anesthetist in Dalat," Adam explained.

"Nice to meet you," Brian said.

"I...I just got back to the States. B.J. and I were the last to leave. I have a four-hour layover." She turned back to Brian. "So I thought I'd look up your father and make sure he's okay. He left the mission so hurriedly I...I didn't get to say goodbye.'' A tinge of color stained her cheeks.

"I'm fine,'' Adam said, and his voice was suddenly cold and hard.

"I can see. I'm sorry I barged in on you this way. I...I should have called, I guess.''

She looked uncomfortable. So did his dad. There was something going on here, undercurrents he couldn't understand. This might be a good time for him to make an exit. "I have a phone call to make. It was nice meeting you,'' he said again, smiling at her once more, hoping she'd smile back. She did.

"It was nice meeting you, too, Brian, but please, don't hurry off on my account. I truly did only stop in to see if your father was all right, and to thank him.''

"For what?'' Brian asked. He wasn't flirting with her, not really—she was too old for him. But it was hard not to want to coax her to smile again.

"For seeing that Vo and My Lei found sponsors here in the States.''

"Vo and My Lei?''

"Yes, a Vietnamese man and his daughter. Your father operated on the little girl—''

"I'll tell you about them later, Brian,'' Adam broke in. "Don't you want to make your call?''

"Yeah, sure I do.'' He tried one more smile, but this time she didn't smile back, only nodded a little distractedly. "I'll use Camilla's phone to call Mom.'' Brian left the room wondering just what had gone on between his dad and this woman in Vietnam. Maybe if he worked it just right, he'd find out, but he doubted it. His dad never talked about his love life—if he had

one, and besides, right now Brian had more important
things on his mind—like changing the entire course
of his life.

THE DOOR CLOSED behind Adam's son, and Leah
wished she'd left the office with him. Why had she
given in to the impulse to come here and see for herself that Adam was all right? He obviously was. And
he obviously wasn't happy to see her. She said the
first thing that popped into her mind. "Your son is a
very good-looking young man. Very nice, too."

"Yes, he is."

"I'm sorry I interrupted your visit."

"It's okay," Adam said. "Can I get you something. A cup of coffee?"

"Yes, thanks." She wanted to refuse, but he might
think it odd—their love of coffee was one thing they
had in common. But she wouldn't have more than a
swallow, not now. Because now she was pregnant.

She'd bought a pregnancy-test kit as soon as they
landed in Frankfurt and confirmed what she'd suspected almost from the moment she'd awakened
alone in her bed that morning. She should never have
made love to him without protection when she knew
she might be ovulating, but she hadn't been thinking
with her head that night, only with her heart.

Adam walked to the credenza on the far wall. He
slid open one of the paneled doors to reveal a wet bar
and an insulated carafe and cups. "You like cream,
as I recall."

"Yes."

He turned back with the coffee. "I'm sorry. I
should have offered to take your coat."

"I prefer to keep it on. I haven't adjusted to the temperature change yet. It's snowing, you know," she said, making a little joke of it. He didn't smile and she asked, "Do you know if the others all reached home safely?"

He took her backpack and set it on the floor, then gestured her to a seat in the big leather chair in front of his desk. She sat because it was more awkward to stand. Then he handed her the coffee mug and leaned one hip against the side of the desk.

"Roger Crenshaw sent me an e-mail a day or two ago saying as much. He's elected himself unofficial social secretary of the group."

"That's nice."

"And why did you stay behind?"

"B.J. asked me to help move Ahn Lyn to a hospital in Saigon. A friend of his there has promised to get her permission to go to Paris for therapy on her leg."

"I imagine that permission cost B.J. a bundle."

"I imagine it did." She looked down at her coffee cup, then made herself meet his eyes again. "And you must have been busy pulling strings and unsnarling red tape to get Vo and My Lei asylum so quickly."

"There are all kinds of places to go for help. You just have to know where to look."

He didn't seem to want to talk about Vietnam, so she changed the subject to one he was probably no more willing to discuss. "Are you really okay? Your hand was shaking like a leaf when you handed me my coffee."

He scowled down at her. "You don't miss anything, do you?"

She refused to be cowed by the anger she heard in

his voice. There was too much at stake. "I've been worried about you. You left without a word."

"I'm sorry about that."

"Where did you go?"

"I walked until the sun came up and then I hitched a ride to Saigon and wrangled my way onto a flight home."

"I'm impressed. That must have taken some doing."

"It did."

"And you're really okay?"

"Yes. And sorry as hell for what I did to you."

"You didn't do anything to me." That was a lie, a bald-faced lie, but Adam wasn't the only one avoiding the truth at the moment.

"I took advantage of your kindness and your generosity."

"Adam, please. Don't trivialize what happened with platitudes and clichés."

"God, Leah, I didn't mean to sound that way. You saved my life that night, but it doesn't change anything."

Inside she was in turmoil, but she refused to let him see how deeply he had wounded her with his cool words. "I know. Your life is here. Dr. Adam Sauder soon to be chief of neurosurgery."

"Where did you hear that?"

"B.J. told me."

"I should have known."

"Congratulations."

"I've worked hard for this position."

"Chief of neurosurgery at St. Barnabas is a long way from a small practice in Slate Hollow, Kentucky—almost a different world.'' Why had she said that? It sounded almost as if she was asking him…for what? To leave all this behind and go there with her? Deep down, wasn't that what she really wanted? For him to make a commitment to her—and to the baby he didn't even know she was carrying? She looked around for a place to put her coffee mug. She was shaking so hard she was afraid she'd spill it. Finally she set it on a corner of the desk. When she looked up again, Adam was staring across the room at the door.

"Leah, Brian is coming to live with me. We just made the decision. I want to make sure he gets his feet under him. We've been apart for a long time. This might be my last chance to make up for the lousy father I've been in the past. I have to concentrate all my energy on Brian.''

His energy, not his love. His words took her breath away. Adam wanted no more human contact than that. He would never allow himself to feel another's anguish—or joy—as long as he suffered from PTSD. He would never open himself to love and to being loved. Not by Brian, or her and certainly not by their baby. The thought sent a stab of pain from her brain to her heart and lower to her womb, and once more she realized how close she was to caring too much for this man. The decision she'd agonized over for the past ten days was made for her in an instant.

"I understand,'' she said. "I really have to be going now.'' She couldn't be in the same room with this stranger any longer. She grabbed her backpack from beside the chair and stood up. "I won't take up any more of your time.''

"Leah." Adam set his mug down so hard coffee splashed onto the polished wood. She jumped as if a gun had gone off next to her. He pushed away from the desk and reached for her hand. "If there's ever anything I can do…"

Leah took a step backward, avoiding his touch. She wasn't made of stone, even if he appeared to be. "There's nothing you need to do for me." *Or our baby.*

No, she thought frantically, the reality of the situation finally hitting home. *My baby. Mine alone.* "I'll be fine. Goodbye, Adam. God bless."

Leah. Wait. He didn't say the words aloud, but he wanted to. He wanted to shout down the corridor for her not to leave. He should go after her. She was serenity and bedrock in a world edging closer and closer to chaos. He could talk to her, tell her things he'd never told another living soul. He couldn't just let her walk out of his life—the way he'd walked out of hers.

Adam made it as far as the chair where she'd been sitting before he stopped himself from following her out the door. He wasn't so lost in his misery that he didn't know right now he wanted her for all the wrong reasons. She didn't deserve that. She deserved to be loved and cherished for herself alone, not because she could buffer him from the terrors of his past and the uncertainties of the present. It was better this way. A clean break.

He could only deal with one problem at a time, and Brian had to come first, before his own wants and needs. On that thought his son entered the room.

"I saw her leave," Brian said, closing the door

behind him. He ran his fingers through his hair, hair the same dark brown as his own. "Can you give me a hand here, Dad?"

Adam pulled himself together. Leah Gentry was gone out of his life. "Is it your mother?"

Brian nodded. "She's on the phone in Camilla's office. I told her what I'm going to do. She's...she's crying. Would you talk to her? Calm her down enough so I can explain this is the right thing for me?"

"I'll do my best." Denise Carlton wasn't going to be easy to convince. She wouldn't take kindly to him getting involved in their son's life now, when he'd been a long-distance father for the past eight years. And she had a point. Hell, since Brian was ten he hadn't been there for him at all, but maybe she would understand he wanted to change that.

Years ago, before she'd pulled up stakes and gone to Boston, Denise had stuck it out until he'd drawn so far inside himself no one could reach him. But she knew he loved Brian with all his wounded heart, even if he didn't always show it, and because she was a good woman, he hoped she'd give him one more chance to be a father to their son.

He turned back to his desk. "I'll put her on the speakerphone. We'll both talk to her at once."

A look of relief spread over Brian's face. "Thanks, Dad. I knew you'd come through for me."

Adam picked up the phone. Leah's coffee mug was still sitting on his desk, a faint smudge of lipstick visible on the rim. He turned his back on the mug and sealed away any lingering thoughts of the woman who had so recently held it in her hands.

She was part of his past now, just another painful memory. But he had a suspicion she would be equally hard to forget.

CHAPTER SEVEN

LEAH REACHED UP to rub the tight muscles at the back of her neck. She had another headache, a dull, throbbing pain that circled the back of her head. She'd taken a couple of Tylenol, but it hadn't gone away, and it wasn't likely that it would unless she could relax and put her feet up. Even standing in the bright April sunlight flooding through the window did nothing to unwind the tension in her arms and shoulders, or lessen the pain.

"You're hurting again?"

"Just a little headache." Leah moved across the small room to the high tester bed where the old woman lay. Sixty years ago, Aurelia Cade had probably been a very attractive woman; now she was as brown and wizened as a winter apple. Her face was a mass of wrinkles, her hair, what was left of it, was gray and wispy, and her body little more than skin and bones. Aurelia was dying of cancer. Leah and Aurelia had been friends since Leah had first come to Slate Hollow. Now she visited her as often as she could.

Leah smoothed back Aurelia's hair from her forehead and adjusted the prongs of the nasal oxygen catheter to a more comfortable position. "How's that?" she asked.

"Better. Seems like I can't get along without this stuff night or day anymore. It's a nuisance, and the tank hisses and keeps me awake."

Leah looked at the gauge on the oxygen bottle and gave the valve a turn that moved it barely a fraction of an inch. But the slight hissing that bothered Aurelia diminished, and the old woman smiled. "Thank you, dear."

"Now, why don't you get some rest."

"I'll have eternity to rest soon enough," Aurelia said tartly. "And don't try to tell me it's the weather change causing your headache. There's rain coming—I can feel it in my bones. But that ain't what's wrong with you. It's your blood pressure acting up again, isn't it?"

"I don't know. I haven't had a chance to take it. I came straight here when I got off duty." Leah had been attending a seminar on biological weapons at the University of Kentucky medical center. Until she'd become pregnant, she'd planned to volunteer for a special medical unit that trained reservists to deal with chemical- and biological-weapon attacks. That training, like her army career, was now on hold.

"You need a nap morning and afternoon, and sassafras tea," Aurelia said, reaching over to pat Leah's hand when she bent to tuck Aurelia's arm back beneath the quilt. Aurelia was a wise woman, something of a healer in her own right, as had been her mother and grandmother before her.

"I know. A cup every morning." Leah's blood pressure had become elevated at the end of her first trimester, at first she'd been able to keep it within safe limits with diet and exercise. But over the past couple of weeks the readings had risen steadily, and Caleb had put her on a mild diuretic.

"And the pill Doc Owens prescribed for you—it can't hurt none. But no more soldiering." Aurelia made a face at Leah's khaki fatigues and boots. "It's not fitting. You're a mama now, not a soldier."

Leah sat down on the straight chair beside the bed. The sunny room was scrupulously clean. There were pots of herbs and crocuses on the windowsill. A bowl of dried mint by the bedside almost, but not quite, masked the smells of sickness and approaching death. "I'm done soldiering. My medical leave was approved this weekend. I'll be getting the official paperwork any day now."

"Good. I don't want anythin' happening to the wee 'un you got in your belly." So far Aurelia and her great-granddaughter, Juliet Trent, along with Caleb Owens and his wife, Margaret, were the only people who knew she was pregnant. Margaret and Caleb had known almost from the beginning, but she'd told Aurelia and Juliet only a few weeks ago. In a small town like Slate Hollow no pregnancy stayed secret very long, and Leah hadn't wanted to take the chance that the teenager would hear the news from someone else.

"I promise that I'm taking the best care of him I know how." Leah reached out and patted Aurelia's hand beneath the faded Drunkard's Path quilt. Today was a good day for the old woman. She was alert and talkative, and the new combination of medications had her pain under control. Good days were rare now, and Leah and Juliet savored each one.

"Him," Aurelia snorted derisively. "Your little 'un is a girl. Going to be the perfect match for Juliet's pup. It's a boy. She's carrying that baby way too low for it to be a girl.''

Leah giggled. "My mother says it's the other way around—boys are high and girls are low." A twinge of guilt stung her heart. She should be having this conversation with her mother, not Aurelia. At Christmas, when she'd last visited her parents, she hadn't been ready to face the reality of her condition. But now it was April and her parents and brothers had a right to know about the momentous changes in her life. She was going to have to make time for a trip to Florida to break the news very soon.

''What makes your mama such an expert?'' Aurelia challenged her.

''She has three sons.''

''What do your brothers think of you being in the family way by some man they don't even know?''

Leah was used to Aurelia's blunt way of talking. She'd answered this question before, but Aurelia had forgotten. ''If they knew, they'd threaten to hunt him down and march him up here in front of the business end of my daddy's shotgun to make an honest woman of me. You know that already.''

Aurelia chuckled and then started to cough, gasping for breath. ''Them's real men, your brothers. You're gonna have to tell 'em sooner or later.''

''I know. I will, soon. You're talking too much,'' Leah said, lifting Aurelia's head to give her a sip of springwater from the glass on the bedside table.

''Bet your daddy would be marching right alongside 'em,'' Aurelia said, but her voice was weaker, her speech slower. The pain medication was beginning to work. Leah checked her watch. Good. The dosage was holding. She didn't want to increase the medication any more than necessary to keep Aurelia comfortable. The time would come soon enough when she would need much more.

"He'd be standing right there beside the preacher," Leah agreed.

"If he knowed who the daddy was, that is," Aurelia prodded.

"If he knew."

"You ain't told no one?"

"There's no need. He's not going to be part of my baby's life. Just like Cash Dentrell isn't going to be a real father to Juliet's baby."

"That's 'cause he's nothin' but white trash," Aurelia said. "Damned Dentrells is all no good. I'm glad my Lizzie never lived to see what a poor mama her Justine was to Juliet." Aurelia had taken Juliet to live with her when Juliet's mother, Justine, and her boyfriend had taken off for parts unknown four years ago.

"Juliet's a good girl. She'll make a good mother."

"I thank the dear Lord every day that she's got you to help her and the little 'un make their way in life. I just hope I'm here to see him born. Promise me you'll help make that happen." Aurelia's skeletal hand came out from under the quilt and grasped Leah's fingers. "Promise me."

"I promise." Leah smiled down at the old woman. "If the Lord's willing to have you stay with us till Juliet's baby's born, I'll do my best to make you as comfortable as I can."

"That's good enough for me."

"It's a deal then."

"What's a deal?" Juliet came into the room carrying a wooden tray with a steaming teapot and two cups sitting beside a small glass vase of daffodils. She was a tall, pretty girl with the red-gold hair and blue eyes of her Scottish ancestors.

"I'm gonna stay alive until your young 'un is born, and Leah's gonna help me."

Juliet's eyes darkened with apprehension. "Oh, Granny, I wish you wouldn't talk about dying that way. You're going to be here for years yet." She set the tray on the table under the window and bent awkwardly to give her tiny great-grandmother a hug. She was in her ninth month, and her large belly made movement difficult for her.

"Don't go crying, girly. Dying comes to us all. My time's comin' but I ain't ready to go just yet. I'll be around a spell."

"You said you'd be here for the baby. You promised."

"I always keep my promises." Aurelia closed her eyes, exhausted.

"Juliet, is that sassafras tea I smell?" Leah asked.

Juliet smiled at her. "Yes, it is. I saw you rubbing the back of your neck a while ago. It's your blood pressure again, isn't it?"

"I'll have Caleb check it as soon as I get back to the clinic."

Juliet settled into a bentwood rocker on the other side of the bed. She rested her cup on the bulk of her stomach and bit into a cookie, watching her great-grandmother with an anxious eye. "She's asleep," she whispered. "That's good. She needs the rest."

Juliet wanted to be a nurse. She'd told Leah that when they'd first met five years ago, on Leah's first day in practice with Caleb. Juliet had come to the clinic with a black eye and a broken wrist from a "fall down the stairs." Her mother said she'd been rough-housing with her new stepfather, which was how she'd described her most recent live-in boyfriend. Two months later Juliet had another "accident," this one resulting in a cracked jaw and a concussion. Caleb had called the sheriff and the child-protection agency right then and there. Juliet's mother and boy-friend had left town one step ahead of the law.

Leah pulled a straight-back chair close to Juliet's and sat. The teenager poured her a cup of tea. "Here, this'll help your headache."

"Thanks." Leah took a sip. It had been a long day. She'd been up since five, attended the final seminar on biological weapons and then made the drive from Lexington straight to Aurelia's century-old cabin near the top of Pine Mountain. And always in the back of her mind were thoughts of the future, of her parents and brothers—and of Adam—and the secret she was keeping from them all.

They sat quietly for a few moments. Juliet watched her grandmother sleep, then turned to face Leah. "I got a letter from Cash today," she said abruptly, her voice pitched low enough to avoid waking Aurelia.

Two months earlier Cash had joined the army and left Juliet to face her pregnancy alone. Leah thought Juliet was better off without him, but she didn't tell the girl that. She wasn't in the best position right now to be counseling the teenager on affairs of the heart.

"What did he have to say?" Leah whispered back, trying to ignore her aching head to concentrate on Juliet's words.

Juliet put her half-eaten cookie and her teacup back on the tray and rested her hands on her distended belly. "He says he doesn't know how he can send me any support money for the baby, because the military doesn't pay much. He said I should've been more careful and I wouldn't have gotten pregnant."

"It takes two people to make a baby, Juliet, and the law says Cash has to take responsibility for fathering your baby and pay support."

"I don't have the money for a lawyer to fight him on it."

"We'll get this worked out. Don't worry about it today."

"I'll try not to. You always seem to know all the answers. That's the difference between your having a baby and not being married and me. You knew what you were doing. I just wanted Cash to like me, so I let him talk me into having sex. How could I have made such a stupid, stupid mistake?"

"Juliet, don't upset yourself over what's past and unchangeable. You made a mistake, yes, but it's the same one many women before you have made." Leah felt like a hypocrite. She had acted just as impulsively and heedlessly, and ended up in the same condition.

"Cash said he'd heard that some couple from Lexington wanted to adopt the baby. I guess maybe that lawyer they sent around to talk to me talked to other people, too, and figured out who my baby's daddy was. He said he thought it would be a good idea. We could both get on with our lives without a baby to worry about. He's probably right—it would be better for the baby. If I had an education and a good job like you, it would be different. Then I could raise him by myself.'' Juliet began to cry, silently. Big tears ran down her cheeks.

"Juliet, I'm so sorry.'' Leah felt like more of a hypocrite than ever. Juliet had accepted her explanation that she'd met a man she cared for, but their lives were too separate to allow them to be together, so Leah was going to raise their baby alone. Juliet had assumed that Leah had planned her pregnancy, and coward that she was, Leah had let her go on thinking that way.

"It's okay. I knew he was never coming back here to be a father to our baby. I don't want him to, the rat, but I don't want to give up the baby. Do you think I can keep him and still go to school? If I don't get the scholarship, I'll get a job. I can do it, Leah, can't I?''

Leah's pounding headache worsened suddenly, almost blinding her with its intensity. She hesitated a moment too long before she answered. Juliet's eyes filled with tears again. She brushed them angrily away with the back of her hand. "You think I should give my baby up, too, don't you?''

Leah fought to clear her thoughts. "No, Juliet, but I think you can't make that important a decision so quickly. Let's wait and see if you get the scholarship and then we can find good day care and a safe, clean place for you to live near the university. Let's concentrate on taking care of you, so your baby is born safe and healthy. We'll talk as much as you want, as often as you want, and whatever decision you make I'll stand by you, okay?''

Juliet nodded. "Okay. It's just that most days I want to keep him, but once in a while I think it would be better for the baby to be with two parents who will love him and give him everything he needs and wants.''

''That's perfectly normal.''

''You don't think that means I wouldn't be a good mother?''

''No. I think that means you realize what an awesome undertaking raising a child alone will be.''

''Well, if I do keep the baby, and oh, most days I want to so badly…well, we can learn about being mothers together, can't we?''

''Yes,'' Leah assured her. ''We'll learn together.''

''The tea didn't help your headache, did it?'' Juliet asked softly.

Leah realized she was rubbing the back of her neck again. Her head was throbbing. Dark spots danced before her eyes. ''No, it didn't,'' she admitted. Her heart was hammering against her chest. Anxiety skittered along her nerve endings. She really needed to lie down, unwind. It was bad for the baby, her feeling this way.

''You don't look too good,'' Juliet said bluntly.

''I'll be fine, but I do think I'll call it a day.'' Leah stood up and the room swung in slow circles around her.

''Leah?'' There was alarm in Juliet's voice. She reached up and took the half-full teacup Leah was holding from her hand before she dropped it. Leah barely noticed.

She made it to the small kitchen at the back of the cabin, then dropped into a chair and laid her head on the scrubbed pine table. The room was still spinning and waves of nausea washed over her. Instinctively she put her hand on the gentle swell of her belly. Juliet saw the protective gesture, recognized it for what it was and acted.

"I'm calling Doc Owens," she said, heading for the telephone hanging on the kitchen wall.

"No, Juliet, I just need a minute to rest. It's a dizzy spell, that's all." Leah tried to stand up. The room rushed away from her down a narrowing tunnel. She laid her head back down on the table. Slowly the dizziness faded. She sat up and managed a smile. "There, it's passed. I just stood up too quickly, that's all."

Juliet laid her hand on Leah's shoulder. "It's too late. I already called Doc Owens. He's on his way to pick you up."

"GOOD MORNING."

Leah opened her eyes and blinked against the bright band of sunlight that fell across the bed. She lifted her head, took a look around the unfamiliar room and then down at the oversize T-shirt and shorts she was wearing—red and gray with a big block *O* for Ohio State, Margaret Owens's alma mater. She remembered putting them on and lying down to rest—about midnight. "Don't tell me I've been here all night."

"You have," Caleb Owens said. He walked farther into the room, smiling his cat-who-ate-the-canary smile. He was a small man with a big presence, built solid and low to the earth. Caleb was nearing sixty. His hair was gray now and mostly gone on top. He wore what remained long, tied in a ponytail with an old leather thong. He favored plaid flannel shirts and blue jeans; Ben Franklin glasses perched on the tip of his nose. You might be fooled into thinking you were dealing with a small-town doctor who was twenty years behind the times—until you looked into his eyes. There you saw the wisdom and expertise of thirty-five years of medical know-how and you were reassured. Caleb was her employer; he was also her friend and mentor. But that didn't mean she wasn't upset with him.

"You tricked me. You said that sedative would only put me out for a couple of hours."

"A couple, eight, what's the difference?"

"A lot." Leah turned her attention inward, taking inventory. Nothing hurt. Her headache was gone. Her heartbeat had returned to normal. The baby moved, a series of light flutters that brought a smile to her face. "I have to go to the bathroom," she said, and sat up. Everything still felt fine, except for the pressure on her bladder. She wasn't dizzy or short of breath. Her blood pressure must be back within the normal range.

"Good, that means the diuretic's working. I'll check your vital signs when you get back, and then Margaret has breakfast ready for us." He motioned toward the bathroom with the hand that held his stethoscope. "There are towels in the cabinet and a toothbrush on the sink, and your fatigues are in there, too. Margaret washed and dried them for you. Your dog tags are in your purse, in case you've noticed they're missing."

"I did notice. And Margaret didn't have to go to all that trouble."

"I know that." Caleb smiled. Margaret was five years older than he was and had retired from teaching third grade at Slate Hollow Elementary at the end of the last school year. She wasn't taking to retirement any better than Leah's father was. "I'll meet you in the kitchen. Take your time."

"Thanks."

Fifteen minutes later she was washed and dressed with clean teeth and combed hair. She walked into the sunny kitchen at the back of the house and greeted Margaret, who was making pancakes at the stove. Margaret was small and plump with short, curly black hair that never showed a strand of gray, thanks to Bette, down at the Cut and Curl beauty shop.

The older woman waved her into a chair by the window. "Go sit in the sun while I fill your plate. There's a pair of cardinals at the feeder."

"I see them," Leah said, and did as she was told. Forty feet behind the feeder the yard ended in a steep upward slope that contained a rock garden. In the summer it was covered in wildflowers and now held beds of tulips and narcissus, and purple and white crocuses. Gardening was one of Caleb's passions. He sat down beside Leah and took her blood pressure while Margaret stood by with two big bowls of oatmeal. Leah's stomach growled. Caleb unwrapped the blood-pressure cuff from around her arm and took the stethoscope tabs out of his ears.

"Much better," he said.

"But you're putting me on more medication, anyway."

He nodded. "We tried it your way. You didn't play by the rules. Eat your oatmeal." Sometimes Caleb seemed to forget that Leah wasn't his daughter.

"Caleb, I don't have time to spend half the day in bed. I—"

"Do you want to lose this baby? Maybe have a stroke?" he asked.

"No."

"Then you'll do things *my* way from now on."

"What's *your* way?" she asked suspiciously, although she knew very well what he would prescribe.

"Medication to keep your blood pressure down. There are a couple of new ones that are safe for pregnant women. We'll see which one you tolerate better. If you have to drink coffee, make sure it's decaf, take regular rest periods and cut down on work hours."

"Caleb, we can't keep up with all our patients now."

"We'll manage."

"I'm a single mother, remember? I can't afford to start babying myself."

"I'd say you can't afford not to. Your reserve unit's up for rotation to Bosnia, isn't it?"

"Yes," she said, knowing what was coming.

"I'll get in touch with your CO. Have you put in for medical leave?"

Leah was one step ahead of him on that front. "I've already informed them of my pregnancy. My medical leave starts at the end of the month. I'm thinking of resigning my commission. If I was married, it would be different."

Caleb looked down at his bowl of oatmeal and not at her. "You've stood your watch, Leah. You have a child to think of now."

"A child for whom I have sole responsibility." Her voice cracked a little. She took a spoonful of her oatmeal to cover the lapse. It was rich and hot and sweet with brown sugar, but it stuck in her throat like glue. Why had she said that aloud? It sounded as if she was uncertain of the choice she'd made to raise her baby alone.

"We'll always be here for you," Margaret said. "You're like the daughter we never had. You know we only want what's best for you and the baby, and since you haven't told your parents, Caleb and I have felt like, well, we should stand in their place." Something in Margaret's voice alerted Leah. She put down her spoon.

"Thank you, Margaret. I've taken comfort knowing you've both been here for me these past few months. I love you both, too." Their steadfast support had made the early frightening days facing the reality of her situation easier to bear.

Margaret sat down and patted Leah's hand with her plump, liver-spotted one. "I'm glad you know we have your best interests at heart. We were worried about you last night—your blood pressure was dangerously high. Caleb wanted to put you in the hospital, but you were so adamant." Leah's recollection of the hours after she'd left Aurelia's place were hazy, but she hadn't believed herself or her baby to be in danger. Now, seeing Margaret's worried face and Caleb's set jaw, she began to suspect otherwise. "High enough that you could have had a stroke. Thank God, you're better now," Margaret said, patting her hand once more.

"*Now* is the operative word. Stress has a lot to do with your condition, Leah. I shouldn't have to tell you that. Mental and emotional well-being are important in a healthy pregnancy.'' Caleb spoke in the tone of voice she'd heard him use countless times before—to a patient who was resisting his medical advice.

Leah's heart beat a little faster. Margaret, usually so straightforward, wouldn't quite meet her eyes. ''What are you getting at, Caleb?''

''Just remember we were worried sick about you and the baby,'' Margaret interrupted.

''Caleb!'' Leah prodded impatiently.

''You need help, Leah. Support. Emotional, if not financial, and I know what you make, so that's a factor, too. You're spreading yourself too thin. I know you're worried about your parents' adjusting to retirement. I know how much time you spend with Juliet and Aurelia.''

''They need me. Juliet's carrying a burden no teenager should have to bear.''

''I'm not saying you shouldn't do what you can for the girl and the old woman, but you don't know when to stop. That's always been your problem.''

''Picking up strays,'' Leah said, half to herself.

''We'll help Juliet all we can,'' Margaret interjected. ''You know that.''

''As your doctor my first responsibility is to you and *your* baby. Oh, hell. I've never done anything so damned unprofessional in my life, but I don't regret it.'' Caleb stood up and ran his hand over the top of his head. ''I wasn't thinking like your doctor. I was thinking like a friend—more than a friend. I did what any parent would do, Leah. What your father would have done if he were here.''

''I take it you're trying to tell me you went behind my back to tell my parents?''

"Not your parents, dear, although we tried to reach them, but they're out of town. The manager of their apartment said he didn't think they were due back for another two or three days. We thought it was for the best, Leah. Please understand."

Leah listened to Margaret's words with a sinking heart. She knew what she was going to say next. "How did you find out who the father is?"

"You're due the third week of August. It doesn't take a genius to figure out you got pregnant while you were in Vietnam. I called B.J. He told me in his opinion it could only be one man."

Margaret looked at her husband, then back at Leah. "Caleb called Adam Sauder last night. He's already on his way."

CHAPTER EIGHT

ADAM SHOVED HIS SUITCASE into the closet and shut the door. He looked around the motel room trying to decide what to do next. Making decisions, even the smallest and most everyday kind, was becoming more and more of a chore. He should have stopped somewhere along the interstate and gotten a room; but he wouldn't have been able to sleep, so he kept driving. He'd left cold, blustery Chicago late the evening before, bisecting the moon-washed farmlands of Indiana, meeting the sunrise as he skirted Cincinnati and headed south into the hills of Kentucky. He'd thought of Leah often over the long, cold winter and regretted letting her walk out of his office and his life that December day, but never once had he imagined she was pregnant and keeping it a secret from him.

Brian knocked lightly on the connecting door and then opened it. With raised eyebrows he surveyed the spartan furnishings and the TV on a shelf on the wall. "Exact clone of my room," he said, shaking his head. "The Hideaway Inn. Your Home Away from Home. I don't think so. But the view is awesome. Have you checked it out?"

Adam hadn't. The curtains were still drawn over the window behind the cheap, plastic-topped table and chairs. Brian opened them and Adam was treated to a view of hills and valleys marching off into the distance. Mist rose like smoke in the early-afternoon sunshine. The trees covering the hillsides were cloaked in spring greens, darker and fuller on the valley floor, pale and new on the higher slopes. A small river ran behind the motel, its clear waters tumbling over rocks, its banks lined on the far side with willow trees.

"Kind of makes up for the Bates Motel decor, doesn't it?" Brian said.

"We could ask for rooms in the new addition." The Hideaway Inn was undergoing extensive renovation and remodeling. A whole new wing had been added on the highway side of the building and had just opened for business, the manager had told them.

"Nah, I'd rather stay here and keep the view."

"Then we stay."

"I bet there are some decent rapids on that river. Wonder if anyone does any kayaking around here."

"We'll ask around."

"It can wait. We're not here for R and R." Brian was silent for a moment looking out the window, then he turned back to Adam. "If you have calls to make, I'll disappear for a while."

His son had been with him when Caleb Owens's call had come the night before. Brian had left him alone to talk to the older man in private, but he'd known something was up. Later Adam told him Leah Gentry was carrying his baby and there were complications with the pregnancy, and that was all he knew. He hadn't expected Brian to insist on coming to Kentucky with him, but he had. "You'd do the same for me," he'd said, grim-faced.

"Owens isn't coming after me with a shotgun," Adam reminded his son now.

"I wouldn't be so sure." Brian didn't smile back. He hadn't smiled once since Adam had told him about the baby. These past months he'd been making headway in his relationship with his son but not much else in his life.

"I should check on Leah's condition before I go see her."

"Why don't you just ask her yourself how she's feeling? How hard could she be to find in a burg this size?"

Brian had a point. Adam didn't want information about Leah filtered through a protective friend. He wanted to confront her face-to-face. Hear from her own lips why she'd hidden the knowledge of her pregnancy from him all these months. "Okay, I will."

"Dad...you won't just swallow her story whole, will you? I mean...well, maybe it isn't your kid. Maybe she just wants to find a rich dad for her brat."

"Brian, get this straight—I slept with Leah Gentry. We didn't use any form of birth control. It was not quite five months ago, and according to what Caleb Owens told me last night, Leah is eighteen weeks pregnant. It's my baby."

Brian looked defiant. "She wouldn't be the first woman to try a scam like that."

"Not Leah."

Something in his voice must have warned his son to drop the subject. "Okay, I'll take your word for it, but I still want to see for myself. That's why I came along. If this is your baby, then it's my half brother or sister, just like Megan. I don't want to be a stranger to him. I want us to be family.''

Adam didn't know how to respond. He had no idea yet what part he himself was going to play in the baby's life. Obviously Leah had intended that he'd never know about the child. She may be just as adamant that he and Brian have *no* connection.

''I'll talk to her about your concerns.''

''Yeah. It would probably be awkward if I'm there the first time you two see each other.''

''I think it would be best.''

''How's this—you take the Cherokee and I'll do the grand tour on foot. I figure I'll be back here sacked out on the bed in half an hour, tops. If I don't get lost or caught in rush-hour traffic, that is.''

''I don't think that's likely to happen.''

''Joke,'' Brian said. ''It was a joke. Slate Hollow's not quite the center of the universe.''

Adam had thought Slate Hollow would be a dying mining town, but he was wrong. There was an air of energy and bustle to the small community that he hadn't expected. Leah's hometown might be off the beaten track, but it wasn't behind the times.

''Let's leave the Cherokee. I'll walk with you. I need the exercise after the long drive.''

''Have you got her address?''

''It's 114 Huckleberry Street.''

Brian rolled his eyes. ''Huckleberry Street. Figures. Remember, Dad, I'm here if you need me.''

LEAH WATCHED ADAM and his son approach her house from behind the veil of her lace curtains. She'd been home for less than an hour. She'd barely had time to change out of her fatigues into something more comfortable, let alone have time to order her thoughts and armor her emotions. Briefly she considered not answering the door, but that was the coward's way out and would only delay the inevitable confrontation. She watched the two men without their knowledge as they stood talking in the benign April sunlight. Aurelia had predicted the weather would change, but so far the rain had held off.

Leah had been expecting Adam, but not his son. She had only seen Brian once, that day in Adam's office, and the entire unsettling episode was a blur in her memory. She remembered him having dark eyes, and Adam's square-jawed profile, but little more. She studied him now from the safety of her living room. He had his father's physique and mannerisms. Would her baby look like him when he grew up, if the baby was a boy? She smiled, thinking of Aurelia insisting the baby was a girl. Time would tell. She hadn't had an ultrasound yet, and when she did she wasn't going to ask the sex of the baby. She preferred to wait and be surprised.

Leah caught herself up short. She'd made that decision when she'd had no one else to please but herself. Would Adam expect to be consulted now? Would he want to know the sex of the child before it was born? Did he even care?

He must care, she thought, or he wouldn't be standing outside her door less than a day after he'd been told he was going to be a father.

Brian nodded at something his father said, then turned and walked on down Huckleberry Street toward the river, his hands thrust deep into the pockets of his jacket. What did Brian think of her pregnancy? Judging by his body language just now, she would say he was not pleased about the news of a new half brother or sister. He was another unknown quantity to factor into the equation of her future. Her heart began to race and she took a deep breath. Giving in to incipient panic wouldn't help her or the baby. Adam came up the brick walk and knocked on the door.

She tugged on the hem of her oversize T-shirt and stopped herself from pulling it away from her stomach. The gesture had become a habit over the past several weeks, one that was soon going to be a futile exercise. She felt the baby move inside her. Her nervousness must have communicated itself to the little one.

She opened the door at his knock. "Hello, Adam." She was pleased to discover her voice was steady.

"Hello, Leah."

"Come in. I've been expecting you." She realized with a shock that he'd lost weight over the winter, and the stress lines between his nose and mouth seemed to have become permanently etched into his skin.

"Thank you."

"I saw Brian through the window. I didn't expect him to come, too. Does that mean he's still living with you?" She held out a hand to take his coat.

Adam shrugged off the invitation, as though he needed the layers of leather and padding to insulate himself from his surroundings. "Yes. He's laid off his construction job right now, and he decided I needed some backup."

"He isn't happy about the baby, is he?"

"Actually he seems pleased to know he'll have another brother or sister. Leah, why didn't you tell me about the baby?"

"I'm not certain I can answer that right this moment."

"Is the child mine?"

She lifted her chin and her eyes met his. "Yes," she said simply.

He ran his hand through his hair. There were threads of gray in it now that she hadn't noticed in Vietnam. "Of course it is. I'm sorry I asked."

"You had every right to. We can do blood tests if you…" She forced herself to keep her hands at her sides. With every fiber of her being she wanted to cross them over her stomach, protect her baby and her heart from the coolness in his voice, the emptiness in his gaze.

"No, that's not necessary. It's just that it's been so long since there's been a woman in my life." He stopped speaking for a moment, then began again. "My ex-wife and I tried to have another child for several years after Brian was born, but she never conceived. I thought it was me."

"And I should have known better. I think the charge of carelessness can be laid at both our doors." She motioned him to a chair in front of the fireplace.

"I've been sitting behind the wheel all night. Do you mind if I stand?"

"No, of course not." She didn't like him towering over her, but she saw he was far too restless to sit still. She sat down and by habit tugged at her shirt.

She caught herself doing it, looked up and found he was watching her.

"What does your family think of your being pregnant?" he asked, moving around the room, stopping by a picture of her parents and brothers taken the last time they'd been together, two years before.

"They don't know," Leah admitted.

He turned around. "I was under the impression you were very close."

"We are. But my parents are having some problems of their own right now, and my brothers are based on two different continents." She caught herself sighing and straightened her shoulders. "The timing just hasn't been right, but time is running out." She tried to smile and almost got it right. "I have got a lot of explaining to do, and soon."

He stopped pacing and turned to face her. "Only if you're ready to, I'd think."

This time her smile was genuine, if rueful. "You've never lived in a small town, have you?"

He shook his head.

"It will be everyone's business, at least until the next little bit of scandal comes along."

"Scandal?"

"I'm exaggerating. Let's say until the next bit of news comes along. Don't worry. No one's going to have me shunned or ridden out of town on a rail. I won't be the only unmarried woman with a child in Slate Hollow."

Adam frowned down at her. "I know enough about Caleb Owens from B.J. to know he'll stand by you, but—"

"These people are my friends," she said with conviction.

"And you intend to stay here and raise the child alone."

"Yes." This conversation was terribly awkward. Did they have to plan the baby's entire future now, in the space of half an hour? She couldn't deal with so much so quickly. Not today when her head felt like a block of wood on her shoulders, and she was so shaky she went weak in the knees whenever she stood up. She felt the familiar tightness in the back of her neck, but resisted the effort to try to massage it away.

"Are you feeling okay?"

"I'm fine." At least he hadn't asked her if she'd considered terminating the pregnancy. For some reason she took comfort in the thought that at least he knew her well enough to realize abortion wasn't an option for her.

"How long have you been having trouble with your blood pressure?"

"Almost since the beginning. But yesterday..." She let the sentence trail off into silence. It had been a frightening few hours. "Yesterday it went off the charts."

"And today?"

"It's within normal limits." *Barely.*

"I'm glad to hear that. I'll check with Owens about the dosage of your medication."

"That's not necessary." A spurt of anger energized her. "The only thing you contributed to this pregnancy is motile sperm. Your involvement ended there."

Adam blinked at her plain speaking. "Because you chose to keep our child a secret from me," he said quietly.

Less than twenty-four hours ago she'd believed she would never see him again. She wasn't prepared to have him walk back into her life and demand his rights as a father. Leah stood up too quickly. The blood drained from her head. She took a step forward and held out her hand, searching for something to break her fall.

In a heartbeat his arms were around her. "Leah, what's wrong?"

She looked up into his eyes and thought she saw fear and concern in their depths. Or did she only wish it was there? She closed her eyes. "Nothing. I...I'm just a little dizzy."

"You're white as a ghost." He scooped her up in his arms, just as he had once before. She laid her head against his shoulder, felt the softness of old leather beneath her cheek, the beating of his heart, the strength and heat of him, and couldn't stop remembering all that had happened between them in Vietnam.

"Where's the bedroom?"

He stood with her cradled in his arms until she answered. "The door on the right." Her house was small and square. A living room extended across the front, and the kitchen, bath and bedroom were also downstairs, which was bisected by an open stairway leading to a loft above. She'd had a skylight installed in the loft so her living room was always flooded with sunlight, but her bedroom was cramped and shadowed, only a small single window above the bed letting in light. Adam laid her down on the coverlet, then sat beside her, his hip against hers. She edged a little away from him so their bodies didn't touch.

If her rejection of his nearness affected him, he didn't let on. He picked up her wrist and felt her pulse. "It's racing like a freight train. Do you have a blood-pressure cuff?"

"In the drawer." She lay quietly while he took her blood pressure, fighting back tears. What if it was too high again? Caleb would put her in the hospital or confine her to bed. What was she going to do then? She had some money put away for emergencies, but she couldn't afford to be bedridden for five months. Tears clogged her throat and, try as she might to hold them back, they welled up and spilled down her cheeks. "What is it?"

"It's okay, Leah." Adam took the tabs of the stethoscope out of his ears and unwound the cuff from her arm. "It's 128 over 82. Not bad considering what you've been through in the past twenty-four hours. What about your blood sugar?"

She answered without looking at him. "It's okay. I checked it this morning. Are you sure you read the gauge right?"

"Want to double-check?" There it was, that rare hint of laughter in his voice she found so irresistible.

Leah shook her head, not trusting herself to speak.

"Does the baby feel okay to you? Active? Moving around?" He shifted slightly as though to reach for her.

"Yes, the baby's fine." She laid her hand on her stomach. She didn't want him to touch her there, to make a connection with their child. She wouldn't be able to keep him at arm's length if he did. It would be too easy to let herself start to rely on him.

"All right, I'll take your word for it, but something caused you to nearly faint into my arms."

"It must have been the aftereffects of the sedative Caleb gave me. I don't respond well to drugs. I'm the cheapest drunk you've ever seen."

He laughed softly then, low and rumbling. The baby kicked as though he, too, had heard the laughter and liked it. "I'll remember." He reached over and wiped the pad of his thumb across her cheek. His touch was as warm as his laughter. "Leah, tell me what's wrong."

"Everything," she said, unable to censor the words. "Just everything."

"You don't mean everything. You mean my being here, don't you?"

"Yes. No." She covered her eyes with her arm. "I mean everything. Having something go wrong with my body that might put the baby in danger. Having to tell my parents about the pregnancy when they've got enough of their own problems. Trying to imagine what my brothers will say when they find out their baby sister's knocked up and not getting married. But mostly it's you. I didn't want you to know. I never wanted you to know."

"But I do know and there's no going back now."

"What do you want from me, Adam?"

"What do you want from *me?*" he asked in return.

"To be left alone."

"That's not an option."

"No, I suppose it's not. I'm sorry. I'm just too tired and fuzzy-headed to make important decisions tonight. Please, Adam, just go back to your motel and let me consider the changes in our situation.'' She couldn't hide the exhaustion that tinged her words and didn't try.

"I'm not leaving you alone. If you don't want me here, tell me who to call.''

"Margaret, Caleb's wife. She'll come.''

The mattress shifted as he stood up. ''Get this straight, Leah. You consider all you want, but I'm not leaving Slate Hollow until I'm sure you and the baby are both healthy and going to stay that way. It's my baby, too. You're going to have to come to terms with it. I'm here to stay.''

CHAPTER NINE

FOR THE NEXT TWO DAYS Leah was the perfect patient. She let Margaret bully and pamper her. She slept for hours at a stretch. She ate enormous meals and spent time sitting on a garden bench outside the back door between rain showers, thinking of nothing more taxing than where to set the birdbath this year. Adam had stayed out of her way, although she knew he was still in town, because now and then through her bedroom door she heard his voice, talking to Margaret, or Caleb when he stopped by.

Then this morning, awaking clearheaded and alert, she'd decided it was time to take back control of her life. She called her parents to find that her dad had gotten a new job he liked, and her mother, sounding more like her old self, had said she was learning how to paint in watercolors, something she'd always wanted to do. Leah had listened to updates on her brothers and their lives, and then, when her mother asked what was new with her, she took a deep breath and told Christine Gentry her news.

It had been easier than she'd thought. Her mother had been surprised and a little dismayed, but took the announcement in stride. Her dad, listening on the extension, had been silent for a long moment, then told her he loved her and agreed with her decision to keep the baby. He also wanted to know if she intended to marry the baby's father. She told him no.

She knew her mother would tell her brothers the news as soon as she could track them down. It wasn't in Christine's nature to keep secrets from her family, and Leah resigned herself to probing calls from all three of her siblings in the very near future. She told her parents she loved them both, would come to see them the first weekend she could get away and then hung up, amazed at how much better she felt to have that hurdle behind her.

Caleb had taken her name off the surgery schedule, so she wouldn't be going back to twelve-hour stretches in the OR for several weeks. She felt rested and less anxious. Her headaches and racing pulse had disappeared. Unfortunately Caleb had forbidden her to drive her Jeep. Until he was certain the medication he'd prescribed had her blood pressure completely under control, he didn't want to chance her having a dizzy spell while she was behind the wheel. She had agreed, reluctantly. But it didn't mean she intended to sit on her hands for the rest of the week.

She was worried about Aurelia and she wanted to check on her and Juliet. The Lexington lawyer representing the couple who wanted to adopt Juliet's baby was not above pressuring the girl when no one was around to keep her in check. Caleb had offered to take Leah up the mountain himself that evening, but she wanted to go now.

She stepped out onto the front porch of her house, her arms wrapped around her to ward off the damp chill of the April day. The sky was gray and heavy with low-lying rain clouds. The tops of the hills beyond the river were hidden in mist. The red emperor tulips lining her front walk were the only bright note of color in a mostly gray world.

A black utility vehicle pulled to a halt in front of her house. A man got out. For a moment she thought it was Adam and wished she hadn't convinced Margaret to go home after lunch. She wasn't ready to face him alone again. She thought she might never be. But it wasn't Adam coming up the crushed-stone walk. It was Brian.

"Hello," she said.

He stopped at the foot of the steps. Leah studied his features for signs of his father. His hair was as dark as Adam's, but up close she could see auburn highlights. His eyes were brown, not as dark as his father's, but like the brown of his leather jacket, and there was a line of freckles across his nose. "Hi, I'm looking for my dad. Has he been here?"

"Not today," Leah said.

"He told me he was going for a run, but that was before lunch. I thought…"

"He might have come here, instead?"

"This seemed like the most logical place to start looking."

"I'm sorry. I haven't seen him."

"He's been gone a long time." There was a hint of worry in his voice.

"It's possible that he left the road to follow one of the old logging trails."

"Yeah, I thought of that." He looked off toward the hills. "It'd be easy to get lost up there or step on a stone and twist your ankle."

"If you like I could come with you to look for him."

"Are you well enough to be out riding around with me? I don't want you doing anything to hurt the baby. It's my half brother or sister, you know." His eyes flickered to her stomach before settling on her face.

"I'm fine."

He frowned a little, the same way Adam did. "If you're sure you're okay, I'd be grateful for the help."

"Good. Wait a moment while I get a sweater."

When she emerged from the house five minutes later, Brian was waiting where she'd left him. He walked her to the shiny black vehicle and opened the passenger door. She thanked him and settled herself in the seat while he climbed behind the wheel. "Which way?" he asked. The powerful motor roared to life as Leah fastened her seat belt.

"Straight ahead until you get to the river and then take a left. There's only one road in and out of town, if you haven't noticed."

"I've noticed," Brian said. "I know this town by heart already, and I've only been here three days."

Leah laughed at the forlorn note in his voice. "You've never lived in a small town, have you?"

Brian shook his head. He eyed the swirl of white water as they neared the river. "Does anyone do any kayaking around here?"

"Not that I know of. At least not around town. But there's a canoe livery about five miles farther out in this direction, over near the state forest campgrounds. You could ask there." It had started raining again. Brian turned on the wipers and Leah watched them slide back and forth across the windshield.

"I don't know if we'll be around town long enough to do that, but thanks for the tip."

"If you're here long enough to check it out, just tell the owner I sent you. His wife is one of my pain-management patients."

"Pain management? I thought you were an anesthesiologist."

"I'm a nurse/anesthetist, but Dr. Owens and I also work together with a number of patients to control and alleviate the pain they experience from a variety of diseases and conditions."

"You mean like cancer?"

"Yes, cancer, and diabetic wounds, kidney disease, arthritis, spinal injuries...."

"I didn't know that about you."

Leah turned her head and watched him in profile. That was the way he looked the most like Adam. He had the same high forehead, strong nose and angled jaw. "I don't see any reason you should have."

He took his eyes off the road for a moment and returned her scrutiny. "You're right. My dad never spoke of you once after that day in his office last December. It never occurred to me that you and my dad were an item." He almost smiled. "Actually I did wonder for a minute when I met you if there wasn't something there. It was kinda in the air."

Leah felt her skin grow hot. She didn't want to talk about that day. "Your dad wouldn't want to run along the highway—there are too many trucks along this route. He would have turned off here." She pointed to the left, to the road leading up Pine Mountain.

"Why didn't you tell him about the baby?"

"It was a mistake, my sleeping with your father," she told him truthfully. "I've been confused about the best way to handle my pregnancy. It was just easier to keep the baby my secret. In retrospect I realize it's a course of action I shouldn't have taken."

"He had a right to know about the baby. Father's have rights, you know."

"I didn't say I'd done the right thing. Anyway it's a moot point now. Your father and I will have to come to some kind of agreement about the baby's future." And what was that agreement going to be? What part would Adam play in the baby's life? She didn't want a long-distance relationship with someone her child saw only on birthdays and every other Christmas. No father at all was preferable to that. She'd convinced herself of that months ago.

Brian flexed his hands on the steering wheel. "I have a little sister already, you know. I'm pretty good at being a big brother. Family's important to me."

"We'll try to work something out, Brian, but it's going to take some time."

They traveled in silence for a mile or two up the narrow, winding road. The pavement was slick, but Brian was a good driver. Leah tried to relax, although she couldn't help wondering what she would do or say if Adam had come this way, and they caught up with him along the side of the road. Talking to Brian about keeping the baby a secret from his father had made her feel anxious and uncertain again. She had so many decisions to make. Decisions that, right or wrong, would affect all of them for the rest of their lives.

The last half mile to the top of Pine Mountain was steep and winding. They met no cars coming from the direction of Danner's Mill, the town on the other side of the mountain, or a lone figure running along the side of the road. Brian pulled off the pavement at a turnout where, on a clear day, you could see for miles in every direction. But today the clouds obscured the view and the turnout was deserted. Brian rested both forearms on the steering wheel as he stared out into the mist. "I guess my dad didn't come this way."

"He must have gone in the other direction out of town. I'm sorry."

"It's not your fault." He put the Cherokee in gear and started back down the mountain. "He's probably back at the motel by now, anyway."

Leah couldn't help feeling relieved they hadn't found Adam. She wasn't ready to confront him yet. "Would you do me a favor?" she asked Brian.

"If I can."

"Would you mind dropping me off up here a ways? I'd like to check on one of my patients."

"I guess I can do that." Brian sounded doubtful.

"It's very close by. You don't have to wait for me. It may take a while."

"I'll wait. I'm not getting in trouble with my dad and what's-his-name, Dr. Owens, by dropping you off out here in the middle of nowhere."

"It's not quite the *middle* of nowhere," Leah said, making a joke. "But you can see it from the top of the ridge. Turn here," she directed, as they approached the turnoff to Aurelia's place. The road was fairly smooth in front of Naomi Dunn's, the neighbor who stayed with Aurelia at night, but once they'd passed her driveway it narrowed; the ruts got deeper and the puddles bigger. Brian shifted into four-wheel drive. Muddy water splashed onto the windshield as they passed Old Man Perkins's cabin. He'd been in a nursing home in Lexington since Christmas. No one else lived on the road, and Aurelia couldn't afford to have it graded and stoned. "I'll pay to have your car washed," Leah said as they bounced through a particularly deep puddle.

"No way. This is the kind of driving this baby's made for." Brian grinned over at her. "This must be awesome in the winter."

"It's terrifying in the winter."

Just then they came to the plank bridge over the stream. It was flanked by redbud and hawthorn trees, their rosy pink and white blossoms subdued by the mist. "Wow! Are you sure this thing's safe?" Brian asked, looking down at the tumbled boulders beneath the bridge. The water had risen with the two days of rain. It was only about a foot below the planking and running fast out of a small ravine to their left.

"Just take it slow and steady." Leah had been over the bridge a hundred times, but she always held her breath. The bridge was very old and not all that stable anymore. She often wondered how they would get the county emergency-services unit up here if Aurelia needed to be taken to the hospital.

Brian drove the Cherokee cautiously onto the bridge, crossed it and then gunned the engine as they shot up the steep bank on the far side, topped the rise and came abreast of Aurelia's one-hundred-year-old homestead. Brian turned into the overgrown yard and parked by Aurelia's old pickup truck. "Quite a defensive position they've got here," Brian remarked, looking up at the limestone ridge rising almost from the back door of the cabin, then noting the unobstructed view of the creek and the road beyond to be had from the front porch.

"Aurelia Cade's father was a moonshiner back in the twenties. It was good business to know who was coming up to the front door before they saw you."

"A moonshiner. You mean like Elliot Ness and the whole prohibition thing?"

"Yes."

"Awesome!"

"Aurelia can trace her family back to Daniel Boone." Brian whistled in appreciation and Leah smiled at his enthusiasm. She led the way up the sagging front steps and knocked on the heavy wooden door.

"Leah, is that you? Come in," Juliet called out.

"Hi, yourself." Leah motioned Brian to follow her through the pine-paneled main room, with its massive fieldstone fireplace, and on into the kitchen.

Juliet was sitting at the table, her schoolbooks spread around her. "You didn't drive yourself up here, did you?" she asked. "I thought Caleb was bringing you out tonight."

"No, I didn't drive myself. I'm following doctor's orders, as I recommend all my patients do. Someone offered to drive me." She stepped aside so Juliet's view of Brian was unimpeded. "Juliet Trent, this is Brian Sauder—my baby's half brother. Remember I told you about him the other day when you called?"

"It's nice to meet you, Brian. Welcome to our home."

Brian shook the hand she offered and smiled back. "Thanks."

"I'll go see how Aurelia is," Leah said.

Juliet disengaged her hand from Brian's and looked at Leah, blinking as though she'd just stepped from a dark room into the sunlight. "She's sleeping. The visiting nurse was here when I got home from school. She left some notes for you and Doc Owens."

"Good. I'll go check them, but I won't disturb Aurelia if she's sleeping. Do you mind entertaining Brian for a few minutes?"

"No. I...I'll take him out with me to gather eggs."

"Eggs?"

"Yes, eggs. You know, the kind chickens lay," Juliet said tartly.

"I know about eggs," Brian said defensively, and then grinned.

Juliet stood up and Brian's mouth fell open. He recovered quickly and hurried to open the door leading to the backyard. "We'll be right outside," Juliet told Leah. "Just holler if you need me to help with Granny."

Leah made shooing motions with her hands as Juliet waddled across the kitchen. "I promise. And, Brian..."

"Yes, ma'am?" He carefully avoided looking at Juliet's belly or Leah's.

"Be careful of the rooster. He doesn't like any other males in his henhouse."

JEEZ. HE DIDN'T THINK he'd ever seen any woman so...so pregnant. Juliet Trent was as big as a house. He was the first to admit he hadn't spent a lot of time around pregnant women, but he wasn't certain Juliet's shape was entirely normal. She looked like she'd swallowed a beach ball. She lifted a basket off a hook outside the back door and turned to find him standing there like an idiot.

"You look like you've never seen a pregnant woman before," she said.

"You're not a woman—you're a girl." Seventeen at the oldest, he guessed.

She angled her head toward a half-collapsed shed backed up against the side of the hill, surrounded by a sagging wire fence. Half a dozen scrawny brown chickens scratched in the stony dirt. A white rooster with a big red comb strutted importantly among his harem. "When you're nine months pregnant and you don't even know where your mom and dad are, and the father of your baby took off for boot camp without even calling to say goodbye, you're a woman."

"Sorry," Brian said, feeling foolish.

She put her hand on the small of her back, stretching her lilac-colored sweater over her distended stomach. A curl of hair worked its way out of the barrette that held it back from her face. She blew at it impatiently, then tucked it behind her ear. "It's not your fault I got myself knocked up. C'mon. You hold the basket and I'll get the eggs. Like Leah said, watch out. Lancelot, there, doesn't appreciate any other male invading his territory."

The inside of the old shed was dark, and it smelled. Juliet rummaged around in a couple of bins filled with straw and came up with two eggs. She dislodged two scrawny brown hens from their nests, setting them unceremoniously on the floor, and found a couple more. Brian stood his ground and hoped the indignant hens didn't do anything on his shoes.

"There," she pronounced. "I've got them all."

They walked back out into the pale sunshine, which had temporarily chased away the rain. Brian looked down at the four brown eggs in his basket. They seemed awfully small. "These are it?"

Juliet peered into the basket. "The hens are getting too old to lay good eggs. But Granny's woken up to a rooster crowing outside her window all her life, so I'm not getting rid of these chickens until I have to." Her voice broke on the last few words, and Brian was appalled to see a tear work its way out from under her sandy lashes and slip down her cheek.

"Hey, don't cry. I was just teasing about the eggs."

"It's not the eggs," she said fiercely, grabbing the basket out of his hands.

She whirled around so fast the chickens started clucking and fussing and flapping all over the yard. The rooster, apparently thinking Brian was the cause of the disturbance, charged at him. He had to do some fancy, broken-field running to get out of the pen without getting pecked. He scuttled through the gate and shoved the wobbly wood and wire barrier shut behind him.

"Man, you're right. He's one mean rooster."

Juliet laughed, and he was almost glad Lancelot had come after him. She had a pretty laugh, all tinkly and light. "Leah told you he was a mean 'un, Rich City Boy."

"My name's Brian, not Rich City Boy."

She stopped laughing abruptly. "You don't have

to be nice to me just because I'm Leah's friend." She stood there holding the basket in front of her like a shield.

"I'm not—"

Juliet cut him off. "I'm not asking for anyone's pity. I'm going to graduate from high school with honors in three weeks—if this little guy stays put until then." Her mouth softened into a smile for a moment, then hardened again. "In the fall, when Granny's stronger and can take care of herself, I'm going to nursing school somehow. I might even be a nurse/ anesthetist like Leah. Just because I made one dumb mistake in my life letting Cash Dentrell talk me into having sex with him doesn't mean I'm going to do anything as stupid again."

Brian waited until she'd run out of breath and out of words. "I'm not pitying you and I'm not passing judgment on you. I think you're pretty brave to be planning to raise a baby on your own and go to school. A lot of other girls…well, they would have made different choices, I think."

"Maybe they would, but they're not me. I'm not giving up my baby, do you hear?" She stopped, out of breath, and another tear rolled down her cheek.

Brian didn't know what to say. Even if she had money for day care and school, it would be a real load. And from the looks of this place, Juliet didn't have the money. But to give her baby up for adoption so she could go to school? What a hell of a choice. He didn't know what to say, so he took the basket out of her hand. "Do you have a handkerchief?" he asked.

"There's some tissues in the kitchen. But I'm not crying. It's just all the dust and feathers and stuff."

"Sure." He nodded.

"And I told you, you don't have to be nice to me because I'm Leah's friend."

"Okay, I won't." He grinned and held the door open for her. They heard voices from another room as they walked inside.

"Granny's awake," Juliet said, and her face lit up, but Brian could see a deep sadness in her eyes, and he realized, even though she'd told him her granny was going to get better, in her heart she knew the truth. "Would you like to meet her?"

It was a peace offering, and Brian accepted it as such, although he never felt very comfortable around sick people. "I'd like to meet your granny very much."

CHAPTER TEN

"HEY, DAD?" BRIAN'S VOICE came to Adam over the sound of running water.

"I'm in here," Adam replied, wiping the last of the shaving cream off his face.

Brian's reflection appeared over his shoulder in the bathroom mirror. "I *thought* I heard your shower running. You're back. I was almost ready to send out a search team. Where have you been?"

"Running." Almost far enough to guarantee he'd be so exhausted he could sleep. "I checked on you when I got back, but you were sacked out on the bed so I didn't wake you."

"Something about the air here, I guess," Brian said with a shrug. His image disappeared from the steamy mirror. He'd gone into the bedroom. "Or getting up so early in the morning." The landscapers working around the Hideaway Inn were on the job at 7:00 a.m. sharp. "How about something to eat? I'm starved."

"I could go for a bite," Adam said as he finished in the bathroom and joined his son.

Brian was sprawled in one chair, his feet propped on the other, looking out the window at the fading view of the river. "What sounds good to you?" he asked.

"You choose."

"Well, there's the pizza place next door or the burger joint out by the highway. Or the diner on the town square. I checked the special on their menu board today. It's fried chicken, mashed potatoes and gravy and corn bread, with strawberry pie à la mode for dessert."

Adam pulled on a sweatshirt. "From the attention to detail you gave the menu, I'd say you've already made up your mind."

"Well, yeah, I could go for the fried chicken."

"I could go for that myself." Adam was surprised to find he was hungry. He usually didn't care when or what he ate, or even *if* he ate most days.

"Then let's go." Brian stood up and grabbed his coat off Adam's bed. "It's nearly seven. They'll be out of the special if we wait too much longer."

"I'm ready." Adam picked up his wallet and room key, and they headed out into the misty twilight.

Brian had discovered a footpath along the river leading to a small park near the center of town, and with unspoken agreement they headed along it. They passed the Cherokee sitting under a security light and Adam noticed that its tires and sides were covered with mud. "Do a little off-road driving this afternoon?"

"I'll get it washed in the morning," Brian said quickly.

Adam shrugged. "No problem. That's what it was made for. Couldn't resist exploring those old logging roads up on the mountain, eh?"

"Not exactly," Brian said, as they walked abreast along the asphalt pathway. "I was on the mountain, but not off on an old logging road, although I can't say the one I was on was in much better shape. I took Leah to see one of her patients."

"Leah?"

Brian nodded. "I went over to her house looking for you. You were gone a long time."

"I ran farther than I expected." There were lights coming on in the houses they passed. Television light glowed in darkened living rooms. The mist was thickening, and the rush of water over the boulders in the riverbed noisy. The everyday noises from the town and the highway in the distance were blocked out. They were the only people on the pathway, and Adam felt as if he and his son were alone in the world.

"Looking for you was only part of the reason I went to see Leah. I wanted to tell her I hoped she'd let me be some kind of big brother to the baby. I...I ended up driving her up the mountain to this old lady's house."

"I'm glad you could be of help to her."

They'd arrived at a small bridge over a stream that came down the mountain to empty into the river. Brian stopped and, resting both hands on the railing, looked down at the water, although in the near darkness there was nothing to see. Adam turned his back to the river and watched the streetlights of the town flicker to life.

"Leah didn't exactly come up with a visitation schedule for me and the baby, but she said she'd think about it. But that wasn't all that happened. I met this girl. She lives with her great-grandmother—that's Leah's patient. Her name's Juliet Trent. She's seventeen—a senior in high school. The only person she loves in the world is dying and she's pregnant, too, only a lot farther along than Leah. And to top it all off the father joined the army and left her to deal with it alone.''

''That's a lot to handle when you're only seventeen.''

''She wants to be a nurse,'' Brian said, moving off the bridge and heading for the wooden steps that led up the embankment. ''But she doesn't have the money to go to college and pay someone to take care of the baby and her granny. That's what she calls her great-grandmother—Granny.''

Adam nodded encouragement as they topped the rise and crossed the square toward the diner. Brian didn't really need him to say anything, just to listen as he worked through his thoughts. If he'd done nothing else right these past few months, he had at least made enough headway with his son that the boy talked to him. It was more than a lot of parents could boast. It didn't make up for the years he'd missed with Brian, but it helped.

''There's this couple from Nashville—they'll pay for all Juliet's nursing-school expenses and for a private nurse to take care of her granny, if—''

''If she gives up her baby to them for adoption?''

''Yeah. It's a pile of crap.''

''It happens all the time, Brian. It's a perfectly legal arrangement, and in many cases it's the best solution for the mother and the child.''

''But Juliet wants this kid.''

''You seem to have learned an awful lot about her in one afternoon.''

Brian stopped dead in his tracks. ''Yeah,'' he said wonderingly, ''I guess I did.'' They waited for the red light at Main and First, then turned left at Harley's Fine Furniture. "I want to help her, Dad. Do you suppose Grandfather would advance me some money on my trust fund? I don't want her to have to sell her baby to go to school."

Adam chose his words carefully. He didn't want to put Brian on the defensive, but he had no idea what the details of Juliet Trent's circumstances were. Brian was too close to the situation at the moment to evaluate the choices with any degree of balance. Was it better for the girl to give up her child to a couple who would love and cherish it as their own? Or was she mature enough and strong enough to take on the challenge of raising a child and going to college at the same time? It wasn't an easy question to answer under any circumstances, and certainly not when he'd never met the girl.

"That trust fund is meant for your education, Brian," he said as they approached the restaurant. "I'm not sure what your grandfather would say if you asked to use money from it to help a girl you've met only once."

"I figured you'd say that. Could you lend me the money? I've got a little put away, but since I got laid off the construction crew last month…"

"It's possible she and the baby would both be better off if she did give it up for adoption. I'm sorry, Brian. I know you want to help her, but I can't go along with you on this. Not now."

"You really are a heartless bastard sometimes," Brian said angrily. "I thought doctors were supposed to understand about stuff like this. But you never did put yourself in the other guy's shoes, did you? Even when I was little you always stayed a step back from everything and everybody." He dropped his head back and stared at the sky, letting his breath out in a hiss. "The money's there—more than enough. What's so wrong with wanting to use it to help someone in a real jam?"

"It's a worthy ideal, but money often creates as many problems as it solves. Juliet may not be capable of raising a child and going to school at the same time. It's a tremendous burden. I know, because I was in med school when you were small. Can you assure me after a three-hour acquaintance that she's a mature and focused enough individual to meet the challenge? If you can, I'll get out my checkbook right now."

"You know I can't. But she wants to keep her baby. She cried, Dad." Brian aimed a frustrated kick at the tire of a vintage pickup parked at an angle in front of the restaurant.

"Hey there, son. Take it easy on my truck."

Brian swung around. Adam turned his head to see Caleb Owens and his wife come out of the recessed doorway of the restaurant and walk toward them. "I—I'm sorry, sir," Brian stammered. "I didn't—"

"No harm done. Adam, is this your son?" Caleb asked, extending his hand.

"Yes, it is. Brian, this is Dr. Caleb Owens and his wife, Margaret. They're friends of Leah's. Leah's a member of Dr. Owens's medical practice."

They shook hands all around. "Good to finally meet you, boy," Caleb said. "Wondered when I'd get around to it. Glad you could come down here with your father."

"I thought he could use the support."

Caleb cleared his throat. "Yes, there are quite a few things he and Leah have to work out." He grinned. "So you were admiring my truck, I gather."

"She's a beauty."

"Found her sitting in an old barn up in the hills. Restored her myself. Took me two years. Like to take her for a drive?"

"Sure, I..." Brian looked over Caleb's head through the big, plate-glass window of the restaurant. "We haven't had dinner yet."

"No problem. Margaret can keep your father company for a few minutes while I show you what Carlotta here can do."

"It'd be my pleasure," Margaret said smiling first at Brian and then Adam.

"You call the truck Carlotta?" Brian asked.

"Yeah, a pet name I have for her. C'mon, hop inside."

"Dad?"

"Go ahead. I'm assuming you want me to order you the fried chicken and all the trimmings."

Brian grinned. "And don't forget the strawberry pie."

"À la mode."

"We'll be back in fifteen minutes, Margaret."

"Take your time. I'll tell Delilah to hold the food until you get back. Now come on, Adam. It's too damp to be standing out here when Caleb and your son have given me the perfect excuse to go back inside and have a piece of strawberry pie myself."

IT WAS late that evening when Adam started up the walk to Leah's house. The softly glowing light beside her front door beckoned him. The street was quiet. Nothing like the well-traveled artery outside his condo in Chicago that reverberated with traffic noises day and night. This whole town was quiet. A dog barked somewhere in a backyard a couple of houses down. It was the loudest noise he'd heard in hours. His footsteps on the gravel walk disturbed a mourning dove in the tulip tree at the corner of the yard. Its plaintive cooing sifted through the new leaves and then died away. He paused outside Leah's door. He didn't know what he was going to say to her or what she wanted him to say, but he couldn't stay away any longer.

He knocked and a moment later Leah opened the door. Amazingly enough, she didn't look surprised to see him on her front porch at ten o'clock at night. "I didn't hear a car drive up."

"I walked," he said.

She frowned a little. "It's going to start raining again any minute."

He found a smile. Somehow she made smiling easy for him. "I won't dissolve."

Leah stepped back from the door. "Come in," she said. "Brian must have found you safe and sound when he returned to the Hideaway. If you were still missing by dark, he said he'd call me to get out a search party."

"I was running. I went farther than I thought."

"We looked for you, but we took the wrong way out of town. You must have crossed the bridge and run along the river?"

"Yes, as a matter of fact I did," Adam replied.

"There's not as much truck traffic on that road. How far did you go?"

"To a place called Cade's Crossing."

"Quite a run. The better part of ten miles there and back." She gestured toward a leather armchair in front of the fireplace. He shrugged out of his coat, which she draped over a straight-back chair in front of a small desk as he sat down.

"I was pushing it a little today. I don't often have time for such a long run." The room was filled with shadows. There were small crystal lamps on tables in front of the windows on each side of the door. A lamp in her bedroom shone through the doorway, casting a rectangle of light onto the wooden floor, but only a small fire in the fireplace illuminated the seating area. It was a cozy room with comfortable furniture that beckoned a tired body and mind to relax and unwind.

"I like to walk, but I gave up running years ago. I had enough of it in boot camp." Leah grimaced. She was wearing a denim jumper and raspberry-colored sweater that framed her face with warmth.

"It's a good thing I did run that far. The special at the diner tonight was fried chicken and mashed potatoes and gravy." It seemed to make Leah more comfortable if they just made small talk. He was willing to go along with her, at least for the time being.

"They do have good food there." She moved around the sofa and curled into the corner. She smoothed her skirt with her hand. Her fingers were long and slender. He remembered their softness against his skin.

"Yes, they do. I left Brian sprawled on his bed, swearing he'll never have to eat again." She smiled at the small joke. "Brian told me you spent the afternoon together," he said.

"He was kind enough to take me to see one of my patients after we'd given up searching for you."

"Might that visit have influenced your decision to look for me in that direction?"

"It might have," she said with a rueful laugh. He saw her relax a little more, as they both continued to avoid the dangerous but inevitable topic of the baby's future—their future.

"Brian was very taken by Juliet's situation. The girl's near term in her pregnancy. Do you think the old woman will live to see the baby born?"

"I hope so. She's stubborn and tenacious. But the cancer is very far advanced, and there is only so much we can do."

"I'm sorry." He wondered if the words sounded as meaningless to her as they did to him. Death was a part of life. Leah must have learned her own defense mechanisms to deal with that inescapable part of their professions, as he had. But Aurelia Cade was Leah's friend as well as her patient, and even the best defense mechanisms could be breached if your emotions got the best of you.

"It's hard to say goodbye to a friend," she said very quietly.

"Yes, it is." He changed the subject. "Brian told me Juliet has to decide whether or not to give her child up for adoption. A difficult choice for any woman to make. Doubly so for a teenager."

"I wish I could help her more, but it's a decision she has to make for herself." He imagined that it would be hard for Leah to stay neutral in this situation. She gave so much of herself to everything she did, to everyone with whom she was involved. "Brian said you were feeling much better today. You look...very well." He'd almost said "lovely." The right word, but far too intimate an observation to speak aloud.

"Thank you. I'm feeling much better. I'm sorry, can I get you something? Coffee or a beer?"

"No thanks. I won't be staying long. I just wanted to make certain you were all right."

She chose to answer him, instead of saying he could have made the inquiry over the phone without coming out on such a rainy night. "Caleb says my blood pressure's perfect. So are all the blood tests. Now if he would just tell me it's okay to start driving."

"He thought by Friday—"

"You've been discussing my pregnancy with him again?" Her eyebrows drew together in a frown.

"Yes," he said. There was no use denying it.

She fell silent for a moment, obviously trying to get her temper under control. The fragile rapport that had grown between them during the conversation evaporated in the heat of her displeasure. "Caleb means well, but there's no way I can convince him this is none of his business. He thinks babies should have two parents. He's old-fashioned that way."

"So am I."

"Adam..."

There was a warning in her tone, but he ignored it. "I've been thinking a lot about the future these past couple of days." The baby's future, he meant, not his own. He couldn't see much of a future for himself right now. He only thought about the past. Day and night. Waking and sleeping.

"Yes, I have, too," she admitted warily.

"What conclusions have you come to, Leah?" Adam laced his hands together and let them dangle between his knees. He didn't want her to see him shaking. She would feel sorry for him, and he didn't want that.

"I've concluded you must be a good father. Brian is a very nice young man."

He heard the approval in her voice and it warmed him. He lifted his head to look at her again. He could smile and say thank-you, and Leah, so unflinchingly honest, would despise him for taking credit for the way Brian turned out. "He's been with his mother since he was eleven."

"So he said, but he still thinks a great deal of you. He wouldn't have come down here with you otherwise."

"He wants to be part of the baby's life."

"I hope that's possible," she said carefully.

"I don't want to make the mistakes with this child that I made with Brian, Leah. When he was little, it seemed I was always too busy, too tired, or just plain not there for him. I want it to be different with this baby."

She stood up and moved to the fireplace. He watched as she knelt on the hearth and stirred the burning wood with a poker. Her pregnancy was not advanced enough to make her awkward or unsteady on her feet. Her movements were fluid and enticingly feminine. She rose and turned to face him, pushing at a strand of hair that had worked loose from her braid.

"You won't be making those same mistakes with this child, Adam, because you aren't going to have that kind of father-son relationship with my baby."

He was on his feet in a second. She didn't flinch or try to move away as he came to a halt in front of her. He should have expected this. She had told him as much the first night he'd seen her. She didn't want him in Slate Hollow. She didn't want him in her life now or in the future. But he wanted her. He was drawn to her as he would be to the heat of the fire on a cold day. The rage and fear that were always there inside him, caged in the smallest, darkest corner of his mind he could force them into, howled to be set free.

"I am going to be involved in this child's life," he said, hearing the anger in his voice and fighting to force it back into the cage. For the past three days, since Caleb's out-of-the-blue phone call telling him she was carrying his child, he'd clung to the memories of their night together like a lifeline. If there was any way in the world he could find a door out of the purgatory of his memories, this woman held the key.

"Don't threaten me, Adam."

"I'm sorry. I just wanted…"

She sighed. "I know you'll be involved in the baby's life, but to what extent? Not as a father, a real, come-home-to-us-every-night father. You'll be a birthday and Christmas and two-weeks-every-summer father."

"It doesn't have to be that way."

Leah reached out to him. She let her fingers brush

the sleeve of his shirt. It was the first time she'd willingly touched him since Vietnam. "Yes, it does. This
is my world, Adam. It isn't yours. It could never be
yours."

"I—"

"Adam, don't insult me by saying you would leave
what you have in Chicago for a place like Slate Hollow."

He could see himself doing so very easily. His life
in Chicago was nothing but a sham these days, a
tower of evasions and half-truths that sooner or later
would come tumbling down around him. But he
couldn't tell Leah this, not yet, anyway. It wouldn't
make any sense to her. Adam hesitated a moment too
long answering her, as he struggled to control his
emotions.

"I see no way for us to be together," she said
softly. "I can't give up my home, my friends and my
practice to follow you to Chicago for the same kind
of parenting relationship we would have if I stayed
here."

"We could be a family, Leah. Marriages have been
made for far less noble reasons than giving a child
two parents."

She moved a little farther away from him, into the
shadows. "No, Adam. It wouldn't work."

"I'd do my best to be a good husband and father."
It was a hell of a proposal, but she would reject anything less honest.

"I know you would. You would *try*. But I don't
think you would succeed. I think you've been shut
away from your emotions for too long. I won't subject

my child to that kind of heartache and rejection. I won't submit myself—''

"What the hell does that mean?'' He felt her pulling back from him. They'd connected for a few minutes back there. He'd had a glimpse of what life could be like in this house, with this woman. Quiet evenings before the fire, conversation, companionship and love. He wanted that goodness to keep away the terror.

"I told you before—I always take on the wounded and the strays. When I left home to join the army, I had to stop taking in the four-legged ones. It took me longer to stop taking in the two-legged ones. I'm not going to make any more mistakes with relationships that are doomed from the start. Our child doesn't need a father who is afraid of his feelings, and a mother with a broken heart. It will be better for the baby to have no father than one who's absent physically and a stranger emotionally. It will be better for me to have no husband—''

He crossed to her in three quick strides. "Fine, Leah, I won't talk about marriage again. But I told you that first night I wasn't going anywhere until we had come to some sort of custody arrangement. I'm not asking you—I'm telling you. I'm his father. He's going to know me.''

Her eyes widened in sudden alarm. He reached out to take her by the shoulders, to shake some sense into her. She raised her hand as though to ward him off. "No, Adam. Don't.'' He dropped his hands and stepped back. He shoved his fists in his pockets to hide their trembling. She'd caught a glimpse of the rage at the center of him, and she was frightened.

"I'm sorry. It won't happen again."

"You...startled me, that's all. I'm sorry I sounded as if I was issuing an ultimatum. And yes, please, don't talk about marriage again. But you're right, I can't order you out of my life even if I want to. You have rights." Her lips curved slightly in a mirthless smile. "I have to remember that."

"We have to sit down and work this out, Leah. I want this baby to know he has a father and mother who are there for him."

The grim smile disappeared. "It's going to take me a while to get used to the way things have changed. I don't know what's best for the baby—or for me. Give me a little time, Adam. You said you would stay as long as it takes."

It wasn't much of a victory, but probably all he could hope for tonight. "You're right. It's getting late." He moved to the little desk and picked up his coat. Leah stayed where she was in the middle of the room, her arms crossed defensively in front of her. "I'll leave now, but I'll be back in the morning."

"Brian said he'd drive me to the clinic and then to—"

"I know. He told me. But there's been a change of plans. Caleb offered to let Brian use his pickup so he could have a set of wheels of his own. It was an offer Brian couldn't refuse. He's going in search of kayaking water tomorrow. I'm going to be your chauffeur for the rest of the week, not my son. I'll pick you up at eight."

CHAPTER ELEVEN

THE SUN WAS SHINING when Leah saw Adam pull up in front of her house at eight sharp the next morning. She hoped the return of clear weather was a good omen. She'd spent another restless night. So far the only feeling she could trust was the instinct that warned her she was still dangerously attracted to him and needed to keep him at arm's length until she could decide what was best for the baby. She only hoped she had the strength of will to carry the plan through.

Adam came up the sidewalk to meet her as she closed and locked her front door. She was wearing white leggings and a long, white lab coat over a pink-and-white-striped tunic that pretty much announced itself as a maternity top. She saw where his eyes had strayed and smiled nervously. "Thanks for being so prompt. I hate to be late for work."

His eyebrows drew together in a slight frown. "Are you sure you're up to this?"

"Today's the day I'm going to tell my friends and co-workers about the baby," she said, rushing her words a little.

"And what about me?" he asked.

"I'll introduce you as the baby's biological fa-ther," she said, making no attempt to keep the challenge out of her voice. "If it makes you uncomfortable, you can drop me off at the clinic and go back to the motel."

"I have no objections," he said, then threw out a challenge of his own. "But are you comfortable making the announcement this way? After all, you've kept your secret for a long time."

"The sooner I get it over with, the sooner it will cease to be a nine-day wonder."

"And if I'm introduced at the same time as your pregnancy, the possibility of it being a virgin birth is also laid to rest?" His expression was as sober as ever, but his tone barely masked his pleasure at being able to gently tease her.

He was doing it again, drawing her to him, reaching out to make the connection she both dreaded and craved. She laughed, although a little nervously. "The thought had crossed my mind." This time he smiled. He had a wonderful smile. It was a shame he used it so little. "Would you do me a favor?" she asked.

"Certainly."

"Would you get my emergency kit out of the back of my Jeep? I don't like to go up into the hills without it."

"More house calls?" he asked as she led the way around the house to her garage and showed him the big gray metal box in the back of her Jeep.

"You appointed yourself my chauffeur, so I might as well take advantage of you. I'll be seeing patients at the clinic until after lunch, and then I want to check on Aurelia again this afternoon. We've been working on a different combination of meds for her pain. Caleb initiated the new regimen yesterday. I'll need to check on her at least once a day for the next couple of days.''

''Wouldn't it be easier to admit her for a day or two?''

''We don't like to admit our pain patients unless it's absolutely necessary. Don't you treat chronic-pain patients in your practice?''

''It's not my field of expertise,'' he said curtly.

He opened the door of her Jeep and tipped the seat forward. ''Who does your surgical interventions?'' Adam was referring to neurosurgical procedures that blocked or eliminated pain impulses to affected parts of the body, such as he'd performed on the old man with cancer in Vietnam. They were often methods of last resort when the pain had become unbearable, and Leah fought hard to keep her patients from going under the knife.

''Dr. Peter Assad in Lexington.''

''Good man. I've read some of his papers.''

He picked up the metal box and grunted in surprise at its weight. ''What do you have in here? One of those mobile hospitals B.J. dreamed up?''

Leah shook her head. ''Not quite. But we can't count on a ten-minute response time from the emergency unit up in the hills. It's best to be prepared to act on your own.''

''What have you had to do on your own?''

''Here? Nothing, thank God. But I helped deliver twins in Somalia.'' She had to lengthen her stride to keep up with him.

''Twins?'' He wasn't even breathing hard, although she knew the emergency chest weighed over fifty pounds.

"Goats—twin baby goats. The headman from the village near our aid station brought the nanny in. The first kid was breech. Our chief medic delivered them and I assisted. We were made honorary citizens of the village. The mother was their last producing nanny. It made her kind of a symbol of hope that good times would come back someday."

Adam hefted the emergency case into the back of the Cherokee. "Twins as a symbol of new beginnings." Adam paused and looked briefly at Leah. Then he changed the subject. "Anything else you need?" he asked as she opened the passenger-side door.

"No, I'm as ready as I'll ever be," Leah said casually. She wanted to get under way. New beginnings... Sometimes Adam said things that made her think he understood what she was going through more than she thought he did—and more than she wanted him to.

Adam closed the door for her, and then climbed in behind the wheel. He nosed the Cherokee into her driveway to turn around and headed toward the hospital. Five minutes later he pulled into the parking space with her name on it and switched off the ignition. The clinic opened at nine, so there was plenty of time for her to make her announcement and let everyone get over the excitement before the first patients arrived.

Clint Fackler's bicycle was in its accustomed spot beside the picnic table under the sycamore tree, where they all ate lunch on warm summer days. Clint was a nurse practitioner, a certified nurse/midwife associated with the ob/gyn practice on the second floor.

Leah had already decided to ask him to deliver her baby.

Would Adam want to be with her for the baby's birth? she wondered. How was she going to deal with that when the time came?

Dessie Palmer, the receptionist, was just unlocking the back door. She gave Adam and the Cherokee the once-over, waved to Leah and went inside. Leah felt a twinge of unease. She couldn't help it. Dessie was a sweet person, but she was also the biggest gossip in Slate Hollow. Word of her pregnancy would be all over town by afternoon.

Well, that's what she wanted, wasn't it? Call out the town crier and get the word on the street. *Leah Gentry is pregnant and she isn't going to marry the father of the baby.* Nerves made her next words a little short.

"Let's get it over with," she said.

"KEEPING BUSY?" Caleb asked as he came through the door of the clinic's small staff lounge where Adam was looking at the architectural drawing of a proposed addition to the building pinned to the wall.

"I'm managing to keep myself occupied," Adam told him.

"I see you've found my wish list," Caleb observed, as he poured himself a cup of coffee. He walked over to where Adam was standing. "Two new operating rooms, an outpatient surgery suite, a new radiology department, and office space and exam rooms for four new visiting specialists. We won't have to send our cardiology, oncology or neuro patients to Lexington anymore unless it's an emergency.''

"What will that bring your bed capacity up to?"

"Seventy-five," Caleb replied.

"Do you already have people on board to fill the specialty openings?"

"The bond levy'll be on the fall ballot. I can't do anything officially until it passes of course, but I've been shopping around. We'll move our own oncology and ob/gyn people in. We've got a dermatologist planning to come once a week, and we can make room for her here." He jabbed a finger at the drawing. "As you could probably tell by the wall-to-wall people in here this morning, we're bursting at the seams."

Adam had noticed, even though he'd spent most of the morning shut in Caleb's office playing solitaire on his computer or staring out the window at the kids on their way to school across the street, all the while listening for the sound of Leah's voice, her laughter, as she went about her work. Caleb went right on talking, undeterred by his silence.

"This building was made for four doctors. We've got six crammed in here now, not counting our nurse practitioners."

Adam gestured toward the plans with his coffee mug. "What are these rooms for?"

"Cardiologists in this one, and a neurosurgeon. We're trying to coax Peter Assad here from Lex General."

"I'm familiar with his articles. He's a good man," Adam said, and felt an unexpected pinch of envy. He could almost imagine himself working in a place like this—except for one thing. He would have to deal directly with patients again, one to one, without the buffering layers of hospital bureaucracy that shielded him from too much contact with the human beings he cut and stitched on the operating table.

"I'd like you to meet him someday. How long do you plan to stay around?"

"A few more days at least. I don't want to leave until I'm sure Leah's blood pressure is completely under control." He couldn't stay away from St. B's indefinitely, not if he wanted to stay on the fast track there.

"Another trip, then," Caleb said, as though there was no question Adam would be spending time in Slate Hollow in the future. "Assad's not certain he wants to leave the city, though. It's pretty routine work we do here. None of the fancy stuff he's used to. I imagine you'd feel the same way about leaving St. B's. But the whole thing's a moot point if we don't get the money." Caleb's pager went off. "It's the ER. Excuse me," he said, and walked over to the telephone on the wall.

Adam turned his attention from the drawing to the rest of the homey, cluttered room. Snapshots of staff members and their families were pinned to a corkboard above a round table. He wandered over to look at them. There was one of Clint Fackler, the nurse/midwife he'd met earlier before he headed off to the birthing suites. He had shaken Adam's hand and promised to give Leah and the baby the best possible care. There was one of Dessie Palmer, the receptionist, who had squealed with joy and hugged Leah until she was breathless. But all the while she was making a fuss, there was a gleam in her pale blue eyes that made him think it wouldn't be long before the news of Leah's pregnancy was all over town. A moment later he'd caught Leah's slightly rueful expression and deduced that her thoughts mirrored his own.

Still, as she predicted, no one had reacted with disgust or disapproval. Leah's co-workers were also her friends, and they'd greeted her announcement with surprise and happiness. There were a couple of good-natured hints that they'd noticed she had put on a pound or two, but *never* would any of them have guessed she was pregnant. With him they had been polite and friendly, if reserved. He'd expected nothing more.

His eyes skimmed over most of the other pictures, but the ones of Leah caught and held his attention. There was one of her sitting on the running board of a jeep, with the two baby goats she'd told him about that morning and a group of heartbreakingly thin Somali children crowded around her. The children were smiling, probably without hunger pangs for the first time in their lives. Nearby was another picture of Leah in the snow and mud of Bosnia. Again she was surrounded by children, this time wrapped in scarves and mittens, and again they were all smiling, clearly as delighted to be with Leah as she appeared to be with them.

Looking at those snapshots of Leah in uniform, he realized they shared something they had never talked about—an intimacy with the horrors of war. But unlike him, Leah seemed fortunate enough to have emerged unscathed.

There were yet more pictures of the mother of his

child scattered around the corkboard. One taken at what appeared to be a clinic picnic, one at Halloween with Leah dressed up in a witch's cape and pointy hat, passing out treats. Always there were children with her. She obviously was drawn to the little ones, and they to her. He had never been that natural and carefree with children, not since the day he had strapped all those small, trusting souls into the seats of the C-5A and sent them off to die....

Caleb's voice pulled him from his musings. "Got a patient they sent from the satellite clinic at Cade's Crossing in the ER. Severe arm and shoulder pain and no discernible cause. Want to join me and have a look at her?"

"I'm not licensed to practice in Kentucky," Adam hedged. It had been a long time since he'd walked into an ER exam room to see a patient. Things didn't work that way at St. Barnabas when you were next in line for head of a department. It was rare if he saw a patient at all between his initial office consultation and the operating room. All the interaction of routine exams and paperwork were done by interns and residents.

"Hell, I'm not asking you to operate on the woman. I'd just like your opinion of what might be causing her pain," Caleb said in his blunt way.

"Sure, I'd be glad to," Adam lied.

Caleb grabbed a lab coat off a hook by the door and handed it to him. "Might as well look the part, Sauder. It's not often I get to haul a hotshot headcracker around with me."

Adam slipped on the coat and followed him out the door and through the entryway connecting the clinic to the hospital. Less than a minute after they left the staff lounge they were being briefed on Caleb's patient by a dour-faced ER nurse.

"Her name's Caroline Stead. She's in two. She's complaining of severe left-arm pain that's been going on for about ten days. The attending doctor at the satellite gave her a 'script for pain and when it ran out she came here."

"Thanks, Louise." Caleb took the folder and used it to gesture at the treatment room.

Adam followed him into the small room where a heavyset, middle-aged woman was half-sitting, half-reclining on a raised bed. The overhead fluorescent lights weren't on. The only illumination in the room came from a fixture on the wall beside the bed.

The woman appeared to be dozing, her left arm cradled against her chest. "Caroline? Are you awake?" Caleb inquired, washing his hands at a small sink by the door as he talked. "This guy here is Dr. Sauder. He's visiting from Chicago. What seems to be the problem?"

The woman sat up, her face furrowed with pain. She coughed, using her right hand to cover her mouth. "Sorry, Doctor. I've got this cold and cough that just won't go away. It's been weeks now."

"It's that time of year," Caleb said.

"Well, my cold's been bothering me longer than my arm. They took an X ray of my lungs at the clinic."

"The report's here." Caleb looked at her folder, then glanced at a computer monitor hooked to a retractable shelf on the wall. "Right's clear. Left reads as showing bilateral apical pleural thickening," he said to Adam. "I'll take a look at the pictures when we finish here. Now, Caroline, how did you come to hurt your arm?" he asked, pushing the screen away as he walked over to rest his hand lightly on the woman's shoulder. He moved his hands to both sides of her neck and moved her head from side to side. She remained quiet and composed until he tried to lift her left arm. Then she jerked away with a cry of distress.

"Sorry. I don't know how I hurt it, Doc. Nothing I can recall. It just started bothering me a while back, and it's been getting worse and worse. When it got to where I couldn't sleep at night for the pain, I went to the clinic. They gave me some pills. They make me pretty dopey, but they seemed to help at first. But now..."

"Not giving you relief anymore?"

"No, it's real bad, Doc. I'm not a complainer. I've had four babies, you know. I can handle the pain. The doc at the clinic said maybe I have a pinched nerve from a bad disk in my neck. Said I should come here for more tests. Do you think that's what my problem could be?" She looked directly at Adam for the first time.

Something was wrong. The woman's right pupil was dilated, a normal condition in the low light, but her left was contracted, unresponsive to the light. Clues started falling into place in Adam's mind. He didn't know if Caleb had noticed what he had, so he asked a question of his own. "Mrs. Stead, are you a smoker?"

"I've cut way back," she said defensively, but the

telltale rasp in her voice put the lie to her words. "I hardly smoke half a pack a day."

"But you've been a smoker most of your life?"

She nodded. "Yeah, and I know it ain't good for me. This cough's one of the reasons I cut back. So's it would go away.

"Doc, what can you do for me? I really can't stand this pain no more. I need to get back to my job. And my youngest, he's graduating from high school next month, and we're planning a big party. But it's mostly the pain. It's really starting to bring me down."

"I'll help you with the pain, Caroline," Caleb said, patting her shoulder. "I'll have the nurse get you something right now. But we have to run some more tests before we can decide on the best way to take care of this problem, okay?"

She nodded, lying back against the upraised bed. "Okay, Doc. Whatever you say. I trust you."

"I'll be back to check on you in a little while."

Adam followed him out of the exam room to the nurses' station.

"You saw it, didn't you, Sauder? Her pupils are asymmetrical."

"Horner's sign," Adam said. "Yes, I saw it." Something had paralyzed the nerves regulating the iris of her left eye, preventing it from functioning as it should. The blueprints of the human body weren't always as logical as they could be. The nerves that control the iris of the eye originate not in the neck, but in the upper chest. Whatever was causing Mrs. Stead's pain, it wasn't a ruptured vertebral disc.

Caleb gave orders for the pain medication to the ER nurse. He then picked up a big yellow envelope

How to validate your
Editor's FREE GIFT "Thank You"

1. Peel off gift seal from front cover. Place it in space provided at right. This automatically entitles you to receive two free books and a fabulous mystery gift.

2. Send back this card and you'll get brand-new Harlequin Superromance® novels. These books have a cover price of $4.25 each in the U.S. and $4.75 each in Canada, but they are yours to keep absolutely free.

3. There's no catch. You're under no obligation to buy anything. We charge nothing—ZERO—for your first shipment. And you don't have to make any minimum number of purchases—not even one!

4. The fact is thousands of readers enjoy receiving books by mail from the Harlequin Reader Service®. They like the convenience of home delivery...they like getting the best new novels BEFORE they're available in stores... and they love our discount prices!

5. We hope that after receiving your free books you'll want to remain a subscriber. But the choice is yours— to continue or cancel, any time at all! So why not take us up on our invitation, with no risk of any kind. You'll be glad you did!

6. Don't forget to detach your FREE BOOKMARK. And remember...just for validating your Editor's Free Gift Offer, we'll send you THREE gifts, *ABSOLUTELY FREE!*

GET A FREE MYSTERY GIFT...

YOURS FREE!

SURPRISE MYSTERY GIFT COULD BE YOURS *FREE* AS A SPECIAL "THANK YOU" FROM THE EDITORS OF HARLEQUIN

The Harlequin Reader Service® — Here's how it works:

Accepting your 2 free books and mystery gift places you under no obligation to buy anything. You may keep the books and gift and return the shipping statement marked "cancel." If you do not cancel, about a month later we'll send you 6 additional novels and bill you just $3.57 each in the U.S., or $3.96 each in Canada, plus 25¢ delivery per book and applicable taxes if any.* That's the complete price and — compared to the cover price of $4.25 in the U.S. and $4.75 in Canada — it's quite a bargain! You may cancel at any time, but if you choose to continue, every month we'll send you 6 more books, which you may either purchase at the discount price or return to us and cancel your subscription.

*Terms and prices subject to change without notice. Sales tax applicable in N.Y. Canadian residents will be charged applicable provincial taxes and GST.

from the counter and took out an X ray, held it to the light and studied it for a long time. Adam waited for him to finish. "I wouldn't have noticed her pupils if the overhead lights had been turned on," he said after a while. "Probably why they didn't catch it this morning at the satellite. What's your guess?"

"It's not a guess," Adam said with quiet confidence. He didn't have to look at the X ray to make his diagnosis. He knew. He felt himself shutting down, slipping into automatic clinical mode. "A middle-aged smoker with a chronic cough, a Horner's sign and severe arm pain. I think you'll find a carcinoma. Most likely a Pancoast tumor hiding under the pleural thickening. The arm pain and Horner's sign suggest it's already invaded the brachial plexus."

Caleb studied the X ray a few moments longer. "I think you're right. The radiologist must have read this one while he was asleep. I'll schedule the tests and talk to Baxter about taking over. He's our oncologist."

"Are you going to tell her what you suspect?"

"Yes," Caleb said. "She's expecting to get her neck operated on, or get some kind of therapy and be up and around in time for her kid's graduation. It ain't gonna work that way." He slid the X ray back into the envelope and folded his arms. "Damn, I hate this part of the job. Thirty-five years in this business and I've never gotten used to it, and I never will even if I last another thirty-five years. I've just never figured out the right words to use to tell someone they're going to die." He slapped the envelope down on the counter. "There's no reason for you to wait for me here, Sauder. Go on back to the clinic. Go on back to Leah.'' Caleb walked away, his shoulders bowed by the weight of the bad news he was carrying.

Once, a long time ago, Adam had felt the same way when he had to tell a patient that sooner, rather than later, she or he was going to die. But no more. He didn't feel much of anything now, not empathy, not even love. But with the thought a vision of Leah flashed across his mind's eye, and he knew that was no longer true. What he felt for her proved there was some spark of human feeling still alive deep within him. Right now, he loved Leah as much as he could, but he would never tell her. Because as much as he could wasn't enough.

IT WAS ALMOST TWO O'CLOCK. Adam had disappeared from the clinic nearly an hour earlier. He'd gone over to the hospital with Caleb, Dessie had told her, when Leah asked the receptionist if she'd seen him. Caleb had answered a page from the ER and taken Adam with him. It was anybody's guess how long they'd be over there. But Dessie hoped Caleb would be back soon, because he had patients scheduled for the rest of the day and they were already running behind.

Leah thanked the garrulous receptionist and went into the staff lounge. She poured herself a glass of orange juice from the refrigerator and joined the others already seated around the break table. Clint Fackler was there reading the sports page between deliveries. He looked up, gave her a smile and went back to reading.

"Leah! Congratulations! I just heard the news," Barb Baden, the clinic's ultrasound technician said, reaching up to give Leah a quick hug as she circled the table. "I spent the morning over at the satellite and I just got back. I can't believe it! You—pregnant! You've never said a word about a special man in your life. You could have knocked me over with a feather. But now that I see you in that outfit, I can see they were telling the truth." She grinned with genuine pleasure at Leah's news. "Clint says the baby's father's a neurosurgeon. I'm impressed. I hope I get to meet him."

Leah held on to her smile through the barrage of words. "You will. He's with Caleb in ER. I'm sure they'll be back soon." She was tired, tense and weary of being a good sport about the staff's gentle teasing and endless questions. She felt as though she'd been on display all day, unable for a moment to let down her guard. She realized she'd surprised, and possibly shocked, some of her friends and co-workers with her announcement. It was only natural they were curious about her condition and her relationship with Adam.

She had tried hard not to let it bother her when one of her patients announced flatly that she thought a woman should be married before she got pregnant, not after, or to feel uncomfortable when she came upon Dessie and one of the nurses with their heads together whispering, and neither one would meet her eyes, or when she walked into a room and conversation stopped for a moment before picking up again.

She thought more than once of washing her hands of all of it, leaving and walking the few blocks to her house, getting in her Jeep—Caleb's orders that she not drive for a few more days be damned—and heading off into the hills to check on Aurelia. But her pride wouldn't let her. Besides, she'd had one or two fleeting spells of light-headedness she hadn't told anyone about. They were probably nothing more than a reaction to the anxiety of telling everyone about her pregnancy while trying to work things out with Adam, but she couldn't be certain. She certainly couldn't take a chance on having another spell while she was behind the wheel.

I wish Adam would come and take me away.

The sudden thought was almost as upsetting as the dizzy spells. He'd been very much the man she wanted him to be this morning. He'd been reserved but attentive. He'd also been gracious in his acceptance of congratulations from her friends and co-workers on his pending fatherhood. He'd given no sign at all that the revelation of her pregnancy had recently been as much of a surprise to him, as it was to them. He had sidestepped queries on their plans for the future with wit and humor. He was accepting of the little jokes and the few pointed remarks that came his way from those not inclined to look on single parenthood and long-distance relationships with much tolerance. He listened with equanimity to the advice about how to handle pregnant women and new babies, which almost everyone seemed to feel it was their duty to give him. He asked all the right questions and gave all the right answers.

When he was like this, she could almost forget that he had walked out on her in Vietnam without a backward glance. But she dared not let herself forget that, because of his condition, Adam was not a man to make commitments. He couldn't be trusted to be there for her—or the baby—when the chips were down. She had to remember that and to keep the reality of it foremost in her mind, or she could very easily fall prey to the fantasy of the loving, caring father-to-be she'd seen today.

"When do you want me to schedule your ultrasound?" Barb was asking her.

Her co-worker's question barely registered. Leah's attention had become riveted on the man just entering the break room. Something had happened. She could tell by the set of his shoulders, the line of his jaw, the emptiness in his eyes. She had seen that lost look on his face before and her heart contracted painfully. She wanted to go to him and take him in her arms. She wanted to hold him close and give him the courage to face the horrors he kept bottled up inside him.

Adam's problems couldn't be solved with a wish and a kiss. She knew that was as much a fantasy as the man who'd charmed her co-workers that morning. The reality was the troubled and complex man before her—a man she couldn't trust to not disappear from her life without a backward glance, as he had done before.

"Is this the baby's father?" Barb asked irrepressibly. She looked Adam up and down. "We'll do the ultrasound whenever you want. I can do it right now if you can get away from your patients. That way you both get your first look at the little sweetheart together."

Leah could never allow that. It would be impossible to keep Adam at a distance if he was with her to see the image of their child in her womb, to watch it move and see its tiny fingers and toes and beating heart. She could never deny him anything he asked of her concerning the child after that. She wouldn't be able to fool herself into thinking she wasn't falling in love with him, and she could never bear the pain of waking up some morning to find his demons had driven him away—perhaps never to return.

"No," Leah heard herself say. She saw the shocked look on Barb's face. She knew she had made a mistake. She should have been gracious and turned down the offer with a simple excuse, but she didn't. The words came from someplace deep inside her that wouldn't be denied. "I don't want him there," she said.

CHAPTER TWELVE

BRIAN LEANED HIS ARM on the ledge of the open window of Doc Owens's restored pickup and let her amble along at about forty-five—not that he didn't think Carlotta could do a lot better. He'd looked under the hood. There was plenty of engine under there. But somehow the speed seemed to suit Carlotta's age and dignity, and so he didn't push her any harder.

He grinned. Now he was calling the truck Carlotta just like Doc did. He wondered what his mom would think of him driving the old truck around. She'd probably have a fit, but not Elliot. He was really a pretty cool guy. Brian's conscience tugged at his elbow. He hadn't even called his mom and told her he was coming down here with his dad. He didn't feel it was his place to tell her about the baby. Not yet, anyway. Maybe tomorrow. Yeah, tomorrow would be soon enough.

It had turned out to be a great day. It had stopped raining. The sun was out, at least for the time being, and the air had warmed to springlike temperatures. He'd even been able to sleep in that morning. The landscapers were done with the work and the Hideaway Inn was ready for its grand reopening. He'd slept till ten, had breakfast at McDonald's out on the highway and then taken off in the truck to find the state park and the canoe livery Leah had told him about.

It was right where she'd said it was. The guy who owned it had been friendly and talkative and, wonder of wonders, he had a couple of kayaks. They were older and heavier than Brian was used to, but they floated and that was all that mattered. He'd spent two hours on the river and even found a couple of stretches of white water that weren't altogether sissy. So far it had been a good day, but now he was starving. His breakfast of eggs and hash browns seemed like a long time ago.

Brian turned Carlotta into the parking lot of the pizza joint across from the Hideaway Inn and got out of the truck. He thought he'd try the Red Neck Special this time. It had about every kind of meat you could think of on it: ham, bacon, sausage and venison jerky. A heart attack waiting to happen if you listened to his mom. But what the heck. He felt like living dangerously. Brian was still grinning to himself when he rounded the hood of the truck and saw Juliet Trent sitting on a bench by the door of the restaurant.

She was clutching a ratty-looking book bag under one arm and looked as if she'd lost her last friend in the world. She didn't even glance up when he got out of the truck.

"Hi there," he said.

She raised her hand to shade her eyes from the sun. "Hi," she said. Her eyes were red around the edges like maybe she was allergic to something, or trying not to cry.

"Are you waiting for someone?" he asked, sitting down beside her on the bench.

She slid a little away from him. "I'm just resting," she said. "That's Doc Owens's truck. How did you get it?"

"He lent it to me while my dad and I are here. I left my car back in Chicago."

"What kind of car do you have?"

He felt embarrassed. He hadn't forgotten the aging pickup parked in her yard. "A Lexus," he said finally. "It was a graduation gift from my mom and stepdad."

"Wow," she said under her breath. "Some graduation gift."

Brian sighed, then asked, "Stopping in for pizza after school?"

"No," she said.

"Want to join me for some? I haven't eaten since breakfast and I'm starved."

"I'd better stay here. I don't want to miss my ride."

"Did you walk here from the school?" It was more than half a mile, Brian figured, and she was awfully pregnant to be hiking it so far.

"The truck wouldn't start this morning. I rode the bus and I missed it this afternoon because I had to go to the bathroom. I always have to go to the bathroom." She folded her arms across her chest, and Brian was amazed to see that they could rest on top of her belly as if it were a giant soccer ball on her lap.

"Why didn't your friends pick you up at the school, then?"

She rounded on him. "Because I don't have any friends. I mean, I don't really have any friends coming to get me. I'm waiting for someone who lives out my direction to come in and pick up a pizza, and then I'll hitch a ride home. There—are you satisfied?''

"I'm trying to help, in case you haven't noticed. If you'll wait until I get something to eat, I'll drive you home.''

"Will it take very long? I should get home as soon as I can. Mrs. Dunn will be wanting to get home to her own kids, and Leah's promised to come today.''

"We'll get the pizza to go, and we'll eat it at your place, okay?''

"Thanks," she said. "Why are you doing this for me?'' She pushed at a curl of hair that had worked its way out of her barrette.

Brian took a deep breath. She was without doubt the most exasperating girl he'd ever met. "I thought, after the other day, we were friends.'' She didn't say anything to make him think she felt the same way, which kind of bothered him. "I'm doing it because you're Leah's friend, and I'm doing it because only a real jerk would leave a pregnant woman to walk three miles uphill.''

"Okay," she said. "I don't want anything on my pizza but cheese.''

Brian did the gentlemanly thing and compromised on the pizza. Twenty minutes later they were back on the road with a super-size, half cheese/half Red Neck Special riding on the seat between them. Enough for all of them, because Juliet had called home while they were waiting and found out Leah and his dad were already there.

Juliet leaned her head against the window. She looked tired. Her face was pale and her freckles stood out starkly. He thought about her gathering eggs, taking care of Aurelia and trying to keep up with her studies. He felt ashamed of himself when he compared his life to hers. Here she was pregnant and trying to finish school, and he'd dropped out to "find himself" just because he didn't like his major.

"I should have thought to pick up a couple of salads," he said to get his mind off his own shortcomings.

"There's a head of lettuce and some carrots in the fridge. Nothing fancy but at least it'll be cold and green."

"Sounds great to me."

She turned her head to look at him. "Are you always so darned obliging?"

"I was taught to have good manners and be polite when someone was trying to be nice to me," he shot back.

"I never went to etiquette class." He was horrified to see a tear run down her cheek.

"Don't cry. I apologize. I shouldn't have said that." What was it about women? Why did they always have to start blubbering every time you made the least little critical remark?

"It isn't that," she said, sniffing. "It was the lawyer. She was really why I missed the bus. She was there waiting for me after school."

"Lawyer? You mean the one representing the people who want to adopt your baby?"

Juliet nodded, rummaging in her book bag for a tissue. "She wanted to know if I'd made up my mind yet about giving them the baby."

"You're a minor. I don't think she's allowed to pressure you like that."

"She's always nice about it."

"Don't you have a school counselor or someone you can talk to?"

"Leah. I tell Leah everything."

"That's probably why the woman wants to get to you when you're alone. I've already figured out Leah won't take any bull— I mean, any guff from anyone."

"She said they would help me buy a car this time. Funny that she picked today to tell me, when Granny's old truck just about gave up the ghost for good."

He turned off the main road and they jounced over the ruts toward the Cade place. "It's seems like more than just a coincidence to me."

"Maybe it was, but it doesn't make any difference. I have to make up my mind about keeping this baby or giving him to them."

Juliet, just a kid, really, with no parents to speak of and a dying great-grandmother, was trying to decide whether or not to give up her baby, while he'd spent the day kayaking and driving around in a beauty of a classic truck. Brian felt like the biggest jerk in the universe. To hell with his dad and letting Juliet make her deal with the devil without interference from the rest of them. "Listen, I've been thinking. I'd like to lend you the money so you can go to school and keep the baby."

She stared at him openmouthed, a tear still glistening on her cheek. She wiped it away with the back of her hand. "How do you expect to do that?"

"I'll sell my car."

"Will your dad let you? You're older than me, but not that old. What are you, eighteen?"

"I'm nineteen, almost twenty...well, I'll be twenty in November. That's beside the point. The car's in my name. I'll sell it if I want to." His dad wasn't going to be happy about it. His mom and Elliot would go ballistic, but he didn't care. It was the only way he could think of to help her out of the jam she was in. They were almost to the creek. He slowed the truck, wondering if he would pop the clutch halfway across the rickety old bridge and make a fool of himself.

"You'd do that for me? You hardly know me. I could be a real nutcase for all you know. Maybe I'll run off to Hawaii with the money or something, and give my baby away, anyway."

He stopped the truck just before the bridge and leaned both arms on the steering wheel. "I know you well enough to know you'd never do that." He looked at her with a mixture of respect and concern.

Two more tears rolled down her cheeks, but she was smiling. "No, I wouldn't. Thank you. That's a nice compliment." Her smile died away. "But I can't take your money."

"Sure you can. I've got enough stashed away for an old beater to get me back and forth..."

She looked away from him again, staring off into the distance at something only she could see. "It isn't just the money. Leah would help me with money if I asked her. So would Doc Owens. Or I could get welfare, I guess. No, it's me. What's inside me. I don't know if I can do it all—take care of a baby and go

to school. I'm scared.'' The tears were falling again.
''I don't want to be like my mom. She didn't want
me, not really. She let her boyfriend beat up on me,
and then when Leah and Doc caught him at it, she
hightailed it out of town with him and left me behind.
Wouldn't my baby be better off with those nice people if I turn out to be like my mom?'' She swiveled
to face him once more.

''You're not like your mom,'' Brian said. He
reached over and wiped a tear from her cheek. She
had so many things to contend with. It wasn't fair.
He'd just wanted to make it easier for her. He probably shouldn't have offered her the money, like his
dad said. Dammit, what was a guy supposed to do?
Sit there and watch her cry? But Juliet was right and
he knew it. No one could make this decision but her.
''Trust me. I'd say you're more like your granny. I
think you'll make a great mom.''

''Thank you,'' she said, attempting a smile through
fresh tears. ''I hope I will be, because I want to keep
my baby with me more than anything in the world.''

''WHAT'S THAT MAN OF YOURS up to now?'' Aurelia
asked.

''He's tinkering around under the hood of your
truck.'' Leah turned away from the window. The sun
had dropped below the hilltops on the far side of the
valley and twilight was settling over Aurelia's yard.
The old woman was sitting in her rocking chair, her
hands folded loosely on the quilt covering her legs.
There was no sign of tension or anxiety in her posture
or her voice. The new combination of medication was
working, keeping her comfortable and alert.

"Seems like layman's work for a big-city brain surgeon to be doing."

"He promised Juliet he'd take a look at it before she and Brian went off to the softball game."

"He's a good boy, taking her off for a treat. She doesn't spend enough time with friends."

"She wants to be with you. And she's getting awfully close to term. She tires more easily," Leah reminded her.

"I have a bad feeling about the baby," Aurelia said, resting her head against the high back of the rocking chair. The visiting nurse had helped her wash her hair that morning. It floated around her head like puffs of dandelion fluff.

"What feeling, Granny?" Leah asked. She respected the old woman's feelings and her observations on medical matters, the result of a lifetime of experience.

"She's not carrying it right. That baby should've started to drop. It ain't. And she's all the time got pain in her back."

Leah frowned. "I've noticed that, too, although she hasn't complained to me of any pain."

"Juliet's not a complainer, but I worry about her just the same. I don't want nothin' to happen to her or the little 'un. They're all I cherish."

"I promise you, Caleb and I won't let anything happen to her. I'll speak to Clint Fackler about her in the morning. Does that ease your mind?"

"A little." Aurelia fell silent and closed her eyes. The room was quiet except for the slight hiss of the oxygen tank.

Leah turned back to the window. She couldn't

seem to help herself. She was drawn to Adam's presence, as though they were tethered by some invisible force. He'd taken off his jacket and rolled up his sleeves. He was dressed all in black today, a match for his mood on their silent drive up the mountain several hours earlier.

"Your man's in a world of hurt," Aurelia said.

"I thought you'd fallen asleep."

"I sleep too much these days with all the medicine you give me. Do you know what's gnawing at his soul?"

Leah didn't try to sidestep the question. "I think I do. He was in Vietnam. Even though it was the end of the war, something happened to him there that he can't, or won't, forget and he refuses to talk about it. Going back made it worse, not better."

"And whatever it was keeps him from giving of himself to you."

"And his son."

Aurelia nodded. "And your baby. Is that why you're holding him at arm's length?"

"It's getting late. Do you want me to bring you your Bible to read?" Leah asked, not wanting to answer the difficult question Aurelia had posed.

"You can bring me my Bible, but I don't have to read it. I've read that book every night of my life. I know it by heart, but it's a comfort to have it in my hands."

Leah went to the dresser and picked up the big, worn Bible and set it on Aurelia's lap. The old woman folded her hands around it and smiled. "My granny gave me this the day I turned sixteen. It was her mother's mother's before her. Soon I'll pass it on to Juliet. My granny never learned to read, but it didn't stop her from memorizing most every verse in the good book. I got enough schooling to read and write. My daughter, Lizzie, too—Juliet's momma— she went all the way through high school. But what good did it do her? I want more for my Juliet.''

''I know. I'll do my best to see she gets it.''

''And does well by her baby. He's the last of my blood.'' Aurelia knew nothing about the couple who wanted to adopt Juliet's baby. Juliet had insisted she not be told.

''I promise I'll give Juliet all the help I can.'' Leah could give Aurelia that assurance because she intended to support Juliet in whatever decision she made about the baby's future.

''That's all I ask. I pray for all of us, but mostly for you, Leah. You're my light in the darkness.''

''I feel like a dim bulb today,'' Leah said with an embarrassed laugh.

Aurelia chuckled. ''That's a good one. What are you gonna do about that man in my yard? Send him back to Chicago and back into the hell on earth he's made for himself?''

''I don't know,'' Leah said truthfully. ''Can you tell me what to do?''

''Do you love him? It seems to me you'd have to love him with all your heart to be strong enough to fight for him. If you don't, you ain't doing either of you, or the baby you're growing in your belly, a favor.''

''I don't know the answer, Granny. I don't know if I love him or if I've just picked up another stray.'' Leah stood up and folded her arms under her breasts.

Talking about Adam and her feelings for him made her restless and uneasy. She was as confused as ever about the future. The events of earlier in the day hadn't changed anything or made her choices any easier.

"Then you're not ready to do battle for him."

"He has to fight his own battles, Granny."

"Don't give me any of your emancipated, new-woman malarkey," Aurelia said tartly. "That's not what God made us smarter and wiser for. You have to be there beside him to prop him up if he falters. You have to be strong for him. Having you and the baby and a future for the three of you has to be a rock for him to build a shelter on against the past."

Leah felt the baby move within her. "I was there for him in Vietnam. I let him make love to me without any reservations. He left me without a word. When I hunted him down to tell him about the baby, he told me he needed to concentrate all his energy on rebuilding his relationship with Brian. He didn't say anything about loving or caring for him."

"Men don't often talk about their feelings," Aurelia reminded her.

"I know, but I can't help what I feel. He seemed so cold and distant I turned around and walked out of his office without telling him about the baby." She didn't like remembering that day, and today she had done the same thing. He had come back to her from the ER and she had panicked at the emptiness in his eyes and refused to allow him any closer. How could they ever work past the barriers they'd both thrown up to save themselves from hurt and loss? She couldn't see any way they could be happy together, so it was better to stay apart.

"But he came for you when Caleb called and told him about the little 'un."

"He's an honorable man. It wasn't love that brought him to Slate Hollow. It was duty." She needed to remember that. It made it easier.

Aurelia shook her head. "You're as stubborn as he is. It don't have to be something so terrible that happens to a body to make them afraid of loving another human being. Sometimes it's as ordinary as picking up the wrong couple of strays, animal or human, that can sour you on love. Now I'm tired. I want a minute or two alone to say my prayers, and then you can help me to my bed."

Leah leaned forward and kissed the old woman lightly on the forehead. "Is five minutes long enough to tell God what you have to say? You need your rest."

"I think it will be." Aurelia reached up and patted her cheek. "You're a fighter, Leah. Don't give up."

"I'll do my best, but there are some battles you just can't win. This might be one of them."

ADAM SLAMMED the hood of the pickup closed just as Brian and Juliet drove into the yard. He'd worked his way through the University of Michigan as a mechanic. He'd liked the work then, but quit doing it when he decided to go into neurosurgery. No one wanted to see a brain surgeon with grease under his fingernails.

His son got out of the antique truck and sprinted around to open Juliet's door. She wouldn't let him help her out, but she did accept his hand to step down from the running board. Brian reached back into the truck and pulled out a pizza box, smaller than the one they'd all shared for an early supper, but still substantial.

"Don't tell me you're hungry again," Adam said, wiping his hands on an old towel Leah had given him. Working on the battered pickup had been a godsend. It gave him something to do with his hands and kept his mind occupied. He'd battled hard to come back from the cold, dark place his memories had sent him that afternoon, and so far he'd been successful.

"Starved," Brain assured him. "Want a piece?"

"No, thanks."

"Figure out what's wrong with the truck?"

"Looks like the alternator's bad."

Brian nodded. "That's what it sounded like to me when Juliet described how it was acting." Brian liked to work under the hood of a car, too, Adam had learned over the past months. Far more than what his mother thought seemly. "I'll pick one up in town in the morning, and we can change it tomorrow after I bring Juliet home from school. If you and Leah don't have other plans?"

"I don't have other plans." And if he did he would change them. Father-son projects had been too rare in their lives to pass up the opportunity of one.

"How much is it going to cost to fix?" Juliet asked with a worried frown.

"Zip, zilch, *nada,*" Brian said expansively.

"I can pay to have the truck fixed," she said stubbornly. "We're not a charity case."

Brian opened his mouth to argue with her, but

Adam interrupted him. She was a proud child. Brian would have to take that into account in his future dealings with her. "An alternator will cost you around a hundred dollars," he said.

"A hundred dollars?" Juliet's face fell.

"I'll look for a rebuilt one tomorrow," Brian hurried to interject. "It'll only be about half as much, right, Dad?"

"Sounds about right."

"Well, I guess I could afford that," Juliet said. "And I do need the truck to get back and forth to school. The bus only comes as far as the main road. It's a long walk."

"I'll go to the parts store first thing tomorrow—" Brian held up his hand to halt another protest "—and I'll bring you the bill."

"Thank you," Juliet replied with grown-up dignity.

Leah walked out onto the porch, her arms wrapped around her to ward off the chill of the evening. "How was the game?" she called to Juliet.

The teenager turned to her with a smile. "We won! Six to four."

"That means we'll be going to the regional tournament, doesn't it?"

"It starts next week. But the first game's at Lexington Christian, and I don't think Mr. Fackler will let me ride that far in the bus."

"I don't think it would be wise." Leah was watching Juliet closely, Adam noticed. The teenager was standing with both hands supporting her back, as though to ease the strain of the burden she was carrying. "Are you feeling okay?" Leah asked.

"As okay as I can expect, I guess, but I can't say I won't be glad when this is over." She changed the subject. "How's Granny?"

"She's sitting in her rocker. I think she was hoping you'd be back in time to sit with her for a few minutes."

"I'll tell her about the game," Juliet said as she mounted the rickety porch steps.

Leah reached out and brushed a strand of Juliet's hair from her cheek. "I'll be in to help her to bed shortly."

"I can do it."

"No, I'll help. You shouldn't be lifting anything these days."

Juliet sighed. "Okay, I'll call you when she's ready." She took a step then turned back. "Thank you for looking at my truck, Dr. Sauder."

"I'm glad to help, Juliet."

"Thanks for the pizza, Brian. And thanks for… everything. I'll never forget it."

"The offer still stands."

Juliet nodded. Brian looked as if he wanted to say more, but not with Adam and Leah listening. He lifted the pizza box toward Juliet. "Do you want a couple of pieces of this for a bedtime snack?"

Juliet shook her head. "I couldn't eat another bite."

"Say good-night to your granny for me, and remember, I'll be at the school at three to pick you up."

"You don't—"

"I'll be there at three sharp."

Juliet nodded and went on into the house. Leah came down the steps and walked toward them. "I'd like to thank you for all you've done for Juliet today."

"My pleasure." Brian avoided his father's eyes, making Adam wonder what had happened between the two teenagers that afternoon. "If no one else wants some of this pizza, I think I'll head on back into town with it."

"I'm with Juliet—I couldn't possibly eat another bite," Leah told him.

Adam just shook his head.

"I'm going to call it an early night, Dad. I'll see you in the morning."

Adam interpreted Brian's remark to mean he wouldn't be waiting up for him to come back to the Hideaway, but Adam didn't think he'd be far behind his son in returning to the motel. Leah had barely spoken a word to him since he'd walked in on her and the others in the break room back at the clinic.

"See you tomorrow, Leah."

"Bye, Brian."

His son gave him a half salute, sprinted to Caleb's truck and rattled away over the ramshackle bridge leaving Adam alone with the woman he wanted so much to be able to love.

"I hold my breath every time I see someone cross that thing," Leah said as the sound of the truck's engine died away.

"It needs to be shored up," Adam agreed.

"There's no money for that kind of project, and, well, it won't be much longer that anyone will be living out here." She looked at Aurelia's bedroom window.

"Will Juliet come to live with you?"

"I don't know. We haven't discussed it yet. She's having trouble accepting that Aurelia's dying. There will be time—after—to make those kinds of arrangements." Leah paused a moment and cleared her throat. "I just came out to tell you I'll be ready to leave soon. Aurelia's tired and needs to go back to bed."

"I'll help you."

"That's not necessary."

"Yes, it is. Juliet's not the only one who shouldn't be lifting a lot of weight."

"Aurelia's skin and bones."

"Leah, let me help." She was warier of him than ever this evening, and he understood why. When he had left Caleb and his patient in the ER, he'd felt himself shutting down, as he'd done so often in the past. He knew there was only one hope for him—to find Leah and let her healing presence bring him back into the light. But when he found her, she had seen the darkness in him and reacted accordingly. Still, he'd managed. Just being near her had helped him to fight back against the overwhelming terror of his memories.

"You don't have to."

"I want to."

Her next words hit him like a blow. "I don't want her upset by your...distance."

"What do you mean, Leah?" She might be talking about Aurelia, but she was really talking about herself and the baby.

"I don't want her to see how remote you are because you know you can't help her. If you can't heal her, you want nothing to do with her emotionally."

"I've never done less than my best for any patient."

"Technically, yes, but how long has it been since you've given anything deeper than the surface of yourself to anyone?"

"We're not talking about Aurelia now, are we?"

"No," she said softly, shaking her head. "I guess we're not."

"What is it you want of me, Leah?" He took a step toward her.

"Everything you can't give," she said, then turned and went into the cabin.

CHAPTER THIRTEEN

SHE SHOULDN'T HAVE SPOKEN to him that way. Leah couldn't get the image of Adam's stricken face from her mind as she helped Aurelia get ready for bed. It was a measure of how deeply her words had penetrated his defenses that he'd let his reaction show at all. And her own reaction? How could she defend herself for keeping him at arm's length?

He had tried very hard to be part of their small circle earlier that evening. He had eaten practically none of the pizza, but he'd sat at the table with her and Juliet and Brian with his coffee mug cradled between his hands. He had added bits and pieces to the conversation and treated Aurelia with the respect due her age and condition.

He was trying, but could he succeed? It wasn't for herself alone that she had to ask the hard questions. It was for the baby's sake, too.

"I thought your man would come to bid me goodnight," Aurelia said as Leah tucked the blankets around her. "Did you two have words out there?"

Leah sighed. "Are you able to see through walls?"

"No, but I know you. I can tell when you're struggling with yourself."

Leah sat down on the edge of the bed. "I am struggling. I have to make a decision about what part

Adam will play in the baby's life, and I need to make it soon.''

"Seems to me his role is clear enough. He's the baby's father, isn't he?''

"You know he is.''

"Then he should be your husband, too.''

"Things aren't always so cut-and-dried.''

Aurelia shook her head. "Right is right,'' she said with conviction. "That's the problem with the world today. Everyone wants to make everything come out right for them. They don't think of others. The man has rights as a daddy, don't he?''

"Yes, he does.''

"Well, then, you'd better give them to him.''

"I wish it were that easy.''

"Seems easy enough to me—you just have to decide if you love him.''

Leah still couldn't answer that. She stood up and adjusted the oxygen tubing and checked the gauge. "Do you need a little more oxygen?'' she asked, noting the bluish tinge to the old woman's lips and the grayness of her skin.

Aurelia nodded. "Yes. It's so close in here tonight. The weather's changing for the worse again, isn't it?''

"They're predicting thunderstorms.''

"I knew it. I always know when there's a weather change coming.'' She folded her hands on her chest. "I'll pray the way comes clear for you,'' she said.

Leah bent over and kissed the old woman on the cheek. "Thank you, Aurelia. You've eased my mind. Now get some rest and remember I'm only a phone call away.'' She adjusted the shade on the bedside lamp so the light didn't shine directly into Aurelia's eyes and turned to leave the room. Adam was standing in the doorway.

"I've come to say good-night to Aurelia," he said.

"I thought you had better manners than to leave my house without speaking to me." Aurelia's eyes glittered with satisfaction as she caught Leah's gaze.

Adam walked into the room and leaned over the bed, taking Aurelia's hand in both his strong, well-shaped ones. "Thank you for your hospitality, ma'am."

"You're most welcome. Don't be a stranger, Doctor. I like company. I'm not ready to meet my maker just yet. I still like to hear the gossip and what's going on in the world."

"I'd be pleased to visit again. My son is very taken with your Juliet, you know." The low murmur of Adam's voice was a pleasant counterpoint to the growling of thunder they could already hear echoing among the hilltops.

"And I'm beholden to him for his care of her." Aurelia's voice grew sharper, stronger. "But you tell that young scamp Juliet's too mixed-up in her feelings to be anything more than friends."

"I agree completely. Brian has a lot of hard decisions of his own to make before too long. He isn't ready for more than friendship, either."

"Good. Then we see eye to eye."

"We do. Good night, Aurelia. Sleep well."

"Good night, Doctor. God bless."

"Thank you." He straightened and moved past Leah to the doorway. "I'll wait for you outside."

"Good night, Granny. I'll tell Juliet I'm leaving."

"Don't let the devil get your man," Aurelia whispered, already half-asleep. "He needs saving from his demons, but you'll have to do most of the work."

"Then you'll have to pray for a miracle, I'm afraid."

Five minutes later Leah and Adam were in the Cherokee. They crossed the bridge as night closed in on the isolated glen. "Aurelia doesn't have much time left," Adam said, breaking the silence, as he maneuvered around the biggest puddles in front of the empty Perkins's homestead.

"I know. She's having more and more difficulty breathing. Soon we'll be forced to switch to narcotics for the pain. With her diminished lung capacity…" Leah didn't have to finish the sentence. Adam knew as well as she did that the depressant effect of morphine on the respiratory system would bring the end sooner rather than later. It was a trade-off at this point—time for comfort.

"It's going to be touch and go if she lives until Juliet's baby is born."

"She's due in less than three weeks. Aurelia's determined to stay alive that long."

"And Juliet won't make a decision on giving up the child for adoption while the old woman's alive."

They were quiet for a while as they drove back to town. Leah thought about Juliet and her baby. She was going to lose Aurelia and be alone in the world. Her thoughts swung to her own baby and his father sitting beside her, and she turned to face him. She didn't want to be angry with Adam. They would never be able to come to an agreement on what was best for their baby with hard feelings keeping them from learning what was in each other's hearts.

"I'm sorry for what I said back in the yard," Leah told him. "It was thoughtless of me. But when you walked into the break room this afternoon, it was as if…I don't know, as if you weren't really there. What happened at the clinic today?"

"That's not material to the conversation."

"On the contrary, it's the center of this conversation. Something drove you inside yourself. I want to know what it was."

His fist came down hard on the steering wheel. "Dammit, Leah. If I had the answer, don't you think I would have told you by now?"

They were silent for the rest of the drive into town. Adam reached her house and turned into her driveway. Leah unfastened her seat belt, but Adam was quicker. He was waiting to help her step down out of the Cherokee when she opened the door.

"I'll walk you to the house," he said.

Inwardly she cringed at the lack of emotion in his voice. Aurelia was wrong. She couldn't help him do battle with his demons if he wouldn't even admit to their existence. She opened the screen and unlocked the door while he watched. When she took a step inside, Adam reached out and wrapped his fingers around her wrist.

"Adam, please. I'm tired. It's been a long day."

"Don't turn away from me, Leah. We haven't settled anything. We haven't made any plans. We can't go on like this from hour to hour, day to day, with nothing settled between us."

"There's no hope for us, Adam—not as long as you refuse to admit you even have a problem. Because if what happened to you all those years ago in

Vietnam isn't why you are the way you are, then it's even worse. I fell—'' She pulled herself up short. Telling him she'd fallen in love with him was one weapon she would not give him.

Thunder rumbled overhead as the storm moved farther into the valley and gathered strength and speed. The sky was black, the spring day only a memory. Adam reached out and took her by the shoulders. ''Please, don't go.''

''I have to.''

''Caleb told a woman she was going to die today,'' he said suddenly. ''Do you know how long it's been since I've done that?''

''Adam, what are you trying to say? Surely you've had patients you couldn't help.''

''I don't tell them they're going to die, Leah. I have a chief resident to do my dirty work for me. On the rare occasion I have to deliver the news myself, it's the robot you saw this afternoon who tells the patient or the grieving family their worst fears have come to pass. Caleb is still the kind of doctor I always thought I would be—caring, compassionate, involved, even when he knows it's not in his best interest. I saw today how far removed from that ideal I am. There's nothing left of that part of me. Nothing that can feel another person's pain or happiness. I'm just a shell. It's been getting worse for a long time. But going back to Vietnam—'' He stopped talking so abruptly she heard his teeth snap together.

''Going back made it worse,'' she said.

''Far worse. It's with me night and day now. Before, it was easier to shut away, but no longer.''

''Have you gotten help?''

He shook her, not gently, but with restraint that showed in the locked muscles of his jaw and the tenseness of his shoulders. "I've tried everything, Leah. I've talked for hours to a psychiatrist who's never been closer to war than sitting in the front row to see *Saving Private Ryan*. I've seen therapists. I've tried hypnosis and medications that made me think I was losing my mind even faster than I'm managing to lose it on my own. The nightmares are still there when I close my eyes. The past is still too real. God, Leah, don't send me away. You're my last hope of ever being free of the past."

"You can talk to Brian. Or to B.J." The words forced themselves past the tightness in her throat.

"No, Leah, only you. You understand without my telling you. There's too much locked up inside me. If I let it loose…" He shuddered. "My only hope is to forget it. I've done it before. For more than ten years I was as normal as anyone else, then Brian got hurt. He ran his bicycle into a mailbox. His face was a mess and it was as if—" Once more he stopped talking with an abruptness that left silence hanging between them.

"And that's when it started again for you?" Leah said at last.

"Yes, and all the old nightmares have been with me ever since. But I fought it to a standstill once. I can do it again—with your help, Leah."

She had wanted him to say *with your love*.

"But you're wrong. I can't understand what you won't explain to me." The emptiness in his voice frightened her. His voice was shaking. He was shaking all over. She pushed aside her own panicked warnings of self-preservation. *Leah is always picking up strays.* But this one had stolen her heart. She could make him whole again. She knew she could.

"If you let me stay with you, I can pull enough bits and pieces of myself together to be a husband and father. I asked you to marry me before. Today, I'm asking you again. I'm offering you all of myself that I can give. Isn't it enough?"

It was a question she couldn't answer, but it was a plea she couldn't refuse. He hadn't disappeared today after the incident in the ER the way he had in Vietnam. But that was so little hope to build on! For herself she might take the chance, but with the baby to consider... "Oh, God, Adam. I can't take the chance on you deserting us someday."

"I can't say I love you, Leah. I don't think I know what it means anymore. But I'll cherish you and the baby. I'll be faithful until the day I die." He lowered his mouth to hers and she let her response to the desperate kiss answer without words.

If she hadn't been lost to him before his mouth touched hers, she was when it did. When the kiss ended she was shaking as badly as he was. She led him straight to her bedroom, listening not to the warning voice in her brain, but to the love in her heart.

Adam undressed her quickly and set her on the bed. His own clothes followed hers and then he stretched out beside her and took her in his arms. He bracketed her face with his hands and kissed her again and again, as though he couldn't get enough of her. He settled himself between her legs, resting his weight on his elbows and entered her with no more foreplay.

Leah was surprised by her own readiness. Their

bodies merged, their movements synchronized, and the storm they created with their lovemaking matched the storm raging outside her window. When he climaxed she followed him with her own shattering release. Time ceased to exist for Leah. She didn't know how much later Adam rolled his weight from her and pulled the covers over them both. He held her in his arms and she listened to the beat of his heart slow to normal as he slipped into sleep beside her.

LIGHTNING FLICKERING through her bedroom window awakened Leah. Another storm was rolling down off the mountain. She lay quietly waiting for the thunder. When it came it was still faraway, muted, like Adam's heartbeat beneath her cheek. She was still wrapped in his arms. His hand rested on her stomach.

Leah laid her hand over his and closed her eyes against the awareness that flowed from his skin to her womb. It had taken place while she was unaware, that connection between father and child that she had fought to keep from happening. It didn't matter what she wanted or thought she wanted anymore. Adam was going to be a part of her life for better or for worse. He was trying, she told herself. Today he'd struggled to stay with them, not to lose himself in his nightmare memories. She couldn't refuse him any longer. She didn't want to. She loved him. It was too late to turn back.

She had tried very hard not to move, not to make a sound, but some involuntary response must have alerted him. "You're awake," Adam said, his breath tickling her ear.

"Mmm. It's going to storm again. The lightning awakened me."

"Me, too. It's a long way off. Maybe the storm will miss us altogether. Why don't you go back to sleep? It's hours until dawn."

She drew her fingers along the back of his hand. "I don't think I can. There's so much we have to talk about."

"I'm withdrawing my name from consideration for the head of neuro at St. B's."

Leah's heartbeat quickened at his words, and the baby stirred restlessly inside her. Adam grunted in surprise at the movement, hesitated, then tightened his embrace.

"You've worked your entire career for that position, Adam. You'd be the youngest head of a major neuro unit in the country. Don't dismiss it so casually."

"It's not a casual decision, Leah. It's one of the most important I've ever made."

But was he making it for the right reason? Because he wanted to be here in Slate Hollow with her and their baby? Or because he couldn't face going back to the high-stakes, high-profile medical specialty he'd trained fifteen years to qualify for? "What will you do here?"

"I'm a pretty good mechanic, if I do say so myself." There was a note of gentle self-mockery in his voice that broke her heart.

"Adam, don't make light of this."

He sighed, moving his strong fingers in gentle circles over her skin. "I am serious, Leah. Right now I don't know what I want to do with my life, except that I want to do it here. I have to find peace in my own mind before I can take a scalpel in hand to cut into another human being's brain. If there's anyplace on earth I can accomplish that it's here with you.''

''I'll be here for you.'' Leah turned in his arms. Surely they could have this night to celebrate the miracle of the baby they had made together. Working out the day-to-day details of a life she was now committed to share with him in some degree of intimacy could wait until tomorrow. For a few hours more, Leah was content to let herself be wanted and desired, loved by his body if not his heart. It was not enough for all the tomorrows that stretched before her, but for now it would have to do.

IT WAS DAYLIGHT when Adam awoke again. It took him a moment to realize where he was—in Leah's bedroom, in Leah's bed. When was the last time he'd slept so soundly and so well that he'd lost track of his surroundings? Not for a long, long time. Not since those few, precious hours he'd spent in Leah's arms in Dalat.

And when she had awakened that next morning, he had been gone.

This morning the tables were turned. He was alone in Leah's bed.

A smile curved his lips. She hadn't deserted him as he had her. He could smell coffee brewing and smiled more broadly. That much at least they had in common. An addiction many people shared, but one small brick of compatibility to add to the foundation of their life together.

He pulled on his pants and shirt, and glanced at the

bedside clock. Half-past six. Leah was an early riser. He expected to find her in the kitchen, but instead, she was standing in front of the little desk near the fireplace reading her mail. She was dressed for work in white leggings and a long, mint-green sweater that nearly reached her knees.

She looked up when she heard his footsteps on the hardwood floor. Her hair was held by a large clip on top of her head, tendrils still damp from her shower curling around her cheeks and throat. He couldn't stop looking at it, remembering how last night he had combed the soft tendrils free of her confining braid and buried his face in its silkiness. A slight blush stained her skin, and he knew her thoughts had followed his to the night just past.

"Good morning," she said, not quite meeting his gaze. "You were sleeping so soundly I didn't want to wake you."

He wanted to tell her that was a miracle in itself, but the words wouldn't force themselves past the emotion that clogged his throat. "I wish you had. Your neighbors are going to be waking up to the sight of my truck in your driveway. Exactly where it was when they went to bed last night."

"It will give them something to speculate about over their coffee cups," she said nonchalantly, but the color in her cheeks darkened a shade or two. The good opinion of her neighbors was important to her. It had better become important to him, too, if he intended to make his home in this small, close-knit community.

"It won't happen again."

"It's probably best if you don't spend the night

again. I have trouble thinking straight when that happens.''

"Trouble thinking about what, Leah?''

"Everything.'' She gestured toward the kitchen. "The coffee's hot. It's decaf—I hope that's all right.'' She went back to reading her mail.

"It's fine.'' Adam went into the kitchen to pour himself a cup, but he had no intention of letting the conversation end with Leah's cryptic remark.

Her kitchen faced south. A big window, framed by yellow-and-white curtains, provided a view of her backyard and a garden already green and filled with spring blooms. It was a cheerful, crowded room with plants growing on the windowsill, copper pots and pans hanging from hooks on the wall, a thirties-style, chrome dinette set, and Depression glass plates arranged on a shelf along the wall.

He found a mug sitting by the coffeemaker and filled it to the brim. He was hungry, he realized, and wondered if he could talk Leah into having breakfast with him at the diner. Maybe he'd give Brian a call and ask him to join them, early though it was.

How long had it been since he'd planned ahead to eat a meal? Looked forward to sharing it with…his family?

Leah and the baby and Brian. They were a family now, or would be as soon as he could talk Leah into agreeing to marry him.

When he returned to the living room, she wasn't there.

"Leah?'' She didn't answer and his heart rate kicked up a notch. Had she left the house without him hearing her? Was she so upset by what had happened between them last night that she'd taken off for the clinic on her own rather than talk about it? He spoke more sharply this time. "Leah!"

"I'm up here." He looked up and saw her standing at the loft railing. "There was something I needed to do up here." She disappeared from his view.

He climbed the steep, narrow stairway to the loft and found her standing before the open door of a closet, a garment bag in her hand. On the quilt-covered bed lay her army uniform.

She picked it up. "It came back from the cleaner's the other day. I forgot to put it away. I just remembered it a few moments ago." She turned her back and tried to slide the uniform into the garment bag.

"You're not this upset because you haven't put your dry cleaning away. What's the matter?" Adam came up behind her and put his hands on her shoulders.

She motioned to the letter he'd seen her reading earlier. "My unit's been called up for three months' duty in Bosnia. They'll be leaving July first."

"Does your CO know you're pregnant?"

"Yes. My medical leave should be approved any day now. But it's the first time I haven't been ready to go when I've been called. I've decided to resign my commission."

"Why?"

"I'm an expectant single mother, Adam. Our next deployment could come at any time. I could be called up for any number of emergency situations with only a few hours' notice. I can't leave my child for months at a time. It wouldn't be fair to him or my parents. I can't ask them to take on such a responsibility."

"You aren't going to be a single mother."

"Adam, I'm not sure…"

"What are you unsure of? Last night—"

"Last night was a little unreal. It was hormones, maybe, or a nesting instinct."

"It was like that night in Dalat."

"Yes." She wouldn't meet his eyes.

"Except this morning I'm still here with you."

"It's easier to see all the hazards in the road ahead in the full light of day."

He spun her around. "Is it because I can't say I love you?"

She choked back a little laugh. "It would help," she said. "But no, it's not that. I can't say I love you, either."

"Then what is it? We both agree a child needs two parents. God knows I've learned that lesson the hard way with Brian—I missed so much of his growing up. I don't want that to happen with our baby."

"I don't, either. I don't want my child growing up with a hole in his heart where a father's love should be."

"He'll never have a moment's doubt."

"You stayed away from Brian all those years."

"I told you I made mistakes. That was the biggest one."

"You're saying you promise me you'll be there for our child when he's growing up? I won't wake up some morning to find you gone?"

"I won't run away from you again. I'll be there for you and the baby every day of my life." He wouldn't let the past push him away again. He would fight to stay with her, or die trying.

She was watching him closely. He forced himself to return her steady gaze. "I believe you," she whispered. She lifted her hand to his cheek, her fingers warm against his skin. Her eyes were swimming with unshed tears. "I'll marry you because Caleb and Aurelia and my father are right—a child needs two parents living under the same roof. I promise you I'll do everything in my power to make us a family."

CHAPTER FOURTEEN

"WHEN JULIET TOLD ME a neighbor's dog got into the henhouse, I didn't realize we'd be eating the victim for Sunday dinner," Brian said, grinning at his dad over the chicken-run fence in Aurelia's backyard that they were strengthening against another possible attack.

The dog hadn't actually mauled the chicken or anything, Juliet told him when she called the Hideaway that morning, just run it to death. Juliet and Naomi Dunn, who'd been there to help with Aurelia, had chased the mongrel off in time to save the rest of Lancelot's harem. Naomi had butchered the unlucky hen before she left for church, and Juliet invited Adam and Brian to help eat it.

Leah was there, too, of course. She and his dad were pretty much inseparable these days. Ever since the night his dad hadn't come home until morning. Nothing had been said about a wedding or anything, but Brian hoped they were moving in that direction. He liked Leah, and he liked the idea of him and his dad being part of a family again.

Leah had brought an apple pie she'd had in her freezer, and he'd eaten like a pig. Then before coming out to work on the chicken run, the three of them had cleaned up the kitchen, while Juliet sat with Aurelia, who wasn't feeling well enough today to leave her bed.

"Juliet's a good cook," Adam said as he steadied a fence post so Brian could pound it deeper into the stony ground with a sledgehammer.

"She is. She made that old hen taste like a spring chicken. I'm just glad she didn't have to do the dirty work. I mean cut off its head and take out its guts and everything. It's pretty gruesome work for a girl in her condition." Brian took a swing at the fence post and landed a solid blow, then another and another. His dad didn't blink, even though one slip of the heavy hammer would have crushed his hand. His dad trusted his aim and that made Brian feel damned proud.

"Juliet wasn't brought up thinking chicken only comes cut into pieces on foam trays from the supermarket. I think she could have handled it."

Brian took another swing at the fence post and the satisfying thud of metal on wood echoed off the hillside. "I've never tasted gravy like hers before. It's practically a food group all its own."

"I enjoyed it, too."

Brian and Adam had spent quite a bit of time together over the past few days at the Cade homestead. Working between rain showers, they'd put a rebuilt alternator in the truck and, without letting Juliet know what they were up to, they'd changed the spark plugs and the starter, too. They'd gone to the Slate Hollow lumberyard and bought two-by-fours to replace some rotten porch boards, and Adam had shown Brian how to rehang the screen door.

Brian rested the sledgehammer on the ground and leaned most of his weight on the handle. "Dad?"

"Mmm?" Adam was hunkered down, stringing wire through a hole in the fence, twisting it together so nothing bigger than a field mouse could wriggle through.

"I need to talk to you about something."

For a moment he thought he saw his dad stiffen, then Adam stood up, wiped his hands on his jeans and leaned against the fence post Brian had just made solid. "What is it, Son?"

"Remember when I asked you to borrow money against my trust fund to help Juliet out?" God, was it only a little over a week ago they'd come to Kentucky? It didn't seem possible that Juliet had become so important to him in such a short time, but she had, and there was no way he was going to let her down if he could help it.

"Yes, I remember," Adam said, frowning a little. "And I also remember that I thought we agreed it wasn't a good idea."

Adam's measured response was like a bucket of cold water thrown in Brian's face. He hated it when his dad used that tone of voice, cool and level, like he was a talking robot. He wanted to pick up the sledgehammer and smash something, but that wasn't very adultlike behavior, and he was an adult. He'd put a lot of thought into this decision.

"I didn't agree," he said. "I just didn't want to argue with you anymore that night. I'm worried about Juliet. Did Leah tell you Clint Fackler thinks her baby's not positioned right? It's lying sideways or something, not head down like it's supposed to be."

Brian felt his face getting hot. He didn't know much about women having babies, and he sure didn't know the medical terms his dad would use to describe what was going wrong with Juliet's pregnancy, but he was certainly smart enough to know that a baby lying sideways in its mother's body wasn't going to be born easily.

"Yes," Adam said, "Leah told me."

"Juliet's afraid they'll have to do a C-section."

"It's a possibility if the baby doesn't change position soon."

"That's a serious operation. She said Clint is wondering if she should go to the hospital in Lexington, where they have a special, high-risk baby unit."

"She's not due for two weeks. Things could change."

"But if they don't, it's going to be expensive. I don't think she has the kind of insurance to pay for all that high-tech stuff."

"I don't know the details of Aurelia and Juliet's financial situation."

Brian lifted his hand to his temple and smoothed the faint ridge of scar tissue there the way he'd done when he was a kid. It always rattled him when his dad talked like this, like whoever they were discussing was a stranger neither one of them had met, or worse yet, that Brian was a stranger, someone his dad hardly knew and wasn't too thrilled to be having a conversation with. "I want to help her out, Dad, so she doesn't have to worry about money for a while. So she doesn't have to give her baby away to those people from Lexington just so she can go to school.

It makes me crazy to think she might have to give up her baby to get an education.''

"Brian, I thought—''

He didn't give Adam a chance to come up with an argument that was so balanced and rational he couldn't reject it. He'd made up his mind, dammit, and no one was going to talk him out of what he wanted to do. "I'm going back to Chicago, Dad, as soon as possible. I...well, I was wondering how much longer you were planning to stay around here now that Leah's feeling so much better...."

He let the words trail off. He didn't want to come right out and ask his dad if he was going to marry Leah. And to be really honest, the two of them didn't seem comfortable enough with each other, regardless of how much time they spent together, to be planning on getting married anytime soon. It seemed to Brian there were a lot more things to keep them apart than to bring them together.

He didn't think Leah would want to leave Slate Hollow. She had a lot of friends here and was well-thought-of. He'd been around town long enough to see that. And his dad—how could he give up being the head of neurosurgery at one of the most respected hospitals in the country? His dad was only in his early forties, that made him a boy wonder in the brain-surgeon world. He'd already had articles written about him in big magazines and newspapers. He made a ton of money and operated on famous people from all over the world. It would be hard to give that up, unless he loved Leah so much he couldn't live without her.

And he wasn't sure his dad could ever love anyone that much.

He watched his dad pull off his work gloves and stick them in his back pocket. "Leah and I have a lot of decisions to make," Adam said, "but I will have to return to Chicago soon. Perhaps by the end of the week?"

"Not soon enough for me," Brian said, remembering the pinched, scared look on Juliet's face and the way she'd grabbed his hand and held on for dear life, when she'd told him about the problems with the baby. "I want to go right away."

"Why such a hurry?"

"I'm going back to sell my car. I'm going to give the money to Juliet so she doesn't have to worry about her insurance not paying for the operation, or have to decide whether to sell her baby and go to school, or keep it and work in a car-parts factory for the rest of her life."

"I told you before I don't think it's a good idea for you to give Juliet money. That only adds another layer to an already complicated situation."

"What do you mean?"

"I mean that by giving her money you're trying to manipulate her to make the decision *you* want her to make, just like the couple from Nashville who are trying to influence her in the opposite direction."

"Well, I don't give a goddamn what you think!" Brian yelled, throwing down the sledgehammer in disgust. What was it with his dad? How could he just stand there and talk about Juliet like she was nobody to them? "Jesus, Dad. Don't you have any feelings? Juliet's scared and alone. Why are you so determined to make it as hard as possible for her? I thought you and I were getting on the same wavelength this past week. I thought we were starting to see eye to eye.'' Brian was furious with himself when he heard his voice crack on the last three words. He realized he'd raised his hand to the scar on his temple again, and that made him angrier than ever.

''We do agree on most things.''

''But not the most important thing! Listen to yourself. You sound like we're discussing these stupid chickens or something, not Juliet. When I was little I always thought I'd like to be a doctor like you, but then I smashed my face up against the mailbox. Do you remember?'' He was talking too loudly and he knew it. The hens were still skittish from the dog attack, and they flapped and squawked and headed for the relative safety of the coop. Lancelot was muttering under his breath and stalking back and forth a few feet away, considering whether or not to run the human intruders out of his domain. Brian ignored them all, focusing on his dad, trying to read whatever thoughts were hidden behind the stony mask he wore.

''I remember.'' His dad's face was pale. Brian was too wound up to wonder why he looked as if he'd just seen a ghost standing behind him, instead of Lancelot.

''I used to think I wanted to be a doctor like you because you took such good care of me that day. You picked me up and carried me home. You held me on your lap in the car while Mom drove us to the hospital. You stayed beside me all the way into the operating room so the plastic surgeon could put my face back together, and you were still there when I woke up. But after that you started to change. By the time you and Mom got divorced, I couldn't figure out what had happened to you. I was just a little kid. I always thought it was my fault we weren't a family anymore.'' Brian waited for a moment, the little kid in him hoping against hope his dad would say it wasn't true. Adam remained silent.

''You know why I quit school, Dad? Because I wanted some time to think about being a doctor like you. Yeah, go ahead and laugh. What a hoot! Well, I just changed my mind again. Thanks for reminding me what a jackass you turn into when you get to play God every day of your life.'' Brian turned and stalked off.

Jeez, why had admitted he wanted to be a doctor? He'd never told anyone. *Never.* Well, it wasn't true any longer. He didn't want to be a doctor. Not if it meant turning into a heartless, uncaring monster like his dad.

Adam was yelling something, calling him back, but Brian didn't stop to listen. He was heading to Chicago, and he was leaving today. Now. Even if he had to walk every damned step of the way.

LEAH SIGNED THE NOTES she'd added to the visiting nurse's chart and replaced the chart in the top drawer of the dresser. She'd heard Juliet and Brian's voices in the kitchen, but hadn't paid much attention to them as she jotted down her comments on Aurelia's condition, but now the teenagers' voices were raised in what sounded like anger.

She glanced over at the bed. Aurelia was awake, propped up against the pillows, her Bible in her hand.

She'd had a restless night and was heavily medicated, and didn't seem to be aware of the confrontation in the kitchen. "I'm going to see how Juliet's doing," Leah said as she hurried out of the room.

Just as she entered the living room, Brian raced past, his face dark with anger. He jerked open the front door. "Don't, Brian. Aurelia's trying to sleep," Leah called softly, afraid he'd slam it and startle her patient. "What happened? Where are you going?"

"I'm going home," he said bitterly, then closed the door behind him with deliberate care.

"Goodness, what got into Brian? Did you two have a fight over something?"

Juliet was standing in the doorway to the kitchen, a glass of lemonade in her hand, her lower lip trembling as she tried not to cry. "I...I don't know. I mean, Brian had a fight with his dad, and then, well, I guess we had a fight, too." They heard the truck engine start, then fade, as Brian drove away. "He's really going."

"It would appear so." Leah looked past Juliet toward the backyard. What had happened between Brian and Adam? Everything had seemed fine when the two of them went out to work on the chicken run.

"Leah, what am I going to do? Me having this baby is causing everyone so much heartache. I wish I'd never been born." Juliet started crying in earnest.

Leah took the glass of lemonade and placed it on a table by the door. She put her arms around the distraught girl. The TV was tuned to an early-season baseball game, and Leah hoped the sound was loud enough to prevent Aurelia from hearing Juliet's sobs. "Don't cry. It's not good for the baby," she murmured. "Come on. Sit down and tell me exactly what happened." She led her back into the kitchen.

Adam was still outside. She could hear the thudding of metal against wood as he continued to work on the chicken-run fence. Why hadn't he gone after Brian? What had triggered such a blowup when they'd seemed to be getting along so well the past few days? Or had she been so caught up in her own growing love for Adam she'd failed to notice the tension between father and son?

No, she was certain all was well as little as an hour ago.

"Brian told his dad he was going to go back to Chicago to sell his car," Juliet said with a sniff. "He has a real expensive car. He wanted me to have the money so I don't have to give the baby away or worry about medical expenses or anything. But his dad said he shouldn't do it. They got into a really big fight over it."

The screen door opened and closed. Leah looked up to see Adam standing in the kitchen doorway, his shirtsleeves rolled up, work gloves in hand. "Is this true?" she asked him.

"That Brian and I had an argument over whether or not he should give Juliet money? Yes." There was little emotion in his voice, but there was anguish in his eyes. "I'm sorry, Juliet. I didn't mean to upset you." The harshness in his voice was tempered now with compassion. A surge of hope and love filled Leah's heart. He was trying very hard not to retreat within himself, not to seal himself away.

"I told him I didn't want his money," Juliet said. "That's when he got mad at me. His face went all red and he almost yelled at me. He said, 'Am I the only person here who wants to keep this family together?' Like I didn't know how it was to have a parent run off and leave you just like…'' She looked at Adam with remorseful eyes. "I'm sorry."

"It's all right, Juliet. I did leave Brian, or at least, I let his mother take him away, which amounts to the same thing."

"I'm just so confused, and I'm scared. I don't want anything to happen to my baby, but I'm worried he won't be born right. Or what if I don't know how to take care of him properly? Maybe I should give him away. Maybe he'd be better off with those people in Lexington."

"What are you talking about, girl? Who said anything about you giving up your baby to strangers to raise?" Aurelia was standing in the bedroom doorway, her arms outstretched to keep her balance. Her face was a pasty gray, her breath coming in labored gasps. "He's the last of our blood, Juliet. He's the last of the Cades." The old woman's knees buckled. She sank to the floor, her hands clutching her chest.

"Granny!"

Leah headed for her, but Adam was quicker. He picked Aurelia up in his arms and carried her to her bed. Leah repositioned the prongs of the nasal catheter and increased the oxygen flow, but Aurelia continued to struggle for breath.

"She needs to be hospitalized," Adam said, his fingers on her pulse. "This is more than just overexertion. She's having a reaction to her medication. When did she have her last dose?"

Aurelia was still fighting for every breath despite

the increase in the oxygen flow. "I gave her an injection about thirty minutes ago. She hasn't had any problems with it before now, but I think you're right. Let's take the Jeep. We can get her to the hospital more quickly than waiting for the emergency unit to come all the way up here. I have a portable oxygen cylinder in my emergency box."

Adam helped her wrap Aurelia in a blanket, then carried her out to Leah's Jeep. Leah went ahead and had the small oxygen cylinder and a disposable nasal catheter ready as Adam placed Aurelia gently on the seat beside her. Leah adjusted the oxygen and supported Aurelia's thin body against her, and Adam climbed into the driver's seat.

Juliet got in beside Adam, clutching Aurelia's purse and slippers in her hands. She was still crying as she positioned herself awkwardly sideways so she could hold Aurelia's hand. Adam negotiated the bumpy road off the mountain with skill, but it was impossible to miss every rut and pothole, and Aurelia moaned in pain with every jarring thump. Fortunately there was little traffic this dreary Sunday afternoon, and five minutes after they'd turned onto the highway they had pulled up under the ER canopy.

Once inside the automatic glass doors, the ER staff took over. Leah was prohibited by hospital policy from following Aurelia's gurney into the treatment room, so she stayed with Juliet, who was still crying and distraught. She settled the teenager in the waiting room with Adam and took a moment to call Caleb and apprise him of the situation. He promised to come right over. Then there was nothing to do but wait.

Caleb was as good as his word. Ten minutes later

he waved at Leah and Adam as he passed the waiting room on his way to the treatment area. Juliet had stopped crying and was curled up on the leather sofa at the far end of the room, dozing. Leah covered her with one of the crocheted afghans the hospital auxiliary provided for just such times. She smoothed the blanket over Juliet's shoulders. The girl didn't awaken, but turned her cheek into the folds of the blanket with a little sigh.

Leah was as worried about the teenager as she was about Aurelia. Juliet's medical situation was a serious one. Tests had shown the baby was a transverse lie, with a shoulder presentation. It would be impossible for Juliet to deliver the baby normally. Clint was already making arrangements for her to undergo a C-section in a little less than two weeks. He would tell her the details, he'd informed Leah, as soon as he had confirmed an appointment with the obstetrician at Lex General who specialized in high-risk pregnancies. He'd tried to prepare Juliet for the possibility at her last visit, but the teenager was still hoping against hope that the baby would turn and move into position for a natural birth. Leah knew the chances of that happening now were very slim.

All these things were running through Leah's mind at the same time that another part of her, this part linked even more directly to her heart, was worried about Adam and the fight he'd had with his son. Where was Brian? Had he returned to Aurelia's house to find them all gone? It might be hours before Aurelia's condition stabilized, and there was no way to get word to him of what had happened, other than leaving a note with the desk clerk at the Hideaway Inn.

"Adam?" She kept her voice pitched low so as not to disturb Juliet.

He was sitting with his elbows on his knees, his chin resting on his folded hands, lost in his thoughts. He looked up when she spoke his name. "Yes?"

"You should go and find Brian. Make things right with him." She held out her hands, hoping he would take her in his arms, not shut her out. She dreaded that most of all.

"I don't know if that's possible." He stood up and took her hands in his, but didn't bring her closer.

"Don't say that, Adam. He's your son. You *have* to make things right between you."

"He accused me of shutting him out of my life a long time ago, and he was right."

"Then tell him you're sorry. That you want it to be different now." She saw him pulling away, even though he didn't move a muscle. She remembered what he had told her all those months ago in Vietnam. His parents were dead. He was virtually estranged from his only brother. Brian was all the family he had in the world. She had to make him see how important it was to heal the breach between them.

She moved into his arms. He hesitated a moment, then held her close. She let herself be comforted by his strength and the solidity of his body, then leaned back in his arms so she could see his face. "You don't have to tell him everything tonight, Adam, but at least tell him about the post-traumatic stress. Tell him his bicycle accident started it again for you.

That's what he remembers, isn't it? Your distancing yourself from him after that happened? Give him a reason. He's an intelligent young man. He'll understand. All he really wants is for you to tell him you love him.''

Dear Lord, that was all she wanted for herself and the baby, too.

His voice was anguished. "God, Leah, don't you know that's the hardest thing of all for me to say?''

"Adam, please. For the baby's sake.'' Desperation gave her voice an edge. He winced. She hadn't meant the words as a threat, but he seemed to take them as such.

"I'll do my best to make him understand.''

"Go now. Take my Jeep.''

"Will you be all right here alone with Juliet?''

"Yes.'' She stepped out of his arms. She reached up and brushed her fingers across his cheek. She loved him. She had taken him into her heart. She wanted him to find happiness again. She wanted him to regain his son's trust and love so that her child could benefit from that love, too. "Caleb's here if we need him. Go to your son.''

CHAPTER FIFTEEN

CALEB'S PICKUP was still parked in its usual place beside the Cherokee, and for a minute or two Adam let himself hope Brian's anger had played itself out on the drive into town. He didn't want to lose his son, but it wasn't going to be easy to make things right. He still couldn't attempt to face the past without retreating to that gray nothingness inside that kept him sane.

Adam knocked lightly on the connecting door to Brian's room. He waited a moment, then turned the knob. Brian's things were gone, and his backpack and carry-on, the only luggage he'd brought with him, weren't in the closet. The bathroom was empty of shaving gear. His son had left town, just as he'd threatened.

For a moment Adam just stood there. He didn't know what to do next. Go after him? He didn't have the slightest idea where to start looking. Brian hadn't taken the pickup or the Cherokee, so that meant he'd either just started walking or hitched a ride out of town. It had been a little over two hours since he'd barreled out of Aurelia's yard. He had at least an hour's head start.

A rectangle of white on the table by the window caught Adam's eye as he shut the door to Brian's room. It was a letter, weighted down by the keys to Caleb's truck. Brian had left a note asking him, Adam, to return Carlotta with his thanks. Beneath the letter was a second one, sealed in an envelope with the Hideaway's return address printed on the corner. It was for Juliet, but there was nothing more for him.

Adam headed out to the Cherokee without a thought in his mind except finding his son and talking him into staying in Slate Hollow. If not for Adam's sake, then for Juliet's. He drove out of town along the highway, not really certain how far he intended to go. He couldn't leave Leah without any explanation and follow Brian to Chicago, which was his first impulse. But neither could he sit idly in the hospital waiting room without making some effort to determine his son was all right.

Rain was coming down hard by the time he got to the cluster of fast-food restaurants that lined both sides of the road at the interstate exit. He pulled into the parking lot of the truck stop and went inside. It was a big place with a restaurant and newsstand, a video-rental shop, a barbershop and showers for road-weary drivers. He found what he was looking for tucked away in a corner near the back. The Grey-hound ticket window. An elderly man with a monk's fringe of gray hair and wire-rim glasses perched on the end of his nose, was on duty.

"Has anyone been in here to buy a ticket to Chi-cago in the past couple of hours?"

"No one's bought a ticket here for anyplace to-day," the old man answered. "Next bus through here goes to Charlotte, and that don't leave till ten tonight. One don't go north till Tuesday."

"This was a young man. A little over six feet, dark hair, wearing a leather coat. My son." His voice almost broke on the words. "He probably had a backpack and a carry-on."

"No one bought a ticket here today, I said." The old man was adamant.

"Thanks." Adam turned away. Not finding Brian here was a blow. He'd hoped against hope his son would be waiting for a bus at the station.

"I said no one bought a ticket today. Didn't say no one asked about one."

Adam spun around. "He was here?"

"Six feet tall, dark hair, longer than yours. Gold earring." The old man curled up his lip in displeasure. "Same nose and chin you got. Yeah, he was here. Couple hours ago."

"But you say he didn't buy a ticket?"

"I did, because that's what you asked me."

"Did you see where he went when he left here?"

"Nope. Ain't none of my business what anyone does once they leave this here window."

"Did you see him talking to anyone?" Adam persisted. "Did he get a ride with one of the truckers?"

"Mister, look around. There's been thirty, forty people through here since then. If he hitched a ride with a trucker, I didn't see him do it. He was here, and he didn't buy a ticket."

"You've been a big help." Once more Adam turned to leave.

"'Course, I did tell him there's a bus leaving the Lexington station for Cincy today."

"When?" Adam wanted to reach through the grated window and take the old coot by the throat,

shake him until his teeth rattled. He balled his hands
into fists and then deliberately relaxed them again.
Violence would get him nowhere. The old man held
all the cards at the moment, and there was nothing he
could do but play along.

The ticket agent looked over his shoulder at the
clock on the wall behind him. "Leaves in about fifteen minutes, I'd say. If she's on time."

"Is she usually on time?" Something in his voice
must have alerted the old man he was at the end of
his patience.

"I'll call and check it out if you want."

"I'd appreciate it." It was a twenty-minute drive
to the outskirts of Lexington. Adam had no idea how
the city was laid out, how much longer it would take
to reach the bus station; he just knew he had to try
to catch up with Brian if it was humanly possible.

The old man picked up a phone and punched in a
number. "Yeah, Harry? This is Mel over at Slate Hollow. Your seven-fifteen to Cincy on time? She is.
Good. Glad to hear it. Okay."

"Ask him if anyone matching my son's description
bought a ticket for Chicago in the last hour." Adam
had learned his lesson dealing with Mel.

The ticket agent did as he asked. "He says nope.
No one looking like that's bought a ticket. Sorry."

"Have him paged."

"That's not my job."

Adam reached through the grate and grabbed Mel
by the front of the shirt. "I'm tired of your games,
old man. Give me the phone." He couldn't give up
on finding Brian, not yet. "Harry, this is Dr. Adam

Sauder. Are you certain no one answering my son's description is getting on that bus?"

"Yes, sir, I am."

Adam felt his anger drain away into despair. "Okay, I believe you. If he does show up, you give Mel here at Slate Hollow a call. Understand?"

"Yes, sir."

Adam handed the phone back to the ticket agent. "You call me if you hear from Harry."

"Yes, sir," Mel sputtered.

"Thanks for your help. If he shows up here or in Lexington, you can reach me at Slate Hollow Memorial. I'll be there the rest of the night."

CALEB STRODE into the waiting room at his usual energetic pace. He never seemed to tire, Leah thought, although he must have had a long day. He was a deacon of his church, and the early service on Sundays was at eight. He'd probably been up several hours before that, reading the Sunday paper and catching up with medical-journal articles he gathered off the Internet.

It was a quiet evening in the ER. She and Juliet were the only two people in the waiting room. Adam hadn't returned. He'd been gone nearly an hour. Juliet was still sleeping, curled up on the couch at the far end of the room. Leah went forward to meet Caleb near the doorway, so they could talk without waking her.

"How is Aurelia? Can we see her?" She wasn't a nurse at the moment. She was as worried as any family member.

"Hey, Leah, slow down a bit. Give me a chance

to pour a cup of coffee and I'll tell you everything you want to know."

"I'm sorry, Caleb. It's just…well, I'm not used to being on this side of the equation around here."

"I know. Doctors and nurses make the worst patients. They make the worst family members to deal with, too." He put his hand on Leah's shoulder. "She's going to make it—this time." He looked at the sleeping teenager. "It won't be much longer, Leah. It would probably be a good idea to start preparing Juliet for the eventuality of Aurelia going to the county hospice."

Leah pressed her fingers against her lips to stop them from trembling. She'd known this day was coming, but it was hard to hear the words. "Oh, Caleb, she wants so badly to die at home."

"Juliet's in no condition to be Aurelia's caregiver. There's a waiting list a mile long for home-care nurses, especially for the night shift." Caleb shook his head. "I'm sorry, Leah, but facts are facts."

"Naomi Dunn's a good practical nurse. She'll stay until the end if I ask her. And I'll stay with Aurelia and Juliet at night." Juliet depended on her. Aurelia had been her friend since her earliest days in Slate Hollow. She couldn't desert them now.

"Leah, it might be weeks. You have your own health—"

"It might only be days."

Caleb exhaled a gusty sigh. "Yes. I'll see if I can get you a home-care aide to come in the mornings to help spell you and Naomi, and so there's someone available if…if she's still with us when Juliet's baby comes."

Leah gave him a kiss on the cheek. "I knew I could count on you. Thanks, Caleb. When can we take her home?"

"Late tomorrow morning if she has a good night."

"Fine. I have patients scheduled for tomorrow morning. One home visit I can push back till three. Oh, I forgot. Juliet's appointment with the Lex General obstetrician is tomorrow. I'll—"

"I'll take her to Lex General." Leah hadn't seen Adam approach. He was standing just outside the doorway. His hair was shining with moisture, the shoulders of his coat darkened with rain. He was alone.

"You didn't find Brian?"

He shook his head. "He's left town." Adam stepped into the waiting room and handed Caleb a set of keys. "My son asked me to give you these and to tell you he's most appreciative for the use of the truck."

"Brian's gone?" Caleb asked as he pocketed the keys. "I was under the impression he was planning to stay around town awhile."

For a moment Leah thought Adam would ignore the question. "We had an argument this afternoon," he said at last. "A difference of opinion over what's best for Juliet's future. He's determined to see she has the resources to keep her baby and go to school, or whatever she wants to do. He's gone back to Chicago to sell his car and bring her the money."

"Quite a gesture," Caleb said.

"He cares about Juliet," Leah said. She went to Adam, hesitating only a little. She had committed herself to him. He hadn't yet committed himself to her in the same way, but if she was going to live her life with him, she would not do so at arm's length. She slid her arms around his waist. After a moment's hesitation he enfolded her in his embrace.

"How did he leave town? Did you give him your truck?" she asked. Adam's leather jacket was wet with rain, cool beneath her cheek.

Adam shook his head. "He must have hitched a ride with a trucker. I've been trying my damnedest to find out if he caught a bus out by the interstate, but the old reprobate running the place wasn't much help. I finally got him to call the bus station in Lexington, but the ticket agent there hadn't seen anyone fitting Brian's description."

"Adam, you should have gone after him."

He reached up and traced the tip of his finger down her cheek. "I came back to be with you."

Leah swallowed against the tightness in her throat. He was torn; she could feel the tension in the muscles of his arms as he held her close. "We're okay. Brian should be your first concern."

He brushed a kiss across her forehead. "He's a grown man, Leah. He'll be okay. I'll make my peace with him when he returns."

"Promise you'll try to contact him soon, please, for all our sakes," she said softly.

"I promise. Do you want me to drive you and Juliet to your place?"

"I'm not going home, Adam. Aurelia hates hospitals. I'll stay here with her tonight, and then I'll be staying at her place for…a while."

"I overheard your plans, but tonight you're going

home to rest—both you and Juliet. I'll stay here and watch over Aurelia.''

A BABY WAS CRYING somewhere nearby. Adam shot bolt upright in the chair where he'd kept vigil beside Aurelia's bed. Were the baby's cries echoes of long ago or real, in the here and now? For a moment he couldn't be certain. He stood up and leaned over the rail to study the old woman in the high bed. She was sleeping, her breathing even but shallow, a slight frown of discomfort between her eyebrows despite the sedatives and pain meds she'd been given.

It had been touch and go for several hours after Aurelia's collapse, Caleb had informed him before he left the hospital. Her heart was greatly weakened by its struggle to obtain enough oxygen from her failing lungs. The older physician had prescribed sublingual morphine for the pain, whenever it became necessary. If God was kind, Aurelia would be asleep as her life slipped away.

He heard the baby crying again. Adam stiffened. Time altered for a moment. He was back in Vietnam in the flooded rice paddy. A baby was still alive. A miracle in that scene of death and carnage. Why wasn't someone taking care of her, tending to her wounds? He found himself out in the hall—and back in reality.

The ER was mostly quiet. Slate Hollow was a small hospital. Less than half-a-dozen patients had been admitted through the automatic doors since midnight, and none were serious from what Adam could see and overhear from his place beside Aurelia's bed. There was only a case of heartburn, which might have been a heart attack but wasn't, and a fender bender out on the highway that had resulted in a case of whiplash and assorted scrapes and bruises. There were no spinal-cord injuries, no bullets wounds, no cerebral aneurysm to be tied off and carefully removed from a living brain. Not tonight, anyway.

But perhaps on other nights there were? Adam could see himself walking through those doors, making the life-and-death decisions he'd trained fifteen years to make. If there was anyplace on earth he could heal enough to work again, it was here in Slate Hollow. If only he could forget. But the baby's crying continued, and he couldn't stop himself from following the sobbing wails.

The young ER nurse Caleb had introduced him to before he left at eleven came out of a treatment room a few doors down from Aurelia's. "Can I get something for you, Dr. Sauder?" she asked.

"There's a baby crying." Deep inside, Adam heard the screams of maimed and dying children. He fought to ignore them, to still the tremors. In a matter of months he would be a father again. He would hear a baby crying, his baby and Leah's. He couldn't let it get to him this way.

"Just an earache," the nurse said with a smile. "Always in the middle of the night—new parents and a crying baby. They just can't wait until morning. You know how it is."

"Yes, I know how it is." An earache, an ordinary childhood ailment. If he walked into the examining room now, he would find nothing more terrible than exhausted parents and a fussing, feverish infant. Yet he couldn't take those steps, that leap of faith, so he returned to Aurelia's room, still a captive of the past.

"Who's there?" asked a peevish old voice.

"It's me, Aurelia. Adam Sauder, remember? I'm sitting with you tonight."

"At the hospital?" She moved her head restlessly on the pillow, lifted her arm to peer at the IV inserted in the back of her left hand, touched the oxygen tubing as though to reassure herself it was there, then spoke again. "What time is it?"

"It's very late. You should be sleeping."

"I heard a baby crying. It's not my Juliet's baby, is it? I've lost track of time. The little 'un hasn't come, has he?"

"No, it's another baby—with an earache."

"Why is there a baby here? Isn't this the place they put dying old women?"

"We're still in the emergency room, Aurelia. It's a baby with an earache, that's all." Because she was going to be discharged without being formally admitted to the hospital, she hadn't been transferred to a conventional room, but remained under the care of the emergency-room staff.

"Cut a twig from the hickory tree outside my bedroom. Hold the branch over the fire until the sweet oil runs out. When it cools down some, put a couple of drops in the baby's ear and he'll be right as rain by morning."

"I'll tell them, Aurelia," Adam promised. "But you need to go back to sleep."

"I don't want to sleep. I want to talk."

Adam scanned the monitors beside the bed. He had long ago become inured to the sound of their beeps and blips, and the eerie green glow of their screens. He touched the screen pad of the computerized nursing chart and checked the display. The readouts were as good as could be expected. Aurelia was one tough lady. He smiled down at her. "All right, let's talk."

"I was dreaming," she said.

"That's the medication," Adam told her. "Sometimes it causes you to have bad dreams."

"Not a bad dream exactly, but a sad one. I saw my Juliet walking off into the hills above the house. Her and her baby. But she was alone, and sad. I called out to her, but she didn't hear me. There was an angel beckoning to me to follow her. I wanted to be with Juliet. But...I wanted to go with the angel, too."

"Perhaps the baby crying triggered your dream."

She shook her head. "It's the dying. I'm gettin' preoccupied with dying, but Juliet still needs me. I can't go and leave my poor Juliet alone, no matter how much pain this cancer eatin' away inside me brings. To think she's having to make such a terrible decision all on her own. To give up her own flesh and blood to strangers because I can't do what's right by her." A tear rolled down her cheek. "I've failed."

Almost against his will, he reached over and folded his hands around Aurelia's cold, skeletal fingers. "I promise you, Juliet will not have to give up her child to keep a roof over her head, nor will she have to sacrifice her education to keep him with her."

"Thank you. You're a man of your word. I believe you and it comforts me."

"Now get some sleep."

"Not quite yet. I haven't had my say. Leah loves

you.'' She paused to get her breath. "She loves you with all her heart. Do you love her back?"

"I don't know, Aurelia," he said truthfully. "I care for her, but I lost the knack for loving a long time ago."

"You can get it back if you open your heart to Leah and that baby you've got comin'." She turned her hand palm up beneath his and squeezed weakly.

Adam didn't answer.

Aurelia closed her eyes, whether in determination or exhaustion he wasn't sure. "I have the faith. Go to Leah and let me rest so I can do some hard prayin' that'll make you see the light."

"I'm staying here with you."

"No. Go. I can't sleep with a strange man in my room." Aurelia opened her eyes and smiled, and he saw a fleeting glimpse of the strong, loving woman she must have been. "Go on. Let me rest so I can go home bright and early tomorrow."

THE CLOCK ON THE MANTEL struck one as he stepped into Leah's living room. She'd left the front door unlocked for him, as though she knew how badly he needed to be with her, if only for a little while. He stood quietly just inside the door, getting his bearings. The smell of wood smoke drew his eyes, for a moment, to the pale flames of a dying fire in the fireplace. The glow of a night-light came from the loft where he assumed Juliet was sleeping. He took off his damp jacket, hung it over the back of the desk chair and turned to see a figure in white standing in the shadow of the stairway.

"Adam? Is that you?" Leah's voice was little more

than a whisper, barely audible above the sound of raindrops on the roof.

"Yes."

She moved toward him. "You're soaking wet."

"I walked from the hospital."

"Oh, Adam, it's raining. Let me get you a towel."

He reached out and circled her wrist with his hand. "No, don't bother."

"Why did you leave Aurelia?"

"She sent me away. She said she couldn't sleep with a strange man in the room."

His words caused her to laugh, a low chuckle that almost brought a smile to his lips, as well. "How like her. Is she comfortable?"

"Yes. She was sleeping when I left. I asked the nurse to keep an eye on her until I get back."

"It was a near thing tonight."

"I know."

A sigh sifted past her lips. "I talked to Juliet about arrangements for hospice care. It was hard on her. But I still hope we'll be able to grant Aurelia her wish to die at home."

"So do I."

"You must be hungry. When was the last time you ate?"

"I honestly don't remember."

"Can I fix you something?"

"No, I'm fine, thanks. I just wanted…" What did he want? To be with her, to hold her in his arms, to feel the movement of their child inside her, to lose himself in her serenity. All those things and more. He wanted to tell her he loved her. But when he opened his mouth to say the words, the cries of dying children pounded in his ears, and the screams he never let himself utter all those years ago fought to be free. "I can't stay, but I wanted to make sure you two were okay."

"Juliet's sound asleep, but I'm worried about her. She's uncomfortable, and she's retaining a lot of water. I'm glad she has an appointment at Lex General tomorrow. I think the sooner they deliver this baby the better."

"Would she be more comfortable if Margaret went with her, instead of me?"

"Possibly," Leah said. "But I'll be more comfortable with you there. I love Margaret dearly, but she isn't a doctor. You are. I'd go myself, but I've neglected my patients more than I like these past couple of weeks."

"Then it's settled. I'll be here at ten to pick her up."

"I think she wants to stop by the hospital and see Aurelia first."

"Of course. Shall I meet you there, instead?"

He sensed her smile more than saw it in the darkness. "Yes. Maybe that's best." It was cool in the darkened room, and he saw her shiver.

"I shouldn't have come here. It's the middle of the night and I got you out of bed." He opened his arms. "But God, I needed to see you."

She closed the small distance between them in the blink of an eye. She went into his arms and he held her close. "I'm glad you came even if you can't stay."

Adam kissed her silky hair and found the strength to force the screams in his mind aside. "I wish I could, but we've got your reputation to think of, and there's Juliet..."

"I'd rather she didn't find us in bed together in the morning."

"Me, too." He cradled the back of her head in his hand, increased the pressure of his mouth against hers. When the kiss ended, he rested his chin on the top of her head until the beating of their hearts slowed and steadied. He stepped away. "If I kiss you again, I won't be able to leave."

She took a step back, too, smiling a little. "My willpower isn't any stronger than yours."

"Aurelia said I should take the risk of loving you and the baby we've made together."

Leah lifted her fingers and pressed them to his lips. "Not tonight, Adam. Don't try to force yourself to say the words."

"You deserve so much more than what I can give you right now."

"I love you," she said simply. "I can wait."

CHAPTER SIXTEEN

BRIAN STARED DOWN at the cashier's check in his hand. He'd gotten a good deal on the car, but now what was he going to do with the money? It had suddenly occurred to him, while he was imagining himself handing it over to Juliet with a flourish, that the IRS wasn't going to think it was such a magnanimous gesture. They were going to consider it income, and tax her on it. Big time. And him, too.

There had to be some way to shelter the money. He needed to save as much as possible for Juliet and the baby, the way he'd intended to in the first place. But how? He couldn't call Elliot and his mom, not today. Elliot might understand, but his mom was still plenty steamed about what he was doing. There had been half-a-dozen messages on the answering machine when he'd arrived at the condo two days earlier, all from his mom, each one more frantic than the last.

He'd phoned her right away, even though he was dead on his feet. He'd spent eighteen hours on a bus on top of hitching his way to Cincinnati in an eighteen-wheeler with a guy who liked to talk politics and religion way more than Brian did. His mom had been happy to learn he was okay. He'd spent a good couple of minutes talking to his little sister, Megan, all the time thinking in the back of his mind that pretty soon he'd have another little brother or sister to talk to. But oddly enough, when he thought of doing things with little kids, even Megan, he thought of Slate Hollow as the place they'd be, not Boston.

After his mom came back on the line, he'd fended off questions about whether or not he was ready to return to Harvard. Then he'd taken a deep breath and told her why he'd called. She hadn't been happy to hear what he intended to do with his car—and why— and grilled him until he'd told her the whole story. And once he'd started telling her about Juliet and her baby, well, he'd ended up telling her about Leah and *her* baby.

That revelation had gotten his mom's mind off his selling the Lexus, but not for long. Then Elliot had come on the line and he'd had to tell the story all over again. His mom had called twice since then, trying to get him to change his mind and come back to Boston, but he'd held firm. The last time she'd told him he was as stubborn as his father and hung up the phone without another word. He was going to have some serious fence-mending to do the next time he saw her.

Brian got up and walked into the kitchen. He laid the check on the central island and opened the fridge. It was empty, or darned close. He should have thought to get some groceries before the guy who bought the Lexus came to drive it away. He grabbed a jar of peanut butter and one of pickles, and sat down on a stool. He scooped peanut butter into his mouth with a spoon, pulled a pickle out of the jar with his fingers and stared at the cashier's check. He supposed he could take it with him to Slate Hollow and then ask Caleb, or his dad, the best way to handle it.

Except he remembered some of the not-so-upstanding citizens he'd come across on the bus trip north. He wasn't sure he wouldn't get his pocket picked or his luggage stolen on the way back to Kentucky. Maybe he should deposit the check in his bank account here. But then, he might have to fill out a bunch of forms, which would start the whole tax ball rolling.

Maybe he should just call his dad, tell him he was sorry for the things he'd said on Sunday and ask his advice.

He washed down the peanut butter with a can of soda and went to the phone. After all, what he was trying to do for Juliet was more important than his hurt pride. He called directory assistance and got the number for the Hideaway. The clerk said his dad had checked out a couple of days ago. For a moment Brian felt a squeeze of fear around his heart. If his dad had checked out a couple of days ago, where was he? Then he grinned, feeling like a fool. He'd gone to stay with Leah of course.

He tried there next. No answer. She didn't like answering machines, he'd remembered her saying, and so didn't have one. He stood there, looking out at the bright spring afternoon and wondered what to do next. Then he realized what time it was—a little after four. Maybe Leah and his dad were both at Aurelia's place. He punched in the numbers and waited a little nervously for the call to go through. It was going to be awkward apologizing to his dad over the phone. Maybe it would be better to have hopped the bus back to Slate Hollow and told him in person. He almost hung up the receiver, but just as he made the decision, the connection clicked through.

"Cade residence," Leah said.

He smiled. He couldn't help himself. It was good to hear her voice, with its faint hint of the South. He missed her and his dad—and Juliet—more than he'd imagined. "Hi, Leah. It's Brian. Is my dad there?"

"HE'S ON HIS WAY BACK," Adam said, replacing the phone in its cradle. "He'll be here late tomorrow afternoon."

"He's taking the bus back?" Leah came from Aurelia's bedroom, where she'd gone to give him privacy for his conversation with his son. Her arms were folded under her breasts, as though to give herself comfort. Her manner was serene, but he knew her well enough to detect the underlying concern in her eyes. Aurelia was slipping away from them.

"Yes. I told him Juliet's C-section was scheduled for a week from tomorrow, so he's taking the first bus out." He pulled Leah in his arms. They were alone for the moment. Juliet was outside, checking to see if Lancelot's traumatized wives had started laying again. "He apologized for what he said last Sunday. I told him I was sorry, too…but the conversation was still awkward."

"It's hard to apologize over the telephone, Adam. You've made a good start. It'll be easier when you're face-to-face."

"I hope so. I don't want my relationship with Brian, and someday my grandchildren, to be limited to twice-a-year phone calls."

"You can't have the kind of relationship you want with secrets between you," she said.

"I know, Leah. God help me, I know." Coward that he was, he changed the subject. "Brian wouldn't let me send him money for a plane ticket. He's determined that every cent he got from the sale of the car goes to Juliet."

"How did he know you were here?" Leah laid her head against his shoulder and slipped her arms around his waist. She accepted his diversion, but he sensed her disappointment. He had squandered another opportunity to unburden himself, more frightened of the terrors locked inside him than of the specter of losing his son.

He forced the memories away and focused his attention on the feel, the warmth, of the woman in his arms. "He called the Hideaway and learned I had checked out. When no one answered at your place, he figured we were all out here." They had given up any pretense of maintaining separate residences after Brian had left, but they had yet to be alone together. Leah was spending the nights at Aurelia's bedside.

"Of course. A perfectly logical explanation. I'm not running on all cylinders this afternoon." Leah looked up at him and smiled, but this did nothing to hide the dark circles under her eyes, the faint stress lines from nose to chin.

"You're spreading yourself too thin," he said, his voice edged with concern. Luckily her blood pressure had remained within normal limits. If it hadn't, he would have insisted that different arrangements be made for Aurelia's care, even if doing so made him the heavy.

Leah blinked away a sheen of tears. "It's only going to be a few more days, Adam. I don't think she'll be here when the baby's born."

"You know these last days will be the hardest." He almost added that Aurelia was so heavily medicated now he doubted she would even realize where she was if they moved her to the hospice, but he held his tongue. Leah would know and Juliet would know, and the anguish that would cause them both did not outweigh the benefits of a few more hours of sleep.

"I'm taking care of myself. Don't worry. If…if it gets to be too much, I'll do what has to be done. For the baby's sake, for Juliet's sake."

He bent his head to kiss her lightly, the merest brush of his lips, because there was no time or place to be more intimate. "I'll be here for you." It was all he could offer.

"Thank you." She bracketed his face with her hands and kissed him back, then smiled up at him. "You're pleased Brian's returning so soon, aren't you?"

"I meant what I said, Leah. I want to make things right with him."

"I know you do." She made small, circling movements on her stomach with her hand, as much to soothe herself, Adam thought with a deep sense of disappointment for not being the man she deserved, as to reassure the infant sleeping inside her. "I want that, too—for all our sakes," she said.

"IF IT DOESN'T STOP RAINING soon, I'm going to…" Margaret Owens shook raindrops from a plastic rain scarf and hung it next to her raincoat on one of the brass hooks inside the door of Leah's office.

"Do what?" Leah asked while she went on typing case notes into her computer. She refused to look out the window at the steady downpour that had gone on without stopping for the past forty-eight hours.

Margaret threw up her hands in exasperation. "I don't know. Something. It won't be pretty, and it might very well be criminal."

Leah laughed. "This weather has really gotten you down." A huge low pressure system, drawing moisture from the Gulf of Mexico up into the Ohio River valley, had stalled almost directly over Slate Hollow, and it didn't look as if it was moving out of the area anytime soon.

"Of course, I'm depressed, and worried—the sun hasn't broken out from behind the clouds for a solid week. Have you heard any weather reports at all today?" Leah shook her head without looking up from the computer screen. Margaret went on talking. "The TV station says the National Weather Service has issued flash-flood warnings for the whole county. They've already called out the National Guard up along the Ohio River. There's no end in sight. We could get six or eight more inches before it's over."

Leah felt uneasiness curl through her, and guilt that she wouldn't be available to join her unit and help if the situation got worse. But her duty was to her unborn child now, not to the country she'd served for more than ten years. She looked up from the computer screen into her friend's anxious eyes. "Did you have any trouble getting over Aurelia's bridge this morning?" Margaret had insisted that she stay with Aurelia the night before, so that Leah could get a decent night's sleep.

"We made it, but just barely. The water's almost up to road level. I've never seen the water so high around here. The river's out of its banks. It won't be much longer before half the houses on Hyacinth Street have to be evacuated, and they're already talking about moving people living on Mulberry and Carson out."

Leah closed the patient file she'd been updating and got up to go to the window. Margaret's news had caught her a little off guard. She'd been so busy seeing patients all day that she hadn't ventured out of the windowless exam rooms for at least five hours. It was only a little after three o'clock in the afternoon, but the leaden sky was almost as dark as night. She looked out at the drenched pavement and the sodden lawns of the houses across the street with alarm. Hyacinth Street ran along the river. It was in the lowest part of town and had flooded once or twice since Leah had lived in Slate Hollow, but Mulberry and Carson were on higher ground. As a matter of fact, Mulberry Street ran parallel to Huckleberry—where her own house could be in danger of flooding. If the Slate River was that high, it would be backing up creeks all over the county.

"Do you think we should move Aurelia and Juliet into town?" Juliet wasn't going to school any longer. Leah picked up her work assignments at the end of the day, or Juliet's homeroom teacher gathered them together and dropped them off with Leah at the clinic.

"That's up to you and Caleb," Margaret said. "But to tell you the truth, that's why I stopped by. I don't think it's a good idea for you and that child to be out there alone tonight.''

Leah turned away from the window. She lifted her stethoscope from around her neck and laid it on the desk. It seemed suddenly very heavy. "Adam will be with us.''

"I'm glad to hear that, but he isn't going to be able to hold back the creek water if it decides to go over the banks and take that old bridge with it.''

"He's going to stop by here in a few minutes on his way out to the highway to meet Brian's bus. I'll discuss the situation with him then.''

Margaret was watching her closely. "You and I have hardly had a chance to talk in almost two weeks.''

"I know, but everything's been so hectic.'' Leah smiled at Margaret apologetically.

"Now that I'm here, we have a few minutes. Caleb says you and Adam are going to be getting married sometime soon.''

"Yes.''

"Are you sure that's the best decision?'' Margaret was a blunt, no-nonsense woman. She had been a friend for as long as Leah had known her. She obviously had doubts about Leah's relationship with Adam and she meant to voice them.

"I hope it is.''

"He's a troubled man, Leah. Caleb told me that Adam has indicated he has no intention of returning to Chicago and his position at St. Barnabas. Ordinarily I'd be thrilled to hear that, because I don't want to lose you either as a friend and neighbor or as a member of the clinic practice, but Leah, Adam isn't an ordinary doctor. He's a neurosurgeon with a growing worldwide reputation. That he intends to give that all up…''

''Just to marry me?'' Leah asked, trying to deflect a little of the pain Margaret's plain-speaking had inflected, but the joke fell flat. Her friend had an uncanny knack of putting her finger exactly on all the doubts Leah tried so very hard to ignore. Adam had turned his back on medicine. He had barely set foot inside the door of the clinic since the day he'd gone with Caleb to see the woman in the ER.

''No, that's not what I mean. I mean, he's going to give that all up, period, end of sentence. End of career. He's a young man. What will he do with his life? What will *you* do if it doesn't work out?''

Once more Margaret had given voice to one of Leah's greatest fears. Would he come to resent leaving all that? Perhaps not right away, but eventually, inevitably? ''He's trying so hard to work his way through the past.''

''But what if he doesn't make it? Some Vietnam vets never make a reconnection. What if Adam's one of them?''

Leah looked down at the small stuffed stork one of her patients had given her as a gift. The longer Adam fought against coming to terms with what happened to him all those years ago, the lower the odds became of his ever putting the ghosts to rest. Last night he had stayed with her. He hadn't gotten up before dawn to leave her, but slept in her arms. Even as she held him close she couldn't keep the past away. His sleep had been troubled, but when she asked him about it, he had kissed her into silence, refusing to talk about the nightmares that gave him no respite.

When would those nightmares begin to spill over into his waking hours? What would she do then? Would he grow violent or even more withdrawn than he sometimes was now? That was the picture of the future that frightened her most of all—a withdrawn and distant husband, and a child who would suffer from his father's inability to show the love every child needed. This was one thing she had promised herself she could not let happen. It would be better to raise their baby alone.

"I love him, Margaret, but I made myself a promise. I will put my baby's welfare above everything else, even a broken heart."

"I pray it doesn't come to that," Margaret said. "There, I've had my say and I feel better. With your parents living so far away, I feel it's my duty to stand in your mother's place."

"I know you do, Margaret, and I appreciate your concern." Leah ran her finger over the spindly yellow legs of the little stuffed bird. "I *pray* I don't, but I may need your help in the future. It's wonderful to know that you and Caleb will always be there for me and the baby."

Margaret swept across the room and reached up on tiptoe to give Leah a kiss on the cheek. "I've had my say, but that doesn't mean I'm not rooting for true love and a happy-ever-after for you."

Leah hugged her back, her throat tight. "I know that, too."

"Well, I'd better be on my way home. Caleb's fixing supper tonight and I don't want to be late," Margaret declared briskly. "We'll be at home all evening, so don't hesitate to call us if you need anything at all out there at Aurelia's."

"I won't hesitate for even a moment."

Margaret grew serious once more. "I'll miss Aurelia's friendship. She and I go back a long way. She was almost the first friend I had in Slate Hollow when Caleb and I moved here after he got out of the service. But I'll be glad when this is all over—she's fading fast. And Juliet didn't sleep a wink last night. I almost wish her C-section was scheduled sooner than next week. I want to see that little one born safely into the world."

"We all do, Margaret."

"Has she made up her mind about the adoption yet? I wanted to ask last night, but she didn't broach the subject so I didn't press."

"No, she's still very torn." Leah wondered what effect Brian's return would have on the decision she made.

"At least you've been able to keep that Lexington lawyer away from her."

"Yes, that has taken some of the pressure off."

"Has she asked your opinion lately?" Margaret turned away as she spoke, reaching for her raincoat and little plastic hat.

"No, she's kept to herself these last few days. She spends as much time with Aurelia as she can. She does her schoolwork and she stays in her room."

"It's the weather. It's getting everyone down. Lord, I wish it would stop raining." She opened the door and stepped out into the corridor. "I'll call this evening to make sure everything's all right. And remember, if you need us, we'll be there as fast as we can.''

"Thanks, Margaret.''

Leah sat back down at her desk and stared at the computer. Margaret's words played over and over in her brain, blanking out the information on the screen. What would her life with Adam be like? Was she opening herself to years of heartache and regrets? Would her listening to her heart, instead of her head, cause heartache for their child, as well? The door opened and Adam stuck his head inside.

"Hi there. Are you ready to head out to the bus stop with me?'' He smiled, and for the time being her doubts melted away. When he smiled, he was the Adam she knew he should and could be. The whole man, caring and committed. This was the man she had created a child with, and fallen in love with.

"I'm ready,'' she said, and smiled back. "Just let me shut down the computer and get my umbrella. Margaret was just here.''

"I know. I passed her in the hall.'' He came into the room and shut the door. He was wearing a white shirt and dark jeans, and he'd hooked his jacket over his shoulder with one finger. He smelled of fresh air and rain, and the subtle pine aftershave he always wore.

"She said there are flash-flood warnings out for the whole county.''

Adam nodded. "I had the radio on when I drove over here.''

"Do you think we should move Juliet and Aurelia into town?''

"The weatherman's talking about a break in the

rain for tomorrow. Let's wait and see how the creek looks when we get out there. I imagine Brian will insist on telling Juliet about his gift or loan, or whatever he intends to call it, as soon as possible.''

"I should probably drive myself to Aurelia's then. Brian won't be staying the night.''

"Good idea. I'll stay with you tonight, and Brian can use the Cherokee to come back into town.'' He smiled again.

"You're glad he's coming back, aren't you,'' she said, moving into his arms.

He tossed his coat onto the chair in front of her desk and gathered her close. "Yes, I'm glad he'll be here with us.''

"Even though what he's done will put more pressure on Juliet?''

"She'll make the right decision and you'll stand behind her, no matter what that decision is.''

"And you'll stand behind me.''

His smile faded. "I'll be *with* you.''

He had told her what she wanted to hear, but his smile didn't return, though her persistent niggling doubts did. "Let's go out through the ER entrance,'' she said. "I parked the Jeep on that side of the building this morning because the clinic lot was full.''

"I'm over there, too. The clinic lot is still full.'' He grabbed his coat and slung it over his shoulder, then held the door for her to precede him into the corridor. "After I pick up Brian why don't he and I stop at the diner and get some carryout for dinner tonight? How does that sound?''

"Great.'' They could be any husband and wife leaving the office, planning the evening, except that

Adam wouldn't step foot in the hospital and they were going home to a dying friend. Leah shook off the gloomy thought. It was the weather, just as Margaret said, and it was getting her down.

"The special's chicken-fried steak and scalloped potatoes."

"Sounds marvelous. I'll fix a salad, and there's ice cream for dessert."

"What more could a person ask?" He reached for her hand. He did that more often now, made the first move toward intimacy, and Leah's spirits rose a little.

They paused for a moment under the canopy outside the ER entrance, while Leah fumbled with the clasp on her umbrella. She found the button and popped it open just as a beat-up old station wagon roared into the driveway and skidded to a stop directly in front of them. A middle-aged woman in a blood-splattered blouse and slacks jumped out from behind the wheel and raced around the hood.

"Help me, please!" she sobbed. "My grandson— he fell playing on the slide in the park. I told him not to go outside. It was raining too hard, but he wouldn't listen. He slipped on the top step. I saw him fall. I'm afraid he's hurt bad. Real bad."

She wrenched open the car door and reached inside to lift a skinny little boy of four or five from the seat before Leah could tell her it was best he not be moved until his injuries had been evaluated. The child's clothing was covered in mud and blood. The lower half of his face was hidden by the bloody rag he was holding to his chin.

He was conscious, a good sign, and able to move

his arms and legs, another good sign, but that didn't mean he wasn't seriously hurt.

He lifted the bloody towel away from his face and looked down at it, then began to cry lustily. Blood ran freely from what Leah surmised was a badly cut lip.

His grandmother took one look at his face, turned chalk white and sank to her knees. "Oh, Lordy."

"Catch him," Leah said, dropping the umbrella. Adam caught the little boy before he tumbled to the cement while Leah grabbed the distraught grandmother by her shoulders and steadied her.

"I'm sorry," said the woman. "I never could stand the sight of blood."

"Adam." Leah turned to find him staring down at the whimpering child, the look on his face terribly familiar. The expression of banked terror she had seen when he'd lifted the injured children from the wrecked bus, and before that in the market in Saigon. He was pulling away, retreating into that dark world where only he could go.

"Adam!" She was desperate to have him acknowledge her. He looked up. "Take the boy inside. Get him some help." With the wailing child in his arms, Adam turned on his heel and walked on stiff legs toward the automatic doors.

"I can't stand to see my babies suffer," the woman said. "I'm getting too old for this."

"It's only a cut lip," Leah soothed, guiding her to the ER entrance.

"Are you sure?"

"I'm sure. He'll probably need a few stitches. Why

don't we wait until the doctor's seen him and then worry about what his injuries might be, okay?''

''Okay, but I have to call my daughter. She's at work.''

''I'll show you where to find a phone.'' Leah looked up. Adam was already through the treatment-area doors. He was still holding the child. Just as Leah and the little boy's grandmother entered the ER, he handed him to one of the nurses, then turned toward her.

There was blood on his shirt and on his hands. He looked down at the stains, swiped his hands down his pant legs and balled them into fists. Leah's heart froze in her chest. His eyes met hers once more, but it was as though he wasn't there. He had retreated into himself again, and this time when she held out her hand to draw him back, he walked away.

ADAM STARED AT HIS HANDS. The little boy's blood was gone. He'd found a bathroom at the end of the hospital corridor, washed his hands and vomited at the sight of the blood running into the sink. All those tiny naked bodies, passed to him from nurses who held each under a shower to wash off the mud and blood. ''This one is alive,'' they would say in voices devoid of emotion, drained of any inflection by the unbelievable horror of what they were seeing, what they were doing. ''This one is dead.'' Over and over again. ''This one is dead.'' He would take each small, limp body to the makeshift morgue, lay it beside the last and return for another, and another.

He had carried away eighteen little bodies. Nine-teen, counting the child who had died in his arms in the wreckage. One for every year he had lived. All together, he remembered thinking, the sum of their ages probably hadn't totaled five years more than his. God why did he have to remember it now?

That day had been worse than any of the others. He could remember the shellings and the sniper attacks. He could replay in his mind B.J.'s accident and watching him being taken away in the Evac helicopter, wondering if he'd ever see his friend alive again. He could deal with the gut-tightening memory of watching wave after wave of desperate human beings rushing the runways to try to find a place for themselves on the planes leaving the besieged city, and the brutality of the force necessary to turn them away.

But he never allowed himself to remember the children—except times like today when the terrible images leapt to his mind unbidden. They shook him to the core, and he was still shaking. Still unable to go back out into the ER and find Leah and take her away from this place. If he didn't get a grip on himself, he was going to lose it completely.

He needed Leah. He needed the quiet and serenity of her cozy little house. He needed time to pull himself together, and then maybe with her in his arms to keep him grounded in the here and now, he could bring the terror out into the open and talk about it at last.

He scrubbed his hands over his face, hoping to erase the horror he knew was reflected there. He walked down the corridor toward the examining room. Leah was nowhere to be seen. He heard the little boy still crying and clamped his jaws together to keep his teeth from chattering. With every muscle in his body protesting, he headed for the sound. A young man in green scrubs whom Adam had never seen before stepped out from behind a desk.

"May I help you?"

"Leah Gentry—is she with the little boy they just brought in?"

The male nurse gave him the once-over. "She's in there."

"I need to speak to her."

"I'll see what I can do." The nurse disappeared into the exam room, closing the door pointedly behind him. Adam waited one minute, two. The boy's frightened screams increased in volume and intensity. The sound scraped across his nerve endings like a dull scalpel blade. Five minutes and still no Leah.

The nurse returned. Adam headed toward him. He just wanted to see Leah, let her know that he was here, that he hadn't turned tail and run out on her.

"No shots!" the little boy's screams reached a frightened crescendo. Panic fought with Adam's rage to be free of the past.

"I'm sorry. She can't talk to you now." The nurse continued to block the door, as if he thought Adam would try to push past him. "You can't go in there."

The rage dissipated. The panic won. Was Leah truly too involved with the injured child to talk to him? Or was she deliberately avoiding him? If she was, he couldn't blame her. She had told him often enough that if she had to choose between him and his demons and her child's well-being, the child would always come first. There were others to help with the little boy, the nurse standing in front of him for one.

Leah was not coming out, not now and not as long as he was there.

Adam pivoted and walked away. "You're right," he said. "It's not where I belong."

CHAPTER SEVENTEEN

LEAH HALTED HER JEEP at the approach to Aurelia's bridge. It was raining so hard the windshield wipers could barely keep up. She stared at the torrent sweeping out of the ravine, and a chill skittered along her nerve endings. The racing waters of the creek swirled just inches below the railroad-tie decking. Debris had backed up against the supports and piled up along the banks. She had never seen the creek so high. The water seemed to be rising even as she watched, spilling over onto the road and threatening to block her way.

She rested her forehead against the steering wheel and closed her eyes, marshaling her courage. Crossing the bridge in good weather was always a challenge, and today it looked like sheer folly. She gunned the engine, then rolled down the window just in case. If the worst happened and she drove off the bridge into the water, she didn't want to be trapped inside. She felt the decking shudder slightly as it took the Jeep's weight. She tightened her grip on the wheel and kept going. Just once she glanced nervously at the water a little way below her and then didn't look again. Thirty seconds later her front wheels hit solid ground and a moment after that she was back on the road, fishtailing a little as the wheels strove to gain purchase on the muddy incline. She'd made it one more time.

Leah had expected to see Naomi Dunn's pickup parked in its usual spot by the porch, but it was gone. Naomi was a good soul, but timid, and she hated crossing Aurelia's bridge even on a bright, sunny day. Leah wouldn't be a bit surprised to learn she had asked to leave early, possibly even at Juliet's urging.

She parked the Jeep and hurried onto the porch, holding her sweater over her head to keep off the rain. She'd lost her umbrella to a gust of wind at the ER entrance. The last she'd seen the thing, it was rolling away across the hospital parking lot over an hour ago. It had taken longer than she'd anticipated to detach herself from the fortunately only slightly injured little boy and his grateful grandmother. Adam was nowhere to be found in the hospital or the clinic, and she had resisted the urge to go looking for him. His turning away had made her decision for her. Her child's welfare had to come first. Better to raise her baby alone than subject him to the kind of rejection that would result from living with Adam.

"Juliet?" she called, hanging her sweater on the rack beside the door. She was determined to do her best to keep her own troubles hidden from Juliet. The teenager had more than enough to deal with right now without becoming Leah's confidant on matters of the heart.

"I'm in here." Juliet appeared at the doorway to Aurelia's bedroom, her hand, as usual, on the small of her back to ease the strain of the awkwardly positioned baby.

"Where's Naomi?"

"I sent her home. She was so nervous and upset after the weather bulletin about the flash-flood warning, I couldn't stand to be around her." Juliet sounded testy, no doubt because of the weather and her grandmother's worsening condition, as well as her own physical discomfort.

"Naomi's a good soul, but you're right. She's not—"

"She's a wimp," Juliet snapped. Then her voice caught on a sob. "Listen to me. Naomi's been a brick and I'm being a bitch. I'm so glad you're here. Granny's very uncomfortable, but I was afraid to give her another pill. Will you come look at her right away?"

Leah crossed the room, turning on lamps as she went. The gloomy afternoon was fast giving way to twilight. The room was cool and damp. Leah wished she could light a fire to banish the chill and some of the gloom, but with oxygen in use in the next room, a fire was out of the question. "Why don't you go turn up the thermostat? It's chilly in here." She brushed Juliet's bangs from her forehead. "And when Aurelia's more comfortable, you can sit with her while I make us something to eat."

Juliet lifted her hand to her tangled hair. "I...I think I will." She looked over Leah's shoulder. "Is Adam with you?" she asked, then betrayed the real intent of her question. "Did Brian get back yet?"

"I don't know."

Juliet's face fell. "Oh, I was expecting him and Adam to be with you."

Leah knew she had to tell Juliet the truth, or at least a portion of it. Brian's return to Slate Hollow was important to the girl. Perhaps more important than Leah had allowed herself to believe. "I don't know where Adam is. We...we had a quarrel and left the hospital separately. I don't know if he and Brian will be coming out here this evening."

Juliet grabbed Leah's hand between her own. Her forehead creased in a frown. "Oh, Leah, I'm sorry you and Adam quarreled. What was it about? Not that Brian is bringing me the money from his car, was it?"

"No, of course not." Once more Leah felt a stab of remorse. She was so caught up in her own misery she had neglected to realize Juliet's inner turmoil. "It was personal, a problem that has nothing to do with you or the baby."

"I'm glad." Juliet looked down at their clasped hands, then back at Leah. "Not about your argument, but because it didn't have anything to do with me and Brian. He's been a real friend. I was starting to think every guy must be like Cash, a total creep, but not Brian. He's called me a couple of times this week. Wasn't that sweet? I mean, it's been kind of lonely out here and..." She trailed off, coloring slightly. "Well, you know."

"I know," Leah said. It had probably been inevitable Juliet would develop a crush on Brian Sauder. He was as close to a knight in shining armor as she was ever likely to encounter.

"Selling his car—it's a great thing to do, even if it makes it harder for me to decide what's best for the baby, not just for me."

"You want to keep the baby, don't you, Juliet?" Leah had forced herself to remain so carefully neutral

she'd failed to consider how devastating giving up
your child to another woman to raise would be. Now
she was pregnant herself and she knew. The teenager
was proving, with her efforts to keep up her schoolwork and her adherence to Clint's strictures on her
diet and activities, that she was capable of great
strength of purpose and commitment to a goal. As
young as she was, she would be a good mother.

"More than anything," Juliet said simply.

Leah decided to quit straddling the fence. "I'll
make us some soup and sandwiches, and we'll sit
down and talk about how to make it work."

Juliet's eyes brimmed with tears. "You don't know
how long I've been wanting to hear you say that, but
every time I tried to bring up the subject, you always
had a good argument about why I should make the
decision all on my own. It's been so lonely."

"I'm sorry. I thought I was doing the right thing,
not pressuring you one way or the other." Leah
leaned forward and put her arms around Juliet's shaking shoulders. Their bellies collided and Leah stepped
back, laughing.

"I can do it, Leah. I know I can. I already love
him, and I'll take the best care of him I know how.
I'm going to call that snotty lawyer and tell her to tell
her clients to go…to go away." She laughed again.
"First, though, I'm going to tell Granny."

But when they walked into the softly lit room, it
was apparent to Leah that Aurelia wouldn't be able
to comprehend what Juliet wanted to tell her. Her
eyes were dulled, her breathing labored. Her fingers
plucked restlessly at the coverlet. Her condition had

deteriorated a lot since Leah had left her the morning before.

Juliet lowered herself awkwardly onto the chair beside the bed and took one of Aurelia's hands in both of hers. "Granny?" she asked softly. "Can you hear me?"

Aurelia's only response was a slight moan, although she turned her head as though attempting to focus on her great-granddaughter's face. Leah took a pill from one of the containers, and indicated the time and dosage on the notepad sitting beside it on the dresser.

"Granny, it's Juliet. I have something to tell you." She looked over her shoulder at Leah. "She's not answering me."

Leah touched the girl's shoulder, gently urging her out of the way. "Let me give her something for her pain. Perhaps a little later she'll feel strong enough to hear your good news." Juliet stood up and stepped aside so Leah could place the pill under Aurelia's tongue where it would dissolve and be quickly absorbed into her bloodstream.

"She's getting worse, isn't she. She talked to me this morning...but not since."

Leah checked Aurelia's pulse and the setting on her oxygen tank before moving away from the bed to answer Juliet. "We need to keep her comfortable. When she's awake and more alert, she's also in more pain."

Juliet put a hand to her mouth to stifle a sob. "I know, but I'm not ready to say goodbye."

"There'll be time to say goodbye," Leah told her, though she didn't believe it. Juliet was crying in earnest now. "Come with me. Let's get something to eat and then you can come back and sit with Granny and hold her hand. She'll know you're there, and it will help her rest." Leah put her arm around Juliet's shoulders and urged her from the room.

"Okay, but I'm not really hungry. My stomach has been upset all day."

"Well, I'm starved, and you'll feel better with something in your stomach, too."

"I have something in my stomach," Juliet said with a watery little chuckle. "A very big something. I'm going to call that lawyer right now." She preceded Leah into the kitchen. The phone was on the wall beside the refrigerator. She picked it up, waited a moment and, instead of punching in the number, she jiggled the cradle rest up and down. "Rats, the phone's dead. I suppose a tree fell on the lines or something. The way it's raining they probably won't get it fixed till morning at least."

"I have my cell phone in the Jeep," Leah said. "It never works very well up here in your hollow, but you can give it a try."

"I'll go get it." Juliet waddled to the door. She stepped out on the porch, leaving the door open behind her. "Leah," she called, "come here!" There was alarm in her voice.

Leah hurried to her side. "What is it?"

"Look." Juliet was pointing down the slope to the creek. "The bridge is underwater." She clutched Leah's arm so tightly Leah winced. In the short time since she'd arrived at the Cade homestead, the creek had risen enough to spill over the bridge deck. It was raining even harder than it had been earlier, and thunder rumbled ominously in the distance, heralding even more rain.

"The weather report said there was supposed to be two more inches of rain by tomorrow," Juliet said in a worried voice. "We could get trapped up here. Maybe for days."

"We'll be fine, Juliet. The house is built far enough above the creek—it's never flooded before, right?"

"I guess so. Granny's never said. I...I do remember the bridge being underwater before, though, a couple of times when I was little."

"If the water doesn't go back down soon, we'll leave. I think we can still get across, although I don't really want to attempt it."

"But how will we move Granny? I know she doesn't weigh very much, but Clint and the doctor from Lex General both said I shouldn't lift anything. And...well, I don't think you can carry her by yourself."

Juliet was right. Aurelia was far too ill to be moved in less-than-ideal conditions. Leah could drag her out of the house on a makeshift stretcher, but getting her into the Jeep would be very hard, and a fireman's rescue carry—throwing Granny over her shoulder— was out of the question. Aurelia was far too ill to attempt such a thing. It was best they stayed put and rode out the flood. "Let's try my phone first. At least let Caleb and Margaret know we have a problem."

"Or Adam and Brian," Juliet said, moving awkwardly down the slippery wooden steps toward Leah's Jeep before Leah could stop her. In a few moments she was back with the cell phone, but as Leah had feared she couldn't get a signal.

"We're stuck here at least for the night, it looks like."

Juliet's face fell. She was shivering and her face had paled. "Isn't there some way we can get through?"

"I'll try again in a few minutes. The signal comes and goes up here. Don't worry. Now come on, let's get something to eat."

Juliet stayed with Aurelia while Leah prepared grilled cheese sandwiches and heated a can of soup. When Leah called her, she came to the small oak table in the kitchen, but barely ate more than a few spoonfuls of soup and only tore her sandwich into pieces and pushed them around on her plate. "Juliet, honey, quit worrying. The house is perfectly safe," Leah assured her for at least the third time.

"But what if Granny…"

"She's resting comfortably right now, and if she does get worse—" Leah reached out and laid her hand on Juliet's forearm "—it's what she wanted. To die at home."

"Yes, but I just never let myself think about it actually happening."

"It's a perfectly natural reaction to losing someone you love."

"Do you think Brian and Adam have been trying to call us?" she asked, changing the subject, but not before a tear rolled down her cheek and dropped off her chin.

"I'd wager Brian has been."

"Maybe he'll drive up here to see if we're all right when he can't get through on the phone. You know, just to make sure everything's okay."

"Yes, he might," Leah agreed, hoping Adam's son would do just that. She didn't like being marooned on Pine Mountain any more than Juliet did.

"I'm going to see if the phone's fixed," Juliet said, getting up so quickly her chair fell backward on the wooden floor. She picked up the receiver and slammed it down again. "Nothing. Where's your cell phone?"

"Right where we left it in the living room." Leah stood up, too, and righted the chair, then looked at Juliet. Something was wrong. The teenager's eyes were round and huge. Her neck and shoulders appeared tense and she was frowning as if in pain. "Juliet?"

The girl had already left the kitchen. When Leah followed her into the living room she found her doubled over, one hand on the sofa back to keep her balance, the other clutching her stomach. "Oh, God," she gasped. "Leah! What's happening? It hurts."

"How long have you been having contractions?" Leah asked.

"I haven't been having contractions, not real ones," Juliet said. "I mean, only cramps. Those pre-contraction things, whatever you called them."

"Have you had any other symptoms? Any bleeding or spotting?" Juliet's official due date wasn't for another ten days. She might be having Braxton-Hicks contractions, but she shouldn't be in severe pain, and she obviously was.

"I…I've been spotting a little all day. I thought…I thought maybe it was because I've been on my feet so much or sitting beside Granny's bed, instead of resting with my feet up like Clint said I should." She moaned a little and tried to straighten. Her face was drained of all color. She swayed on her feet.

"Sit down," Leah ordered. When Juliet was on the sofa, Leah pushed her gently back against the cushions and propped a pillow under her feet.

"I can't be having the baby already, can I? How will we get to the hospital? Leah, what will we do?"

"Relax," Leah said firmly. "We aren't certain you're in labor, but I think it's time to leave the mountain. We'll go to my place, and from there we'll be able to get you to the hospital in plenty of time. Now just try to be calm and remember your breathing exercises."

Leah picked up the cell phone and was rewarded with a signal, but almost as soon as she'd punched in Caleb's number, it died. "It's still not working."

"I think it's all right. The pain went away. Maybe it was just cramps, or a stomachache." Juliet tried to sit up, but Leah put her hand on her shoulder and held her down.

"Maybe you're right, but we're leaving, anyway."

"But...but Granny?"

"We'll be as careful with her as we can."

Leah hurried into the kitchen hoping against hope the phone would be working. It wasn't. She leaned against the side of the refrigerator and tried to bring her thoughts into order. Assess the risk and the importance of the objective. Make a plan of action. Carry it out. She could deliver Juliet's baby—if the birth was normal, but she could not perform surgery. They must leave Cade Hollow, and soon. Juliet's life and the life of her baby were in danger.

But what of Aurelia? The simple act of taking her

down the mountain could be fatal. Leah made the only choice she could make. If necessary she would sacrifice the few remaining hours of Aurelia's life in order to bring her great-granddaughter and her unborn child safely down the mountain. Leah knew she would do it with Aurelia's blessing.

ADAM RESTED HIS FOREARMS on the steering wheel of the Cherokee and looked out through the rain-streaked windshield. He didn't know exactly how long he had been sitting at the roadside turnout watching the comings and goings in the valley below him, the smattering of lights coming on in the town, as the tattered edges of rain clouds drifted by him like smoke on the wind. It seemed like hours.

Leah was through with him. There was no other way to describe what he had seen in her eyes. If he went back to her now, she would turn away from him without hesitation. She would shut him out of her life and the child's, because he was only a shell of a man, one whose heart was calcified with bottled-up fear and anger, and a bone-deep sadness that had festered inside him for almost a quarter century. Nightmares from the past had finally won the battle for his soul.

He laid his head against the back of the seat. God, why now? Why had those particular memories, the ones he had refused to acknowledge for all that time, come to him today?

He would never set foot in an operating theater again. The past had won. He had nothing left to give to his profession. He had nothing left to give to the woman he wanted to love. It was time for him to leave Slate Hollow.

It was also time for Brian's bus to arrive. Adam hadn't the slightest idea what he was going to do next in his life, except he wasn't going to leave Brian stranded in the rain. If he focused on small things, he could get through the rest of the day and the rest of the night. Tomorrow he'd have Brian drive him to Lexington. He'd fly back to Chicago, and… But that was tomorrow.

Adam turned the key in the ignition and drove back down the mountain toward the town that he'd hoped held his future and possibly his salvation, both of which now seemed to be rushing away from him as fast as the waning day.

MAN, IT HAD BEEN the bus ride from hell. Twenty-two hours since he'd left Chicago, a three-hour lay-over in Indianapolis and two in Cincinnati, then a dozen other shorter stops at towns along the way. He was definitely going back to school. He needed an education to earn a living so he would never have to be without a set of wheels again.

Brian grinned to himself. It was going to take a while to make that vow come true. He didn't have a cent to his name anymore. He'd turned the check over to his dad's accountant before he left Chicago, and told him to figure out a way for Juliet to get as much of it as humanly possible.

He'd worry about getting himself some kind of old truck after he got to Slate Hollow. Maybe Caleb would let him borrow Carlotta again until he could find one. Then, after Juliet's baby was born, and his dad and Leah got married… *Married.* He shook his head and caught sight of his grinning reflection in the bus window. Well, he was going to have to get on the stick and decide what to do with his life. He wasn't really sure he'd meant what he said to his dad on Sunday when they got into that stupid fight. He hadn't ever really admitted to himself before then that he wanted to be a doctor, but since he'd said the words out loud the idea had taken root.

The bus rumbled to a halt at the truck-stop entrance. Brian pulled his carry-on from the overhead rack and headed for the doors. They sighed open, letting in a blast of wind and rain that almost took his breath away. Thunder rolled along the distant ridge, and lightning flashed behind the hilltops as Brian stepped off the bus into a puddle that stretched halfway across the parking lot.

"Bad night to be out," the bus driver said. Brian had been the only passenger for the last two stops, and he and the driver had talked a little to pass the time.

"Yeah, I guess it is."

"There're flash-flood warnings out for this whole part of the state. Just hope I can get this rig into Lexington without having to go through high water. This bus don't like to get her feet wet."

"Good luck."

"Same to you." The driver touched his finger to his hat as Brian got off the bus, ducking his head against the rain coming down in a steady sheet. He sprinted under the wide overhang of the building, but it was raining so hard it provided little shelter. No one came outside to board, and after a few seconds the driver pulled away, heading back toward the highway.

His dad wasn't anywhere to be seen. He'd promised to be here and he wasn't. Brian felt like a little kid again, the way he'd felt when his dad had missed his soccer game or hadn't been able to call him when he said he would because some emergency surgery had come up. That was something else he'd have to think about if he really wanted to be a doctor. How hard would it be to juggle a practice and a family when he had one? And how would he do a better job of it than his dad had?

He'd just decided he was being an idiot standing in the pouring rain having philosophical arguments with himself about his future when his dad's Cherokee pulled into the parking lot and drew up in front of him.

He yanked open the passenger door and jumped inside, heaving his carry-on into the rear seat. "Hi, Dad. Thanks for coming to get me." There was nothing like standing bareheaded in a monsoon to get him past the awkwardness of seeing his dad for the first time since their argument.

"Hi, Brian."

"Wow! Is this some rain or what?" he asked, slamming the door shut and brushing wet hair out of his eyes. "It's like we should be building an ark or something."

"A really big one."

Brian turned his head and tried to figure out the look on his dad's face. It was almost dark now and there wasn't much light coming from the dashboard. "Is something wrong, Dad? Are you still mad at me? I said I was sorry for last Sunday, and I appreciate all your help in getting the money transferred to Juliet—''

''I'm not mad, just tired.''

''Okay.'' Brian wasn't convinced, but he let the matter drop. ''It's good to be back. I can't believe it, but I missed this one-horse burg. Can I bum a ride out to Aurelia's place? I want to talk to Juliet tonight. Or how about if I give her a buzz?'' He grabbed Adam's cell phone and punched in the number.'' The call didn't register so he tried again. ''Is something wrong with this thing? I can't get through.''

''We'll drive back to the Hideaway, and then you can have the Cherokee to head up there by yourself.''

''The Hideaway?''

''I'll take care of getting us our old rooms back while you're visiting Juliet.''

''I thought you'd be staying with Leah.'' Brian felt his face grow hot. ''But I understand if you don't want me in the house.''

''Leah's been spending nights with Juliet and Aurelia. I think I told you that on the phone.''

''I thought maybe she might be a little better...''

''She isn't better. She's dying.'' Brian had hoped never to hear that cold, hard tone in his dad's voice again.

''I'm sorry.''

''So am I.''

They rode in silence for a minute or two. ''Why aren't you coming with me tonight? And why are you getting us both a room at the Hideaway? What's been going on since I went to Chicago?'' He had the sinking feeling he wasn't going to want to hear his dad's answer.

"I'm leaving town in the morning," Adam said. "If you'll drive me to Lexington to catch a plane, you can keep the Cherokee here with you in Slate Hollow."

"You're leaving town?" Brian knew he sounded like a parrot repeating his dad's words back to him.

"Yes."

"Why?"

"I'd rather not talk about it right now, Brian."

"Sure, Dad, whatever you say." His dad had his hands wrapped so tightly around the steering wheel Brian could see his knuckles gleam white in the dash lights. What the hell had happened while he was gone? Maybe Juliet would have the answers. Yeah, Juliet would know. The sooner he got up the mountain the better.

They turned toward the river and found the way blocked by a barricade with a big reflective sign that said HIGH WATER. The next street they tried was blocked, as well. Ahead of them were two or three big trucks painted in camouflage greens and browns. Men in uniform swarmed around them. "Hey, it's the National Guard. Jeez, do you suppose the motel's cut off? It's as close to the river as anything in town."

"I don't know."

Adam turned onto Main Street. Two more Kentucky National Guard trucks were pulled alongside the curb near the little park they walked through when they took the river path into town. Soldiers and townspeople were filling sandbags and piling them on top of the riverbank.

Brian saw Margaret Owens and one or two other people he recognized watching the work. "Dad, pull over. There's Mrs. Owens. She'll tell us what's going on." He didn't even wait for the Cherokee to come to a stop before he jumped out and ran over to her.

"Brian." Margaret gave his hand a squeeze. "Here, stand under my umbrella. So, you made it back safely. Good."

"No, you keep it. I'm already wet. What's going on?" he asked as Adam came to stand beside him. The rain hadn't let up at all. It was coming down so hard the drops hitting his head felt like little stones.

"There's a flash-flood warning. They think the river level will rise at least three feet in the next couple of hours. They sent the National Guard in to fill sandbags and try and keep it from flooding the low parts of town. The mayor's just implemented the town disaster plan as a precaution. Caleb's already at the hospital. I'm on my way to the school to help set up the Red Cross shelter."

"Where's Leah?" Adam asked.

"Why, with Aurelia and Juliet of course. I was hoping you'd come to tell me you'd brought them down off the mountain."

"I left Leah a couple of hours ago," Adam said, "at the hospital."

"Then she's up there alone with a pregnant child and a dying woman." Margaret shielded her hand from the glare of the portable spotlights the soldiers were setting up to shine on the rushing black water of the river. "If the river's this high, Cade Creek is surely over its banks." Margaret's tone was grim.

"Leah's not a fool. She'd get Naomi Dunn to help her bring Aurelia and Juliet down off the mountain if she thought they were at risk."

Brian stared at his dad. Adam's voice was a deep, low growl he'd never heard before.

Margaret shook her head. "Naomi's here in town, at the hospital. She's a volunteer. I saw her with my own eyes just a few minutes ago. Do you have a car phone? Please, call and see if they're all right."

"We tried. There's no answer," Adam said over his shoulder. He was already halfway back to the Cherokee, and Brian had to hustle to catch up. "If you get to a phone, keep trying from this end, will you? Tell her we're on our way."

CHAPTER EIGHTEEN

"I STILL CAN'T GET THROUGH." Brian slammed the phone back into its case.

"Hang on, son. We'll be there in another five minutes."

Adam slowed the Cherokee to make the turn onto Aurelia's road. It was completely dark now. The headlights barely penetrated the silvery curtain of rain. Maple trees writhed in the wind, and pines bowed low with the weight of water on their branches.

Naomi Dunn's place was deserted, no lights showing in the windows as they drove past. It was impossible to tell which of the puddles they splashed through were only reflective sheets of water, or which hid a drop of six inches or more where a washout had occurred. Adam shifted into four-wheel drive, but still the going was rough. He slowed down even more. He couldn't chance sliding off the side of the road into a ditch or running headlong into a fallen tree.

"Man, I can't see a foot in front of the hood," Brian fumed. "How the hell did Leah even get up here? Her Jeep's nowhere near as big or heavy as this baby."

"It was daylight and not raining quite as hard," Adam said.

''What did you fight about, Dad? Why weren't you with her?''

''I haven't got time for this.''

''Make time, Dad,'' his son said in a voice Adam had never heard from him before—a man's voice, not a boy's. ''It wasn't just some kind of lovers' quarrel, was it?''

''No.''

''It was something bigger, wasn't it?''

''Yes.''

''The post-traumatic stress thing.''

''What makes you think that?'' Adam kept his eyes on the road, but inside he had started to throw up the battered remains of his internal barriers.

''You—what's wrong with you. I've been trying to figure it out all winter. Then when I went to your accountant's office the other day to get the money transferred to Juliet's name, he asked me if I knew why you quit coming to the 'Nam vets' meetings. Said he hoped you'd found your peace. That's how you met him, wasn't it? At some meeting for war vets?''

''Yes, a long time ago.'' The first time he'd tried to find his way out of the past. It hadn't worked, and after a few months he'd stopped going.

''I didn't know what he was talking about at first, then I figured it out. Lots of guys who were in 'Nam had post-traumatic stress disorder. I looked up the symptoms on the Net. You've got some of them. But you told me once you were only there for a couple of months at the end of the war. You said you weren't in combat. That you never had to live in a foxhole or crawl through the jungle on your belly.''

"No, I never did." They bounced through another big puddle, and the wheels threw sheets of water up and over the roof.

"But there were other things that happened then, weren't there?"

"Yes, there were," Adam said quietly.

Brian stared out into the rainy darkness. His next words were hesitant but resolute. "I had plenty of time on my hands this week. I called B.J. and he told me some things."

"B.J. talks too much sometimes."

"He's your friend, Dad. He's worried about you. After I called B.J., I got busy and did a lot of reading about Vietnam—all that stuff with the refugees and the pullout. Stuff that started to make sense to me when I put two and two together. Like when I smashed into the mailbox and made a mess of my face—"

"Brian, don't."

"B.J. said the two of you were stationed at Than Son Nhut."

"Yes." The Cherokee nosed into a washout with a drop that jarred his teeth. Brian braced both arms on the dash, but he kept right on talking as they bounced back onto level road.

"You were there when all those refugees were trying to get out, weren't you? I went to the library and watched some of the videos. Jeez, it was awful. Women and little kids getting trampled and beaten by a bunch of thugs who were out to save themselves. People shoving their babies onto airplanes when they didn't even know where they were going or if they'd ever see them again. There was one plane loaded with little kids that crashed.''

Adam didn't answer. He just kept driving.

''You were there when that happened, weren't you?''

Brian was reaching out to him, trying to understand what it was that had kept him so distant. He had missed the opportunity to unburden his soul to Leah, but it wasn't too late to do it with his son.

''I was there, Brian. It—''

''Dad! Stop the car! Look out!''

Adam had already brought the Cherokee to a halt before the words were out of Brian's mouth. A couple of yards ahead of them the road ended in a froth of fast-moving water.

''Shit. Where's the bridge?'' Brian asked.

''Straight ahead of us...somewhere.'' Adam could see the road rising steeply on the other side of the swollen creek, and beyond, the lights of Aurelia's house.

Brian turned his head. ''How much water can this crate handle before she starts to float?''

''I don't know, but I have the feeling we're going to find out.'' Adam opened the door and stepped down into water deep enough to cover his shoes. Brian did the same, swearing as the cold water soaked his Nikes.

''If we misjudge where the bridge is and run off the edge, we're goners.'' Brian shuffled forward a few steps. The water rose to his knees.

''Exactly why you're staying here and I'm taking the truck across.''

Brian rounded on him. "Oh, no, you don't. We're in this together."

"Son, don't argue with me."

"I'm not arguing—I'm just stating my position. I'm not standing out here in the pouring rain all night while you're comfy cozy up at Aurelia's with some of Juliet's cold fried chicken to ward off starvation. I haven't had dinner yet, and I'm not going to walk back to town and maybe get struck by lightning or brained by a falling tree branch. I'd sure as hell rather take my chances with you."

Brian was right. It was at least a mile back to the main road. He'd have to walk even farther, more than likely, before he could hitch a ride on a night like this. Thunder rumbled closer than before. Lightning flickered off in the distance, adding emphasis to Brian's argument.

"Okay, we'll stay together, but we're going to need some help from Leah." Adam leaned inside the Cherokee and pressed on the horn. A minute or two later the door of Aurelia's cabin door opened, the lights of the house silhouetting a slicker-clad figure. A flashlight beam bobbed toward them as Leah picked her way down the muddy slope.

Adam advanced until the water was at his knees. The current was strong, but not as strong as he'd feared. "Leah?"

"Adam!" She stopped just shy of the white swirl of foam that marked the high point of the water on her side of the creek. "Thank God you came. I need your help. Juliet's gone into labor and Aurelia's very low." Her voice almost broke on the last words, then steadied. "We've got to get both of them down off this mountain as quickly as possible."

"First we have to *get* to you."

"Don't try it, Adam. There's at least two feet of water over the bridge. Maybe more. Just turn around and go back to town for help. The phone line's down and my cellular won't work up here."

"We know. And we're not going back to town for help. It'll take too long. We're going to try and make the crossing."

"Adam, no!"

"Stop arguing." He almost smiled at the combative tone of her voice. He could feel Brian's excitement and apprehension as he turned toward him. "Are you ready?"

"I'm ready. But what if we go over the side?"

"If you feel us lose traction jump for it. Understand?"

"Got it."

"Leah," Adam called, "back up and shine your flashlight right down the middle of the road. I'll use it as a guide to stay on the bridge."

"It's too dangerous!"

Lord, she was a stubborn woman—and he loved her for it. He loved her and he was going to tell her so. If she would stand by him, with time he could conquer the darkness inside. With time, and with her love.

"That wasn't a suggestion," he called. "It was an order. Now do as I say."

"What are we going to do about getting them off the mountain if we do make it to the other side?"

Brian asked as he climbed into his seat and lowered his window.

"If we make it over there," Adam replied, "we can probably make it back."

Adam waited a moment for Leah to get positioned, then started forward at a slow and steady speed. He could feel the force of water against his door, feel when the tires left the road and moved onto the planking. It was even deeper than he'd expected, and by the time all four wheels were on the bridge, the headlights were nearly underwater.

"Jeez," Brian hissed. "Water's coming up through the floor. C'mon, Dad. Make tracks."

Adam pressed on the accelerator, felt the engine shudder and miss, then catch again as they surged forward. He felt the front wheels bite into the wet, stony earth on the far side, and then they were thrown sideways as the saturated earth gave way beneath his wheels. He gunned the engine. The back of the Cherokee skidded sideways.

"Out," he yelled at Brian. "Get out! Climb up on the hood and jump clear." Brian scrambled out of the window, his feet on the seat, his hands braced on the roof. "Jump!" Adam yelled.

"Not unless you do!" Brian yelled back. He clung to the side of the Cherokee, half in and half out of the vehicle.

"Jump, dammit!" Adam yelled again. The steering wheel bucked beneath his hands as the back wheels finally found firm purchase on the bridge planking. They lurched forward another yard or two and then got stuck. The back of the Cherokee was filling up fast. "Go!" he yelled. Brian's feet disappeared out of the window, as he climbed onto the hood and jumped.

Adam never saw him land. He shut off the engine and made a grab for the cell phone, but it floated out of his reach as he worked his way out of the driver's-side window. The water was high, lapping against the door handle. He pulled himself onto the roof, then clambered onto the hood. The Cherokee rocked beneath him, and he jumped clear just as it slid down into the creek bed. For an eerie moment the headlights continued to shine from beneath the surface, then they shorted out.

Brian was on his hands and knees in the grass beside the road. Adam reached down and gave him a hand up. "You okay, son?"

"Yeah," Brian said, sounding breathless but unhurt. He came to his feet and slicked his hair back out of his face. He looked toward the creek, where only the roof of the Cherokee remained above water. "Now we're both without a set of wheels."

"And we're trapped on this mountain until Margaret Owens figures out we're not coming back and sends some help."

"You said we'd cross that bridge when we came to it." Brian gave a little bark of laughter. "God, what an awful joke."

"Adam." Leah was running toward him, her flashlight beam bobbing.

"Slow down, Leah," he said, catching her to him, holding her tight against his chest. She went into his embrace willingly, but he could feel her holding back. She had withdrawn her trust. He had seen it in her eyes at the hospital earlier. He could feel it now in her touch. He had to make it right between them somehow, even if it meant baring the most private places of his soul.

"Are you both all right?" She ran her hands over his chest, bracketed his face with her hands.

"We're fine."

"We've got to do something. Juliet's already in the second stage of labor. We've got to get her off this mountain or we'll lose the baby—and possibly Juliet, too."

"Leah, there's no help coming. No one knows we're even up here except Margaret Owens, and she may be too busy with the flood in town to think of us anytime soon."

Leah looked at the black rush of water. "The river's over its banks in town, too?"

"Yes. They've called in the National Guard."

"We're stuck here. Adam, you're—"

"No." He wanted to stop her, but his hands wouldn't move to cover her mouth. He hadn't picked up a scalpel in months. He'd never performed a cesarean section. Hell, he couldn't remember right now if he'd even *seen* one performed. He couldn't do this, not for Leah, not for Juliet. Not even to save his own soul.

"You're going to have to deliver Juliet's baby. I have a field-surgery kit in my emergency case. It's not fancy, but it should have everything you'll need. I don't see that we have another choice."

BRIAN WONDERED if this wasn't all some kind of bad dream. Maybe he was still back on the bus. Maybe those really greasy french fries he'd eaten at the truck stop outside Cincinnati had given him nightmares. He was only dreaming they were stuck on this mountain in a monsoon. His dad's Cherokee and his cell phone weren't really at the bottom of the creek, and he'd only imagined he'd half drowned getting out of the thing before it went under.

He looked down at his still-wet jeans and the old wool socks Leah had unearthed somewhere, itchy and smelling of mothballs, but warm. This was real, dammit. He was sitting here holding Juliet's hand while another contraction tore through her body. This was the third one since they'd gotten here. Brian glanced at the clock. Five minutes since the last one, the same as the one before. Only this one seemed to be lasting longer and hurting more.

Juliet was making little panting sounds. Whooshing noises, like a little kid pretending to be a choo-choo train. Breathing through the pain, Leah had told him. It helped, she said. It would also help if he held her hand and encouraged her, but he hadn't been able to do much of that. She was squeezing his hand so hard he had to bite his tongue to keep from yelping, and if he did open his mouth to talk to her, he started breathing like she was, which made him light-headed.

"That was a bad one," Juliet panted. "I feel like I'm breaking in two."

"It's okay," Brian said helplessly. "It's okay. Just hold my hand." He wasn't ready for this. He'd only *thought* about being a doctor. He hadn't really decided on it yet, and even if he did, it should be years before he had to do anything like this.

"What about Granny? No one's with Granny."

"Brian is going to stay with your granny, Juliet,"

Leah said, coming into the living room from the kitchen where she'd been helping his dad get ready for the operation.

"Will you? I don't want her to be alone for a minute."

Brian wanted even less to be sitting at the dying woman's bedside than he wanted to be doing what he was doing now, but he didn't have a choice. And when you didn't have a choice, you did what you had to do. His dad had gone to war when he was the same age as Brian and seen things that still haunted his dreams. So he could find the wherewithal to sit by a dying old woman's bedside for an hour. "I'll stay with her," he promised. "I'll stay with her every minute until you wake up from the surgery, and then she can see you and the baby."

Juliet nodded. "You're a real friend, Brian. It makes this a little easier knowing you'll be with her." His heart swelled. She trusted him. It felt good.

"I won't let you down, I promise."

"I've got a shot for you, Juliet. It'll help you relax and keep you from getting sick to your stomach, okay?" Leah went on in that same calm voice. If she was worried about what was going to happen, she didn't show it.

"Will it help the pain?"

"Not this one, but soon, honey. I promise. The pain will be gone and you'll have a wonderful healthy baby to hold in your arms."

"I hope so," Juliet said, wincing as Leah gave her the injection. "It seems like this has been going on forever." She reached up and caught Leah's hand.

"Everything's going to be all right, isn't it? It's not going to hurt the baby being born here. Like…this?"

Not once had she mentioned being frightened for herself. All she'd talked about was the baby. Brian was awed by her courage.

"The baby's going to be fine, and so are you. Now lie back and rest, and I'll see to Aurelia before we start, okay?"

"Okay." Juliet lay back against the pillows piled up behind her. Exhaustion and pain had drawn lines on her face, making her look much older than her years.

Brian squeezed her hand and she squeezed back, giving him just a hint of a smile. "I'll see you later, Brian. Tell Granny I love her. I love her with all my heart." The words were already a little slurred. He watched the lines between her eyes begin to smooth out, and as she closed her eyes, the rise and fall of her chest grew more even.

"I think she's asleep," he whispered, detaching his hand from Juliet's and rising to follow Leah into Aurelia's bedroom.

Leah motioned him to Aurelia's bedside. He stood there, feeling awkward and scared, as she took Aurelia's hand between both her own. "Aurelia, it's Leah," she said.

"Your man's here, isn't he?"

"Yes, Aurelia, Brian and Adam are both here."

"You'll take good care of my Juliet?"

"We're all going to go down the mountain, Aurelia. All of us together."

The old woman shook her head a little. "Not me.

Time's short. I'm mighty weary of fighting the Lord's will to take me home to Him."

Leah didn't answer for a moment, and when she did her voice sounded shaky and a little hoarse, as if she was trying not to cry. "Do you need another pill, Granny?"

"I do hurt bad."

Leah walked over to a tall wooden dresser and took a small pill from a bottle. She sat down on the side of the bed and slipped the pill under Aurelia's tongue. "There, now you'll be able to rest. Brian's going to sit with you while Adam and I figure out the best way to get us down off the mountain, okay?"

Another barely perceptible nod. "We're in your hands and His," she murmured.

Leah stood up and said very softly to Brian, "Are you going to be all right with this?"

"She's dying, isn't she?" he whispered. He couldn't take his eyes off Aurelia. Her breathing was quick and labored. One hand was on her chest, moving feebly, as though to help her catch her breath. What would he do if she needed something and he didn't know how to help? His pulse pounded in his ears so hard he could hardly hear himself think. He wanted to turn tail and run.

Leah took his hand. "Brian, look at me."

"I don't think I can do this. I've never seen anyone die...."

"There's nothing you need to do, Brian, except be here for her. No one should die alone."

Brian made himself look at Leah. There were tears in her eyes, but her grip on his hand was firm and strong. He was a man. He had to act like one. "I'll stay," he said.

Leah leaned forward and kissed his cheek. Her damp hair brushed his skin. She smelled of rain and wind and faintly of lemons. "I have to go now and get Juliet ready."

"She's going to be all right, isn't she?"

"We'll do everything we can to make sure she and the baby both come through fine." She led him over to the bed. "Here's Brian, Aurelia. I'll be back in just a little while. You rest now, you hear?"

"I hear. Goodbye, Leah."

Leah kissed her on the cheek. "Goodbye, dear friend." Brian couldn't look at Leah. He was afraid he might cry, too. "May the angels guide you to your rest," Leah said very, very softly, and left the room.

CHAPTER NINETEEN

LEAH OPENED THE OVEN DOOR and used a sterilized pair of tongs to remove the half-dozen towels inside. She placed the towels on a sheet-covered section of the kitchen counter and covered them with another sterilized cloth. The towels and sheets had been in the oven long enough to kill most microbes clinging to them. She'd used similarly treated sheets to cover Juliet and the table where she lay. Her surgical field would never pass muster in a hospital setting, but here it was the best she could do.

She was scared. They were taking a terrible risk operating on Juliet under such primitive conditions, but they had no other choice. At least the electricity had remained steady, despite the phone lines being down and the continuing growl of a thunderstorm off in the distance. She'd rounded up all the flashlights in the house just in case and prayed she wouldn't have to use them.

Leah went back to Juliet. She was lying on her back on the kitchen table, her head slightly elevated on yet another folded towel. An IV bag was suspended from a clip-on pole above her head. The line ran into the back of her left hand. On her right arm Leah had attached a blood-pressure cuff. "Juliet? Can you hear me?" No response. She was unconscious, far enough under for Adam to begin the procedure. The anesthetic drugs Leah carried in her emergency kit were not the ones she would have chosen to use in the operating room, but they were adequate for the job and relatively safe for the baby, as well as Juliet.

If the surgery went quickly with no complications.

But a cesarean section when the mother was already in labor was never just routine. They would have to work fast and make no mistakes. Leah checked the teenager's pulse once more, then pumped up the blood-pressure cuff. She finished the reading and took the stethoscope tabs out of her ears. Juliet's pulse was steady. Her breathing was regular, her blood pressure stable and her color good, but still Leah wished she had instrumentation to back up her observations. As she looked up, she saw Adam watching her from across the room.

''I feel like Doc Adams in a 'Gunsmoke' rerun operating on the pool table at Kitty's saloon. She's under, but I'm flying blind here,'' she said, moving to the sink to scrub her hands.

''We both are at this point,'' Adam answered quietly as he inspected the small array of surgical instruments she carried in her field kit.

''Juliet has faith in you, Adam.'' Leah dried her hands on one of the sterile towels she'd just taken from the oven.

''But do you?''

''I...''

''You can say it, Leah. I see it in your eyes. You're wondering if you can even trust me to go through with this.''

''That's not true.'' But her words lacked conviction

and she knew he heard it. Adam was an extremely gifted surgeon. Her instincts told her Juliet would be in the best of hands, despite his unfamiliarity with this particular surgical procedure. *If he can contain his emotions...* But the sad, terrible truth was she didn't trust him. Would his fears overtake him once again, send him fleeing from the memories that tortured him, leaving her to face Juliet's dilemma alone? She wanted to trust him, but she was afraid. Afraid for Juliet and the baby. Afraid for herself.

Her doubts must have shown on her face. "I won't let you down, Leah. Not this time."

She wanted to tell him she believed him, but the words wouldn't come.

He turned to the sink and rolled up his sleeves, picked up the packet of surgical soap that came in the field kit and started to scrub. Leah opened the sterile packs that held gown, mask and gloves and put them on while he washed. The only sound in the room for the next few minutes was of running water.

Adam turned away from the sink. He took a towel and dried his hands and arms. "The anesthetic should slow Juliet's labor enough for me to make the initial incision and open the uterus. With any luck we'll have this little guy born safely into the world in the next twenty minutes."

"It won't be luck, Adam," she said, hoping he would meet her eyes, but he wouldn't. "It'll be your skill that brings him safely into the world." She prayed her words were true as she held out the disposable paper gown from the pack. He slipped his arms into the sleeves, then donned the sterile gloves.

"I'm ready when you are."

She ran through a checklist in her mind as she scanned the instrument tray she'd readied from her emergency supplies. Everything was there. She had done all she could to prepare. She watched Juliet's breathing for a moment or two more, took a deep breath and moved to Adam's side. "Ready."

"Say a prayer for all of us, Leah," Adam said, and began his incision.

BRIAN STUDIED THE PATTERN of the quilt on Aurelia's bed. It was a complicated arrangement of little blue and gray blocks and triangles. He wondered what it was called? His mother liked quilts; she collected them. They weren't old and worn like this one, which had obviously been made many years ago maybe by Aurelia herself, but colorful arrangements of fabric and thread done on commission by artists from all over the country, purchased as investments and kept locked away from light and dust—and life.

He looked up. Aurelia was staring at him. "How long you been sittin' there, boy? I've lost track of time." She closed her eyes. Brian was glad she wasn't looking at him anymore. There had been something in her eyes, some sort of light maybe, or… He didn't know what to call it, but it wasn't anything he'd ever seen before.

"For a little while. Can I get you something?" There was a glass of water with a straw in it on the table beside the bed. He could manage that.

"Nothing," Aurelia said, and Brian was ashamed to be relieved that he wouldn't have to lift her head and hold the glass to her lips. He was afraid he would hurt her or make her choke. She was so small and fragile-looking.

The clock on the dresser ticked loudly in the quiet room. He strained to hear what was being said in the kitchen, but he couldn't make out words. Only voices, his dad's low, rumbling tones and Leah's replies, calm and steady.

Aurelia reached out with her hand, and he wrapped his fingers around it, very gingerly, fearing he might crush the birdlike bones.

"You've been a good friend to my Juliet."

"I like her," Brian said simply. He wished she wouldn't talk. It seemed as if every word was a struggle, every breath a monumental task.

"I was dreamin'," she said, looking past him toward the doorway, or maybe farther, seeing something he couldn't see.

"What was your dream about?"

"Juliet had the little one in her arms. What a fine boy." She smiled, talking to someone he couldn't see. She reached out her hand. "Bring him here. I'm so glad you're goin' to keep him with you. So much hair, so thick and dark. And a fine name—Cade Adam Trent." Her hand dropped and she clutched her chest, gasping for breath, as though the words had been too much for her failing strength.

"Aurelia." Brian felt panic rise in his throat. He didn't want to be here. He didn't want to see her die, but she was dying. Right here, right now, before his eyes.

She turned her head. Her face had gone from gray to ashen. She looked at him, but he didn't think she saw him. "What a fine boy," she gasped. "And he'll grow into a fine man. You'll help him.'' It wasn't a question. It was a demand.

"Yes, Granny.''

"Praise be.'' She smiled, then coughed, choking a little. Brian stood up. He had to get Leah, had to tell her to come and help, to do something. But Leah couldn't leave Juliet, and neither could his dad. He was on his own. Death was in the room. He could feel the chill of it on the back of his neck.

He sat down again. He had given his word to stay with Aurelia. He held her hand in his, felt her life force flicker and fade away. As he watched, her breathing slowed and faltered and then, with a little sigh, she was gone.

"Granny?''

Of course she didn't answer. Brian sat there quietly for a few minutes more, listening to the drumbeat of rain on the roof, trying not to cry. He laid Aurelia's hands gently on the cover and smoothed her wispy hair away from her face. She had slipped away between one breath and the next. She hadn't lived long enough to see Juliet's baby born.

Or had she?

Brian remembered her words and the smile on her face. She thought she'd seen Juliet and the baby together and happy. He hoped her dream came true.

MAYBE LEAH'S PRAYERS were working, or maybe it was just years of discipline that guided his hand as he enlarged the incision in Juliet's abdomen and exposed the glistening muscular wall of the uterus that still protected the unborn child. His hands had stopped shaking. The chorus of ghostly cries that echoed incessantly inside him these days had almost died away. Almost.

But could he deal with what was coming next? His stomach clenched and he hesitated, scalpel poised. The memories were there again, beating at the walls of his consciousness with furious hands. This afternoon he had given in to the old terror, even if only for a little while. He'd come back to face it, but without Leah he had lost faith again. Tonight he could not afford to, but the fear inside him was very powerful.

"Adam?" Leah had sensed the fear, too. He looked up. She was watching him closely.

"I'm okay," he said gruffly. He had worked through the terror before. He would do it now. Then from somewhere deep inside him he heard an echo of Aurelia's voice bidding him peace, so that he could give life to Juliet and her baby. It was only his imagination, he knew, but the cries of dying children faded a little. They would never be gone, not completely, but maybe with time they would no longer haunt him day and night.

"Are you sure?"

"I'm sure," he said. Something in his voice must have told her he spoke the truth.

"Then let's get this baby born."

He saw movement out of the corner of his eye. Brian was standing in the doorway. His son's face was starkly pale, his expression forlorn. Leah swiveled her head to follow the direction of Adam's eyes.

"Is it Aurelia?" she asked.

"She's gone," Brian said. He focused on what Adam was doing. If possible, his face got even paler. "She died a minute or two ago."

"Just a little while longer," Leah whispered, dropping her head for a moment. When she lifted her eyes to his again, she was blinking hard to keep the tears from falling. "Adam, she so wanted to live to see this baby."

"Somehow, I don't think she's too far away."

Ten minutes later Juliet's baby was born. Adam felt the warmth of the tiny body in his hands, the weight of his head in his palm as he lifted the infant from Juliet's womb and handed him to Leah. The woman who would bear his child. The woman he loved. Their eyes met and held and he knew that soon, soon he could tell her all that was in his heart.

"What is it?" Brian whispered from the doorway. "A boy or a girl? I can't see from here."

"It's a boy," Adam said as Leah cleared the infant's mouth and nostrils with a swab. A baby, a living, breathing miracle. Despite twenty-two years of medical training and experience he had never delivered a baby. It was something he could get hooked on doing.

"And he's perfect," Leah said, looking him over. "Eyes, ears, nose, mouth. Ten fingers, ten toes." She laughed that wonderful joyous laugh that had slipped into his heart the first time he'd heard it, and now helped to heal the ragged edges of his soul. "He's all boy."

"He's not crying," Brian observed a little anxiously.

Adam snapped his finger against the sole of the baby's foot. A kittenlike cry came from his throat. "He's still sleepy from the anesthetic, but he's fine. We need to get him warmed up."

"Can I see him?" Brian asked.

"Even better, you can hold him. Bring me one of those towels," Leah spoke over her shoulder as they cut and tied the cord, and Adam prepared to detach the placenta from the uterine wall and suture the incisions back together.

"Me?" Brian's voice was incredulous. "Oh, no, you don't."

"Yes, you. Now. Front and center," Leah commanded in a voice that reminded him this woman was an officer in the United States Army. She wiped the baby clean with a soft cloth and laid him on the towel Brian held in his outstretched hands. "Take him into the living room and hold him close, and tell him how glad you are to meet him. He's just had a very rude introduction to the world. He needs a friend."

Brian now seemed beyond speech and he only nodded. He held the baby as though he were made of spun glass. "What about Juliet?" he finally managed to ask. The look on his face was a mixture of wonder and discovery.

"She won't be awake for about an hour," Leah explained to Brian, as she handed Adam a suture needle. "When she does wake up, we'll let her see the little sweetheart right away."

"I'll take good care of him till then. You know, just before she died, Aurelia said she saw Juliet standing in the doorway of her bedroom holding the baby."

"She wanted very much to live to see the baby born, Brian," Adam said, remembering the voice he had heard in his mind and in his heart.

"You'll probably think this sounds crazy, but you

know something? I think she did.'' Brian smiled down at the little one in his arms and left the kitchen.

IT WAS ALMOST MIDNIGHT before the rain let up. Leah stepped out onto the porch, straining to see how much higher the creek had risen. It was cold and she wrapped her arms around herself. The baby moved inside her, stretching and somersaulting in a series of tiny thumps and bumps echoed in the beating of her heart.

The door opened and closed quietly behind her, and she felt Adam's arms come around her. She let herself relax against the solid warmth of his chest and covered his hands with hers.

''Are they all asleep?''

''The baby's sleeping. Juliet and Brian are having a discussion about whether or not having initials that spell 'cat' will be detrimental to young Cade's development.''

Leah smiled. ''Cade Adam Trent. I like it, no matter what the initials spell. Besides, someday she'll marry and hopefully the man will adopt Cade and give him his name.''

''I'm sure that's what'll happen.'' She felt Adam kiss her hair lightly.

''She really ought to be resting, though. Maybe I should go back inside.''

''Let them talk. It keeps her mind off Aurelia's passing.''

Leah agreed. ''You're right. It'll be hours before anyone can get up here. It's too dangerous tonight.'' For some reason of atmospherics or just plain luck, Leah had been able to get through to Caleb at the hospital on her cell phone a little over an hour ago. He had promised to send help as soon as possible, but Leah didn't hold out a lot of hope that rescue would arrive anytime soon. They were in no immediate danger, after all, and surely there were others trapped by the rising waters who needed help, as well.

"We'll find a way down the mountain come daylight."

"We...we'll have to make arrangements for Aurelia's funeral. I'm going to miss her." Leah felt a sob tighten her throat and swallowed against the urge to cry.

"It's all right to cry for your friend. Don't hold back."

She turned in his arms. Something had changed in him. She had seen it happen, from one moment to the next back there in the kitchen, as Juliet's and the baby's lives hung in the balance. "Why do you say that, Adam? You've been fighting your emotions from the first moment I met you."

He was silent for a few seconds, as though choosing his words with great care. "I came back to tell you...everything this afternoon at the hospital, but you wouldn't let me."

"I couldn't stand to see the emptiness in your eyes. I love you, Adam. I want to help you deal with whatever memories lie so heavily on your heart, but you push me away. Time and again you push me away."

"Today I ran away not because of the past—it was there like it always was—but because this time, I couldn't hold it back." His voice was harsh with sadness and regret. "I wanted to tell you, Leah. I wanted you to know what's haunted me all these years."

She wrapped his hand in both of hers and lifted it to her mouth. "This time I was the coward. I wasn't there for you. I'm sorry. But tell me now, please, for my sake. For our child's sake."

"You're too young to remember the orphan planes."

"The airlifts at the end of the war when they brought Vietnamese and Amerasian children to the States to be adopted? I've heard about them. I've seen pictures." Her breathing quickened, and she braced herself against a new onslaught of tears. She knew what Adam was going to say, and her heart ached for him.

"I thought we were doing some good there, at the end of a war, where everything else had gone wrong. Getting all those babies and little kids out of 'Nam and back here to the States to new lives with families who would love them. I was glad to help. They were such cute kids. I saw it all, Leah, the day the Baby Lift plane crashed, all the broken little bodies, the death and destruction. I had carried them onto that plane, strapped them into the seats, two by two by two. And an hour later I carried them out of the wreckage and into the morgue.

"There was one little girl..." He was holding Leah so tightly she could barely breathe, but she didn't make a sound or move a muscle. His voice broke and he couldn't go on. There was nothing she could say that would dilute the horror that had held him in thrall for so many years. She just held him in her arms and waited. His words came haltingly, brokenly. "She was so beautiful, Leah, and so terribly damaged, and she died in my arms. I couldn't help her. I couldn't help any of them. There were so many innocent victims at the end, and all in vain.''

''No, Adam, it wasn't all in vain. Do you think you would ever have become a doctor if it weren't for the horror you lived through in those days? I don't.''

''I'm not much of a doctor now.''

''You're a wonderful doctor. You were magnificent tonight. You saved Juliet's life. You gave her son life. Just as you have done over and over again in your career. Just as you will countless more times in the future.''

''I can't do this alone, Leah. I don't know if the flashbacks are gone for good or only banished for the time being, because of your love and Aurelia's stubborn faith. I don't even want to try to find out without you by my side.''

''There won't be any more flashbacks or nightmares, because I promise never to leave your side. I promise never to let you get lost in the past again, as long as there's breath in my body.''

''I believe you.'' He lowered his head and took her mouth with his. She could taste the saltiness of tears on his lips and knew he had begun to heal.

When the kiss ended, they stood quietly for a moment, wrapped in each other's arms. The pounding of Leah's heart intensified, filled the air around her and resolved itself into the thump, thump, thump of rotor blades as a helicopter dropped out of the night sky.

''What the devil?'' Adam asked, the surprised expression on his face thrown into stark relief by the glare of a searchlight playing across the yard from above.

''It's a helicopter,'' Leah said needlessly as the

wind the blades created threatened to tear her hair from its braid. "I never expected…"

The helicopter settled onto the lawn. It bore the markings of the Kentucky Air National Guard. The door to the cabin opened and Brian stuck his head out. "What's going on? I thought I heard…" His mouth dropped open. "I *did* hear a helicopter."

"I think we're being rescued," Adam said, not releasing Leah from the circle of his arms.

An airman in combat fatigues jumped out of the open side of the chopper and ran across the yard. "Ma'am? Captain Gentry?"

"I'm Leah Gentry."

The airman halted at the bottom of the porch steps with a smart salute. "We've come to help you down off this mountain."

"Thank God. We have a postop new mother and infant who need medical attention."

"Yes, ma'am. We have orders to transport you directly to Lexington General. We can take three at a time."

"Adam?" she turned in his arms.

"You go with Juliet and the baby. Brian and I will stay here with Aurelia until they can get back for us."

"I don't want to leave you."

"It won't be for long," he said, brushing her lips with a kiss. "We'll be together again before morning—and then it'll be for the rest of our lives."

EPILOGUE

LEAH STOOD BEFORE THE CRADLE Adam had placed beneath their bedroom window the day before her due date. It was too hot to sleep. The air conditioner had broken down and the repairman hadn't come to fix it yet. The window was open and the scent of lilies and roses, heavy with dew, drifted into the room. Even though the sun was barely over the horizon, the air was already warming up. It was going to be another scorcher of an August day.

She reached out a hand and set the cradle gently rocking. It was old, very old, and it belonged to Juliet. But at four months, Cade had already outgrown it, and so Juliet had lent it to Leah and Adam for their baby. Aurelia's grandfather had fashioned it out of hickory almost a century ago, Juliet had told her, and five generations of Cades had been lulled to sleep by its gentle rocking. It would soon rock the first generation of Sauders.

It had been a busy summer for Leah and Adam. They were going to make their home in Slate Hollow. In another month or so, they would be moving from her little house to a big old Victorian across the river—one of those handyman's specials Adam figured would keep him busy with projects for the next ten years. It had five bedrooms and a big yard just perfect for kids, a kitchen with an acre of counter space and a view of the river from almost every room. Leah had fallen head over heels in love with it the first time she saw it, despite the inadequate wiring and plumbing. Adam had already enlisted her dad and brothers to help work on it. Brian figured he had a steady summer job for as long as he needed it, and her mother had already painted two watercolors for the parlor walls.

Pain tightened across the small of Leah's back and moved around to the front, bringing her rudely out of her reverie. The baby kicked in protest, and Leah knew the little one was anxious to be born. "I'm anxious, too," she whispered. "I hope it's soon." She breathed through the contraction and turned to find Adam watching her from the bed.

"You're up early," he said.

"I'm sorry. I didn't mean to wake you."

"I always wake up when you leave my side," he said with a smile. He smiled often and easily these days. "You're not up early just to watch the sunrise, are you?" he asked, swinging his legs over the side of the bed and crossing to her. All he was wearing was a pair of briefs and for a moment Leah almost forgot she was in labor. He looked tanned and fit and at peace with himself, and very sexy.

He was operating again, flying from Lexington to St. Barnabas two days a week until the end of the year, when he would join Caleb's clinic in Slate Hollow. When they heard Adam was joining the practice, two cardiologists from Nashville had signed on, and Peter Assad was considering leaving Lex General more seriously than before. His decision was a godsend to Caleb's efforts to get the hospital-funding levy passed. It looked like a shoo-in for November.

In addition, Adam had already been asked to lecture at the University of Kentucky Medical Center, and he consulted regularly with hospitals around the country. Obviously, turning down the head of neurosurgery at St. B's in order to practice in a small town in the Kentucky hills had done nothing to diminish Adam's reputation with his peers. There were still some bad times for him, when Leah saw sadness darken his face and cloud his eyes, but they happened less and less frequently. She hoped with time they would cease altogether.

B. J. Walton had visited twice, once for their wedding in early May to act as best man, and again in July to attempt to talk Adam into joining him on another medical mercy mission, this time to Siberia in the spring. Adam had told his old marine buddy he'd think about it but wouldn't commit to going. B.J. had gone away disappointed but vowing to return after the baby was born and renew his request.

Adam may not know it yet, but Leah did. He would go. His sense of commitment to his fellow man was too strong to allow him to deny it. She knew because she felt the same way. That was why they'd agreed she wouldn't resign her commission when her medical leave ended. She was no longer a single mother with sole responsibility for the health and happiness of their child. She had a husband who loved and supported her, and when the call came once more to honor her oath and serve her country, she would go with his blessing.

''You're right. It's not the sunrise—it's the baby.

I think it's time," she said, laying her head against Adam's chest, hearing his heartbeat, strong and steady, beneath her cheek. "The contractions are about eight minutes apart. I want to stop at the clinic before I check myself into the hospital. I have to leave a note for Dessie to cancel my morning appoint—"

Another contraction caught her off guard. Adam held her close as she breathed through it. "That hurt," she gasped.

"It hasn't been eight minutes since the last one, has it?"

She glanced at the bedside clock. "No." A shiver of excitement mixed with a little anxiety shot along her nerve endings. It was her first baby, after all. She had a right to be nervous. "It's only been five."

"Time to go, Leah, and we're not stopping at the clinic," Adam said as he pulled on his pants. "I'll call Clint from the car phone. We're checking you into the hospital now. I'm not going to deliver another baby at home. I'm not licensed to practice obstetrics in the Commonwealth of Kentucky."

"You did a wonderful job with Cade," she said, braiding her hair while he pulled the overnight bag she'd packed a few days ago from the shelf in the closet. She decided not to argue with him, because the last contraction had been strong. Very strong.

"I'm perfectly willing to let Clint do the honors. Now come on. Hurry up."

"I'm ready. Just let me get my purse. Oh, dear, I should call my mother. She and Dad have had their bags packed for a week. Dad's got the driving time planned to the last minute." Another contraction followed hard on the last. "Heavens. Maybe you should tell them to fly."

Adam's face lost a little color. "C'mon or you're going to be having this baby in the front seat of the car."

"My brothers, and Brian and Juliet—we have to let them know."

They had moved Juliet and the baby to Lexington just a few days earlier, so she and Cade could get settled into their little efficiency apartment off campus before classes started. Brian was there, too, camped out on the living-room floor, helping Juliet paint woodwork and put up new window blinds.

"No," Adam said forcefully. "We will call everyone from the hospital."

"Yes, sir." She caught his hand. "I love you, Adam. I've loved you since that night in Vietnam, and I'll love you till the day I die."

"And God, I love you." He pulled her as close as her stomach would allow and dropped a kiss on her lips. "Now get moving, soldier."

"Yes, sir." Leah took his hand and together they walked out into the brand-new summer's day.

"GET THE PHONE, WILL YOU? I'm right in the middle of this," Brian called from the tiny bedroom of Juliet's apartment where he was attempting to hang a curtain rod. The sun was in his eyes and he was getting hungry. It was already an hour past lunchtime, but he wanted to get this done so Juliet didn't have to stumble around in the dark when she got up to feed Cade in the middle of the night. The apartment house sat right on the street, and anybody walking by could look into the bedroom.

Privacy issues aside, the place wasn't bad. It was close to the campus, and the Baptist preacher, from back in Slate Hollow, had a niece with a toddler of her own living nearby who would baby-sit Cade while Juliet was in class.

Brian would be around to help her, too, because he'd transferred to the University of Kentucky. He was going to give premed a try. He might never be the kind of neurosurgeon his dad was, but he intended to give medicine his best shot.

And he was paying his own way. It hadn't seemed right to take money from his mom and stepfather for tuition after he'd sold the Lexus they'd given him and refused to return to Harvard. Besides, he wanted to see if he could make it on his own, the way his dad had done. He'd worked in construction all summer to earn his tuition money. Of course, he wasn't such a fanatic about this making-it-on-his-own stuff that he'd turned down the secondhand Ford pickup his dad had given him, so he didn't have to borrow the new Cherokee all the time.

"I've got it," Juliet sang out from the living room, and then a moment later, "Brian! Come here!"

The excitement in her voice made him jump, and he banged his elbow on the window frame. He climbed down off the bed, edged his way past the dresser and crib, and walked into the living room, where Cade was lying on the floor on one of Aurelia's quilts. "What's up? You didn't have to yell."

Cade waved his little arms when he saw Brian, and Brian took a moment to drop to his hands and knees and tickle his belly just where he liked it. He was a good baby. He slept all night and wasn't colicky or fussy. Juliet seemed to be handling motherhood pretty well, and Brian wasn't doing so badly as a substitute big brother, either.

Everything Aurelia had told him that night had come true—and something even spookier had happened. Juliet had had the same dream. She called it a miracle and said it helped her feel not so bad that Aurelia had died before she could see Cade. And maybe she was right.

"Brian, quit making him laugh. He'll spit up. Come here! It's Leah. She's got something to tell you."

"What? Is she having the baby?"

Juliet laughed and shook her head. "She's had the baby!" She gave him a quick, shy kiss. Their first. "Congratulations! You're a big brother again, and I'm going to be a godmother."

"But what is it?" Leah hadn't wanted to know ahead of time whether the baby was a boy or girl, so they'd all been playing guessing games.

Juliet held out the phone. "It's a girl of course, a beautiful little girl. Just like Granny said."